SEDUCING
the COWBOY

USA TODAY BESTSELLING AUTHOR
KENNEDY FOX

Each book in the Bishop Brothers World can
read as stand-alones but if you wish to read
the others,
here's our suggested reading order.

BISHOP BROTHERS SERIES
Original Bishop Family

Taming Him

Needing Him

Chasing Him

Keeping Him

SPIN-OFF'S
Friends of the Bishops

Make Me Stay

Roping the Cowboy

CIRCLE B RANCH SERIES
Bishop Family Second Generation

Hitching the Cowboy

Catching the Cowboy

Wrangling the Cowboy

Bossing the Cowboy

Kissing the Cowboy

Winning the Cowboy

Claiming the Cowboy

Tempting the Cowboy

Seducing the Cowboy

Out of all the prayers I've prayed
You're Heaven's answer
Out of all the hell I've been through
I never thought you'd be out there
But thank God you were right there, 'cause

"Never Til Now"
-Ashley Cooke, Brett Young

PROLOGUE
PAYTON

SEVEN YEARS EARLIER

I STARE at the empty glass of whiskey sitting in front of me. I'm the only person in the bar besides the owner. Some sad-ass country song plays on the jukebox, and when I glance down at my knuckles, I see the broken skin and red beads of blood pooling on the surface. I wipe it on my jeans, numb to everything that went on this evening.

"So are you gonna tell me what happened?" Of course Benny notices. He's in his late sixties and has run this little hole-in-the-wall since before I was born. My dad used to come here when he was my age. If he were alive, I'm sure he'd say it was the only thing in this town that hasn't changed.

"No." I'm not usually a man of many words, and tonight is no different.

He grabs the bottle of Wild Turkey 101 and pours me another drink—neat, just the way I like it. "This one's on me."

"Thanks," I tell him, biding my time because I know the sheriff is on his way to my mom's house. He might've just arrived.

Tonight, all the pent-up anger I've held against my stepdad finally snapped, and I did what my mother has begged me not to do a million times—decked him right in the face. And I'd be lying if I said it didn't feel good.

Actually, it was *better* than good. It felt fucking great.

For years, Stanley has physically, mentally, and emotionally abused my mother. I've offered to help her leave more times than I can count, and I brought it up again just an hour ago. Her answer never changes.

After Stan picked his tipsy ass up off the floor, he called the cops. Everyone in this town knows he's a piece of shit, but the law is the law, and I hit him first. Instead of waiting at the house for the cuffs to be slapped on my wrists, I decided to go out and get a drink to help me calm down.

"How're things since Edna?"

"The same," I explain, not wanting to think about my cheating ex. I take a long sip, the alcohol burning on the way down.

"That's a shame," he states. "She seemed like a nice girl."

I should've known better than to pursue a relationship with someone I worked with. For some reason, I thought what we had was different. It *wasn't*. Last Friday, I found her fuckin' James in the back of his truck. Now, whenever I have to look at her, I'm reminded of what she did and how badly she betrayed me. "Every day's a reminder that I wasn't good enough and never would be."

"Son, that's not true."

"Oh, it is. Not everyone is destined to get married or start a family. Pretty sure there's nothin' left for me in this shithole of a town."

He looks at me over his glasses. "Then why are you still here?"

His question crashes into me the way my fist slammed into

Stan's nose. I open my mouth before I can put my thoughts to words, then close it.

"This shithole of a town will *always* be here, Payton. Doesn't mean you have to be. Your mama ain't gonna leave Stanley. The woman you thought you'd marry slept with every ranch hand in a twenty-mile radius. And you're still here, hangin' on to hope like something's gonna change. It won't. Trust me. I've been here for sixty-eight years."

I've worked on the family ranch for over a decade, probably longer if you consider all the summers I put in during high school, but that means nothing to Stanley or my mother.

Before I can respond, Sheriff Landau walks in. He sits on the empty stool next to me and sucks in a deep breath. Benny opens a glass bottle of soda and sets it in front of him.

"You know why I'm here," he says, staring forward before turning to look at me.

"To arrest me?" I meet his eyes.

"No. Not this time. But Stanley doesn't want you back on the property."

My jaw clenches tight. "And my mother?"

He doesn't say anything.

I pound my fist on the bar. "She took his side again, didn't she?"

"I'm sorry, son. I wish I had better news." He clears his throat. "Stanley said your things will be on the porch waitin' for you. I'd suggest you let me go with you so there aren't any more altercations. The old fool said some disturbin' things, and I don't trust him."

I scoff. "I'll fuck him up."

"Payton, you know he has guns. They're goin' down to file a temporary restrainin' order on you first thing in the mornin'. I know this ain't fair for him to be runnin' ya off, but since the house and property are in his name, there ain't nothing I can do. Legally, he can say you're trespassing if you refuse to leave."

We sit in silence, other than shitty music playing. "You've got that look in your eye. Now don't be stupid and go ruinin' your future over that piece of shit. I wanted to warn ya because your father was my best friend growin' up. I gotta look after ya the best as I can, and well, I feel like I owe your pa as much. God rest his soul."

I suck in a deep breath, realizing that everything in my life has completely fallen apart.

"You got a place to stay tonight?" he asks.

"Yeah," I lie. I'll sleep in the back seat of my truck just as I did on many nights when Stanley got too drunk and confrontational.

Sheriff Landau slaps a five-dollar bill on the counter and tips his hat at Benny. Then he places a firm grip on my shoulder and pats it.

"Thank you," I tell him before he turns and walks out the door.

"You gonna be okay, kid?" Benny asks after a few minutes of me swirling the last gulp of my Wild Turkey.

"I always am," I say, pulling out my wallet to pay for my other drinks.

He holds out his hand and waves me off. "Your money's no good tonight."

"Happy New Year," I say, realizing it's officially January first.

"You too, Payton. Hopefully, it'll be a fresh start and your best year yet."

I give him an amused half grin because anything will be better than living here.

It's been two weeks since I left home with nothing more than a duffel bag of clothes, two pairs of boots, and my favorite cowboy hat. At twenty-seven, I'm moving away from the only home I've ever known. My mom apologized profusely, but her apologies don't mean shit anymore, not when she hands them out like Halloween candy. I told her I was taking a ranch hand job in Eldorado with over ten thousand acres.

I begged her to come with me, but she gave me the same answer I've always gotten—*I can't*. While I should be angry that she continues to choose him over me, I'm more disappointed that she doesn't trust me enough to keep her safe.

Before I left, I told Benny I was moving and thanked him for everything. He was one of the only adults in my life who listened. Without him, I'm not sure I'd have the courage to leave my idea of home behind.

Edna is already engaged to James, but considering she was pregnant with his baby before we broke up, I'm not even surprised. Even though she seemed more than happy to see me go, I had fallen in love with her. Or at least the version of her she wanted me to see. People warned me about dating someone I worked with, and I should've listened. Catching her ass up with someone I trusted was a hard way to learn a lesson, and it's a mistake I won't be making again.

Between the dramatic break-up and the fight with my stepdad, I experienced an avalanche of emotions in a short amount of time. Some might say I'm running away from my problems, but I need to learn who I am away from my hometown. Eldorado is the beginning of something new.

As I pull up to the bed and breakfast, my nerves get the best of me. It's a beautiful huge white house with a wraparound porch located on the Circle B Ranch. I might've grown up on a ranch, but it was *nothing* like this.

I look at the text message on my phone from Alex Bishop stating to meet him here at nine sharp. It's eight forty-five, but it's forty degrees, and my hands are turning into icicles. So I gather my courage and walk inside.

My stomach growls as soon as I smell fresh eggs and bacon. Clattering plates and chatter lead me to the dining room, where I run into an older clean-cut man with a gentle smile. Laughter wrinkles appear when he grins.

"Howdy. How can I help you?"

"Hey, I'm lookin' for Alex Bishop."

"You must be Payton. I'm John, his brother. I run this part of the ranch. I'm sure he'll be here any minute to give you the grand tour of the place. Welcome aboard." He holds out his hand and gives me a firm handshake.

When I turn around, I'm greeted by a man who looks exactly like him.

"Twins," I mutter with a smirk.

"Jackson," he states with a grip that could crush concrete. "I'm the good-lookin' one. Nice to meet ya."

"The dumb one." John snorts.

"I'm Payton," I tell him.

"Payton!" I hear a deep voice say my name. A blond man walks up, and it's obvious by their facial features they're all related. "Glad you made it." He checks his watch. "Punctual. I like that."

"Yes, sir."

"You hungry?" Alex asks but doesn't even give me a chance

to answer before walking toward the food. "Let's eat and chat, then I'll show you 'round."

"Hope you enjoy the ranch. We need all the help we can get," Jackson says as John busies himself with who I assume is a guest.

As we head to the buffet, my mouth waters as my eyes scan everything they offer.

"You're holdin' up the line. I'm cuttin'," a blond woman who looks a few years younger than me says.

"Go right ahead," I offer, taking a step back, even though she'd already moseyed her way between Alex and me.

She meets my eyes, then stops to take a look at me from head to toe. "You new here?"

"Somethin' like that."

"Who're you related to?" She throws a biscuit on her plate, then smothers it with gravy.

"No one," I respond, intrigued by the spitfire.

She chuckles. "Seriously? I was certain everyone in Eldorado was related to each other."

"I'm from East Texas. Saw the job posting and applied a couple of weeks ago."

"Take it easy on him, Kaitlyn. It's his first day. Don't need you runnin' him off with your sharp tongue. We need the help," Alex scolds, then faces me. "Sorry, she's my niece. Jackson's daughter. And the *loud* fruit doesn't fall far from the tree." He chuckles as Kaitlyn bumps him with her hip and nearly knocks him over.

She sets down a set of tongs and then holds out her hand.

When I take it, she continues. "Kaitlyn Bishop. And before you ask, I'm not married, have no kids, and I'm an oversharer, so get used to it. It's so nice to meet you."

I hold back my laughter because I definitely wasn't going to ask, but I appreciate the intro regardless. "I'm Payton Jamison. Not married or lookin' to be. Also no kids, but I don't typically make it a habit of sharing much. Pleasure's mine." I smirk, meeting her blue eyes that are zeroed in on me. She's cocky. I like that as much as I like honey on a biscuit.

"So how long are ya here, cowboy?" She stacks a blueberry muffin on the side of her plate as confidence oozes off her. I glance down when she walks to the other side of the buffet and notice how great those tan riding pants look hugging her perfect ass. Quickly, I push those thoughts away because it's the last thing I should be thinking about. If she works here on the ranch, she's already off-limits in my mind.

"It might only be temporary, but we'll see," I say, shamelessly staring at her as I become mesmerized by her flirty nature.

"That's what they *all* say. And then they taste the food and never leave." She snickers, lifting her plate. "See ya around, Payton."

Smiling as she walks to a table, I don't think I've ever quite met a woman like her.

CHAPTER ONE

KAITLYN

PRESENT DAY

My BODY HITS the dirt with a thud, and the wind is knocked out of me. As soon as I catch my breath, I get back up. I'm shocked I haven't broken a bone in the years I've been training, considering how many times I've fallen off. Widowmaker stares at me like I'm crazy as I wobble to my feet.

"Such a cunt," I say in an overly friendly tone so he doesn't think I'm scolding him. Right now, we're learning about each other, and I need to build trust when I'm in the saddle. Or these falls when he gets spooked will keep happening.

I've had this black Arabian in my possession since yesterday, and his owner did nothing but praise him. So I got cocky and thought this would be a breeze.

Wrong.

The day did *not* start how I had imagined, and it's only a quarter past seven. The dew from the early spring morning drips down the windows of the training facility. This place would've been a cloudy mess if I hadn't watered the dirt in the arena.

I dust off the front of my shirt and riding pants, then adjust my helmet while trying to fight the urge to scream. Once I'm calm and have walked it off, I look down at my smartwatch.

Ten minutes. That's how long I was in the saddle.

"Havin' trouble?" Dad asks from across the training area.

I scowl at his cheeky grin but keep my tone lighthearted.

"No, sir, this big boy's just bein' a little bitch and spooked at the sound of that helicopter flyin' over. I've had barn cats less jumpy during a thunderstorm."

"Yikes. That's not good."

"I know, but we just got started. New environment and all that. Have a feelin' this one's gonna give me a run for my money, though."

Dad stands next to me with his coffee mug in hand.

"After I fed him this morning, he nearly kicked me in the back of my head. Oh, and don't even dare pick up a rake around him. *Huge* mistake."

Dad holds out his free hand and slowly walks toward Widowmaker. Widowmaker sniffs his hand, then playfully nibbles on his fingers. "You're just a big ole baby, aren't ya?"

At times like this, I swear he's a horse whisperer or something.

"Not the B word I'd use but to each their own."

Dad glances over his shoulder with a knowing grin painted on his face. When he looks at me like this, I brace myself for him to give me *all* the answers. "Today's only his first day, and it might take him a tad longer to warm up to the place, but he'll get there."

"Did he tell you that?" I muse.

"Maybe he did."

"Yeah, well, you know his owner, Susan Henderson. She told me he better be ready before July. I told her I couldn't guarantee such a quick turnaround, and she said if he's not showroom ready by the beginning of June, she'd stop using us to train."

Dad huffs because he knows she's more of a pain in the ass than her horses. "She's been threatening that for twelve years, and after all this time, she's still yappin' like that little Chihuahua she brings everywhere. We don't rush perfection, Kaitlyn. Per the contract she happily signed, it will take as long as it takes. We guarantee a trained horse based on *our* metrics, not anyone else's. If she doesn't like it, I'll blacklist her for runnin' her mouth *again*. I hope you're charging her double."

I snicker, wishing I was brave enough to tell Susan those exact words.

"The only reason she's even allowed—"

"Because Mom likes her and thinks she's nice. Even though she's a ragin' bitch."

"Language."

I roll my eyes. "I'm thirty years old, Dad."

"And as long as you still live under my roof, I'll ground your ass. At any age." He laughs.

"Great. At this rate, you'll be punishing me for saying fuck when I'm fifty." I groan. Living at home saves money, especially since the majority of my time is spent working or hanging out with Payton.

"Well, when you move out, you can cuss all you want in your house. Then your mama and I can finally get some alone time back before we had all you kids," he teases, waggling his brows.

I pretend to gag. "I don't care how old I am, spare me. It's too early to hear you talkin' about doing the nasty with Mom."

"How do y'all think you were conceived?"

"Grandma told me there was a stork, and that's what I'm choosing to believe."

Chuckling, he shakes his head. "Oh, if you only knew. We were hot and heavy back in our early days."

"Gross. Considering y'all are as handsy as you are now, I don't want to imagine how y'all were back then."

He finally turns back to the horse. "When you build the

11

connection with Murderpaws, he won't spook. You know when he starts losing rhythm…"

"What did you just call him?" I arch a brow, holding back laughter.

"After a while, all these *killer* racehorse names start soundin' the same." He shrugs. "You're a pro at this. I'll leave ya to it."

"Thanks. We've wasted enough time this mornin'," I say, moving toward Widowmaker.

I place my foot in the stirrup and pull myself onto the saddle. Leaning down, I pat him, then we return to our warm-up walk before the real work begins.

I've been training horses since I was a teenager, and none of them have been the same, even though the principles and basics don't change. Not sure why I expected this big guy to be any different. He's only four and has a lot to learn.

Each time we pick up our pace, I give him praise so he knows he's done well. We work on the basics of moving in long straight strides. He gets fussy as we take a corner, so I turn him and do it again. When he gets it right, his excitement doesn't go unnoticed.

After an hour of training, I brush Widowmaker, then put him in his stall before getting Danger ready for his session. Keeping my horses on their training schedule is critical. If I fuck up one of my time slots, it will throw off the entire week, and I don't have time for that.

When Mom yells that it's lunchtime, I realize I've lost track of time again. If it weren't for her reminders, I'd skip meals because I get so focused.

After brushing Danger, I head to the front of the facility and wash my hands in the bathroom.

"Headin' to the B&B," I say, poking my head into the office where I catch my parents making out. "Oh, c'mon. Get a room."

"We've got one." Mom reaches over and shuts the door in my face. Even after all these years, they're grossly in love. One day, I wish to have what they do, but at this rate, I'll have more luck being struck by lightning.

"Kaitlyn?" she shouts behind the door before I can walk away. "Don't forget Zach will be late cleaning the stalls after school this week."

"I won't," I reply, then go to my truck.

Zach, my cousin's ten-year-old son, has been a lifesaver. Riley and Zoey, his parents, have encouraged him to get more involved, and since he loves horses so much, I offered him a side job as my official ranch hand helper. Although, he still has to get good grades, and homework comes before chores. His little brother, Zealand, is a few years younger than him and also loves horses. As he gets older, I suspect he'll want to pitch in too.

Several times per week, he helps in the barn to clean stalls and organize the tack room. On the weekends, he does the same but also enjoys hanging around the arena and watching me train. When school lets out for the summer next month, he'll be around a lot more, and I'll find him more stuff to stay busy. The kid loves ranch life so much, but it's all he's ever known. Hell, it's all any of us have ever known.

Walking up the porch steps into the B&B, I can already smell the fried chicken my cousin made. As the head chef, Maize plans all the menus for the guests and ranch hands. It's tradition to eat breakfast and lunch here, and sometimes dinner when I'm feeling lazy.

"Have you seen Gavin today?" Maize asks as soon as I reach for a plate. Her husband, Gavin, works at the training facility and helps break riding horses. He's also a retired bull rider who has trained others to be champions too.

"I saw him earlier, but we really didn't talk. We've been busy as hell today. The stables are full of horses."

"Damn. I'm trying to get all the ingredients together for Kane and Ivy's wedding cake. I need Gavin to run into town and grab me all the vanilla extract they have stocked at the grocery store."

I snort. "How did you run out of vanilla? Isn't that like a key ingredient?"

"Yes. Thank you, Miss Obvious." She places her hand on her hip and playfully rolls her eyes. "But if you must know, I've been making cupcakes for the bride-to-be to taste test. Then the other day, I turned around with a hot pan and knocked the glass jar of vanilla right off the counter. It shattered into a million pieces. I've never cried over spilt anything...until *that* very moment."

I try to hold back my laughter but fail.

She gives me a stern look. "It's not funny. It was imported from *Italy*! And there is no way a replacement bottle will arrive by this weekend, even if I pay for priority shipping. So now I'm gonna have to use some bullshit brand of vanilla *extract*—yes, it's different—which makes me so damn mad I could scream."

"Hey, it's gonna be fine. The wine bar will keep everyone preoccupied, and trust me when I say no one will know the difference other than you and your fancy-ass taste buds. Seriously, you can make a box cake taste like it's gourmet, so I have no doubt this will be just as delicious. The icing is what makes it, and I think they chose buttercream, right?"

Her face cracks into a smile, and she nods. "I guess you're right. I'm just nervous because of everyone's high expectations. It could be the shittiest cake any of y'all have ever had, but everyone would lie and say it's amazin'."

"If it sucks, I'll tell you the truth. How about that?"

"Deal. Speaking of the wedding...how're ya holdin' up?"

"Oh, you mean since I'll officially be the last to get married in the family? And now my brother, who I'd bet five hundred dollars I'd get married before, *actually* beat me to it. I'm happy for Kane but annoyed at myself."

"Just remember a broken clock is right twice a day."

I groan. "I'm a single Pringle with no prospects to mingle. Zero interested parties. What's wrong with me?"

"Nothing's wrong with ya. And there is one interested party.

You just won't give him the time of day." Her brows shoot up just as a firm hand squeezes my shoulder.

"Ready for lunch?" Payton asks. I meet my best friend's bright-blue eyes.

Maize crosses her arms over her chest and grins. She has this stupid idea that Payton likes me, but he's never given me any signals, so I've always pushed it away.

"I can wait until y'all are finished chattin'," he says politely.

"Oh, we're done. Trust me," I say, then walk toward the buffet line.

"I'm just sayin'! You know it's true." Maize laughs as she moves back to the kitchen.

"What's she talkin' about?"

"Nothin'. Don't listen to her," I tell him as I stack two drumsticks, a huge scoop of Grandma Bishop's famous potato salad, and green beans on my plate. I finish it off with a honey butter biscuit. Payton follows my lead.

My stomach growls when we sit at one of the long tables, and I'm thankful Mom reminded me to eat. I would've been hangry.

"How's work goin'?" I ask Payton just as he takes a huge bite of chicken.

"Nothing but a bunch of fuckin'," he says with a laugh, and it causes me to snort. "But that's the business."

Payton works at the stud operation with my older twin brothers, Kane and Knox. It's been super successful, and he's been their right-hand man since the very beginning. I honestly don't know how Knox pulled it off, considering how much trouble he used to get in. But since he married Hadleigh and had a couple of kids, he's a new man. *Sorta*. My brother can still be a raging asshole, but I love him regardless.

"What about you?" he asks.

"Same shit, different day. Though I fell off twice and nearly got kicked in the head this mornin' so that was fun."

"Yikes. Good thing you're as tough as nails."

"That's for damn sure. Nothing I can't handle. I'm gonna have that little pony trained whether he likes it or not. But get this, his name is Widowmaker."

"Fuck," Payton hisses. "Who'd he kill?"

"No one. *Yet*. Probably me, though, if he had the choice."

Payton has nearly cleaned his plate by the time I take a bite of potato salad and goes back to the buffet for round two. That's the thing about these ranch hands. They can eat a person out of house and home. As he picks up one set of tongs to get more chicken, I notice a cute brunette eye-fucking him. He laughs when they go for the same piece.

"It's all yours, sweetheart," he kindly tells her.

She smiles. "Go ahead. I'll take this one. It's bigger. You work on the ranch?"

"Yes, ma'am. Have been workin' on ranches my whole life."

"I can tell." The airy tone isn't lost on me. By the time they make it to the end of the line, she's nearly told him her life story and touched his arm at least three times. Not that I'm counting. Before walking away, she not-so-casually tells him she'll be staying at the B&B for the next week, then hands him her business card. "Call me sometime. Maybe you can show me 'round."

"Sure thing." He shoves the card in his pocket, then returns to the table.

He immediately digs into his second plate. I glare at him, and almost a whole minute passes before he notices.

"What? I got shit on my face or somethin'?"

I roll my eyes and lean forward, keeping my voice low. "You gonna call her?"

"Who?"

Is he really that dense? "That woman who just gave you her number with a side of cleavage."

He finishes chewing, then meets my gaze. "No. Why would I?"

"Because she's cute and obviously interested."

"So?"

"So? Jesus, Payton. We can't both stay single for the rest of our lives. At least you're gettin' hits. I don't think a man has blinked in my direction in two years."

He shrugs. "Then *you* call her. I'm good."

"She's gorgeous. Obviously has her shit together. Professional. And she has a nice ass."

"Didn't notice. The last thing I need to do is hook up with someone from out of town. My luck, she'd be a psycho. I'd knock her up, and she'd want to move to the city or some basic shit, and everything I love about my life would change. No thanks."

His rough confession has me snorting. "I honestly wish some rando would stay at the B&B and knock me up. Then he can go back to wherever he came from. A dream come true."

He chuckles. "Probably need a vacuum cleaner for those cobwebs."

"It hasn't been that long since I've had sex!" I throw my biscuit at him, but he catches it and takes a huge bite before setting it back down on my plate.

"If your cousin sees you wastin' food like that, she'll have your head."

"Wouldn't be the first time." I shrug just as Maize brings out more food.

He looks over his shoulder. "Better behave yourself."

"I know. She's already in a mood about some imported vanilla she spilled or some shit. Don't need to give her a reason to blow a gasket."

"There are three people on this ranch whose bad sides I hope to never get on. She's one of them," he admits.

"And the others?"

"Your grandma."

I chuckle. "And who else?"

"You. Actually, you're at the top of the list."

For some reason, that statement brings me joy. "Well, you know what I always say—don't start no shit, won't be no shit."

"No truer words have ever been spoken."

CHAPTER TWO

PAYTON

I sɪᴛ in the back of the little white chapel on Main Street with the rest of Eldorado to watch Kane Bishop marry the woman of his dreams—Ivy Callaway. The ceremony is perfect, but it's also a reminder of what's still missing in my life.

As far as I'm concerned, relationships aren't in my future. I've lived in Eldorado for over seven years, and I've been single ever since. Though there have been a few interested girls I've hooked up with, it was never serious.

As Kane and Ivy exchange their handwritten vows, I glance at my best friend standing next to Ivy. Kaitlyn may be wearing a smile, but she also has tearstained cheeks. Ninety percent of the time, she keeps herself guarded with a hard shell on the surface, but she's soft on the inside.

She's been vocal about being the only single adult Bishop left. She's her own worst enemy at times. Hell, so am I.

After Kane and Ivy seal their marriage with a kiss, they exit and are followed by the wedding party. As they go outside to take photos, Diesel comes up to me. "Where're ya headin'?"

"To the reception."

"Nah, you're coming with us. We need a lookout." He leads me to where Riley and Ethan are standing in the back of the church. They're holding two large boxes of condoms and window paint.

"We've gotta be quick," Ethan explains, taking the cap off the marker. "Let us know if anyone is comin'."

I nod, watching them and keeping an eye out.

They giggle like twelve-year-olds as they draw gigantic dicks on every window of Kane's truck. Diesel puts his mouth to the end of one of the condoms and starts to blow it up.

"First time you've had one of those in your mouth?" I laugh as Riley adds pubic hair.

"Shut the fuck up," Diesel whisper-shouts. "They taste disgustin', but someone's gotta do it."

"And we played rock, paper, scissors for it, and you lost. So keep blowin'." Riley slaps him on the back as Ethan continues embellishing his artwork.

After fifteen minutes, I get antsy with how long they're taking. "Hurry up." The music is so loud inside the venue we can hear it from here. I know that means the place is nearly full. My stomach growls. "I'm starvin' and wanna get some appetizers."

Ethan and Riley finish, then help Diesel tie ribbon to the end of the blown-up condoms. They secure them to the side mirrors of Kane's truck. When they're done, they step back and look at their handiwork.

"They're gonna kill you." I shake my head. "Their day is gonna be memorialized by huge hairy cocks and condom balloons. And one of you idiots spelled 'congrats' wrong. You're missing an R. Congats? What the hell is that?"

"Shit," Ethan mutters. He uncaps the marker, draws an arrow, then writes an R.

"Kane had this comin'. Plus, it's kinda like tradition."

"One your grandma hates. If anyone says anything to me, I'm tellin' them I wasn't involved."

Riley chuckles. "You're guilty by association. Now tell us if the coast is clear. I want to be inside before they're finished takin' pictures so Kane doesn't suspect a thing."

I do what he says as they ditch their evidence in Ethan's truck. As I round the corner, I see Jackson, Kiera, and Kaitlyn walking down the sidewalk. Kaitlyn looks pissed, and it makes me wonder what her dad said to set her off. He loves to joke around, even if it's at his kids' expense.

I return back to the guys. "People are comin'. Time to go inside."

The four of us enter the venue, and as they find their wives, I make my way to the wine bar. Music fills the room, and I might be one of the only people here over the age of thirty without a date.

After I get a glass of merlot, I scan the room for Kaitlyn. She has a glass of wine in each hand as she chats with Rowan, Maize, Harper, and Hadleigh. I make a mental note to keep my eye on her before she drinks her weight in alcohol.

Diesel's busy making funny faces in the photo booth with his kids. Other members of the family hug and chat with one another.

"Try the hors d'oeuvres," Alex tells me, just as one of the servers passes with something wrapped in bacon. I take one and am not disappointed. He gives me a thumbs-up as he heads toward his grandkids.

Just as I take a gulp of merlot, the DJ announces the entrance of the happy couple—Mr. and Mrs. Kane Bishop. The room echoes with cheers and applause as they move to the middle of the dance floor. While I never would've put the two of them together—just because of the ten-year age difference—it's undeniable how much they love each other and are good for one another. Everyone here knows it too.

"You off tomorrow?" Leo asks me. He's a younger ranch hand who just started at the beginning of the year.

"Just have to go feed the horses in the mornin', but considerin' it's a special night, the boss gave us off."

"What I'd do to work at the stud farm," he says, eyeing the bar, but I know he's not old enough to drink.

"It's hard work. I'm sure you'll get there eventually. Took me a couple of years."

"Yeah, but I don't think I'll be here that long."

I smirk. "Yeah, I said the same thing. Now I can't imagine being anywhere else."

We continue making small talk. When I finish my drink, I excuse myself, and my eyes land on Kaitlyn. She looks like she just finished ripping Knox a new one. He shakes his head as she grabs more booze, then struts toward her grandma's table. At least I know she'll behave over there.

On the way to get a bottle of water, I pass Knox.

"You should probably watch my sister. She's already talkin' shit."

I pop a brow but can't hold back a smile. "She told you off, didn't she?"

"Yeah, and if she downs another bottle of wine, every person in here is gonna get an earful."

"I'll keep an eye on her." I'd already decided to stop drinking because Kaitlyn won't be able to drive. At the rate she's downing the chardonnay, she won't make it to the cake cutting.

"Great, thanks." He lifts his glass of wine before walking off.

I snag a few boiled shrimp to calm my angry stomach, but they don't do much. I need real food.

"Hey, how's my honorary son doin' tonight?" Kiera grins, and when I meet her kind eyes, I notice how much Kaitlyn favors her.

"I'm doing great, Mrs. Bishop. You look lovely. The weddin' has been perfect."

Her smile widens. "It sure was. Now, it's time to eat because I'm starvin'."

I chuckle. "Me too."

"Dinner is startin' in about ten minutes. Gonna make my way to the table."

"Good thinkin'," I tell her, and we head that way. I sit in the first open chair since there isn't assigned seating.

"This seat taken?" a sweet familiar voice asks.

I look up at Kaitlyn. "Nope, all yours."

She plops down and nearly misses her chair, but I catch her before she falls on her ass.

"Jesus Christ, Kate. How much have you had to drink?"

"Three glasses of wine? Four? Wait. Five? I've lost count. A lot." She stumbles over her words.

"You're slurring. You have to give a speech after dinner," I remind her. She was super nervous about it a few days ago, but as long as she's not three sheets to the wind, she'll do great.

With a laugh and a wave of her hand, she confidently says, "I've got this. It's fine."

When a huge plate of chicken Alfredo pasta and garlic bread is served in front of me, I dive in. Kaitlyn drinks water as she eats, and I hope the carbs are enough to sober her up before she has to speak into that microphone. Otherwise, her parents will chew her up and spit her out, and considering she works with them, there'll be no avoiding them.

Once we're finished, the servers pick up our empty plates, and Kaitlyn seems to have snapped back to reality. The speeches begin with Jackson and Kiera, then Knox and his wife Hadleigh speak. I give Kaitlyn a quick nod before she makes her way up front. Before grabbing the mic, she helps herself to a fresh glass of wine.

Fuck.

She glances around the room with a shit-eating smirk. "Saving the best for last, I see."

I can't help but notice how her silk dress hugs her in all the right places, showing off her curves and the perfect amount of cleavage.

"Did y'all know Kane was *always* my favorite brother?" She glances at Knox, who's a good sport and laughs. She gives him the most shit out of the two of them. "Caring, compassionate, and not a complete and total…well, you can fill in the blank. Any word would fit. But seriously, Kane, this isn't a roast for your evil twin brother."

"It should be!" Diesel shouts, and the room roars with laughter.

"This is a celebration of love and commitment. Ivy, you're beautiful, and my brother is so lucky to be able to spend the rest of his life with you."

Kane meets Ivy's eyes before placing a kiss on her cheek.

"See, he knows," Kaitlyn sing-songs. "With that being said, I'd like to make a toast to my brother and his better half. Two of the most wonderful people I've ever had the pleasure to know found love in Eldorado. A miracle, trust me." She holds up her left hand. "No ring on this finger."

There isn't a straight face in the room. If horse training doesn't work out for her, she should consider standup comedy, even if it's at her own expense.

I'm proud of how great of a job she's doing with so much wine in her system. "Now, as Grandma always says, go make some babies. And yes, I'm available to watch your kids whenever you need me. Love y'all. Wishing you all the happiness, love, and laughter in the world. Congrats."

The applause is almost deafening. She returns to the table and finishes her glass, wearing her perfect white smile.

As the wedding planner makes the announcement for cutting the cake, the crowd moves to the other side of the room to watch.

Maize stands to the side with a nervous grin as Kane and Ivy carefully cut into it. Flashes from the professional photographers and cell phone cameras fill the room as they feed each other small bites of cake with their fingers.

"Mmm. This is the best cake I've ever had," Kane tells Maize, and I see her shoulders relax. Kaitlyn has another drink in her hand, which isn't surprising, considering that speech was the last thing on her list.

After we eat our cake, which is so delicious, I go back for seconds, and the lights are dimmed even more. Kaitlyn and I are nearly the only two people still sitting out of three hundred. I suck in a deep breath and look at her.

"Do you wanna dance?" I ask, even though I know dancing really isn't her thing.

"Sure, cowboy. Lead the way," she says, and I take her hand.

Her warm fingers wrap around my neck, and I grab her curvy hips. I try not to focus on her eyes, but she's staring at me with fire in her gaze. I spin her around and zero in on her. "Why are you looking at me like that?"

With a snort, she tries to brush it off, but I see a slight blush creep on her cheeks. "Wait, was I eye-fucking you?"

I smirk, not expecting anything different to come from her mouth. I love that she can hold her own even with her smart-ass brothers. "Probably the wine."

"*Definitely* the wine," she agrees, even though I willingly gave her that out.

Against my better judgment, I pull her closer and rest my palms right above her perfect ass. Leaning in, I bring my mouth to her ear and whisper, "I'm not lettin' you drive home tonight."

"Mm. Are you takin' me to *your* house instead?"

And there she is again, the flirty drunk Kaitlyn who says whatever is on her mind.

"*Woman...*" She's testing my willpower not to provoke her even more just to see what else she'd blurt out.

"What? Am I not your type or somethin'?" she asks with venom in her tone.

Unfortunately, we've been best friends for too long, so her intimidation tactics don't faze me. Instead, I stifle a laugh. "Oh, Kate. You've had way too much to drink, and while I find it adorable, it's also dangerous. You already don't have a filter, but this is Kaitlyn with her balls out."

She chuckles. "That was a good non-answer. You know what they say, a drunk man's lies are a sober man's truth."

I study her, wondering if she has feelings for me like that. At times, I've felt an underlying current streaming between us, but I've always ignored it. The last thing I'd ever want to do is screw something up with her or the Bishops.

She leans in and meets my ear with her lips. Her warm breath brushes against my skin, and I'm trying so damn hard to control myself, but she's pushing me. "Honestly, I just need you to pull my hair, fuck me raw, then knock me up."

I swallow hard and fist the silk material of her bridesmaid dress as the thoughts of doing that very thing nearly consume me.

We're close, almost too close, and for the first time in a long-ass time, Kaitlyn Bishop has made me speechless. And she notices.

"Well?" She turns around, rubbing her ass on my rock-hard cock, and I nearly get lost in the moment. She continues to grind against me, and it feels so goddamn good that I'm tempted to take her into the bathroom and give her exactly what she's begging for.

"I don't know how to respond to that, Kate."

"All you need to say is yes." Kaitlyn spins back toward me, wrapping her arms around my neck. She has me thinking inappropriate thoughts from the way she's looking at me. "Or not."

Before I can say anything, another ranch hand comes over and tries to cut in, but Kaitlyn tells him no thanks.

"I've never seen a woman reject switching dance partners."

"He's too young for me."

"He's twenty," I deadpan.

She leans in and whispers, "I want a *man*, Payton. Not someone who can't even legally buy me a drink."

"Goddamn." I hear Knox say as he spins Hadleigh around. "You tryin' to make babies on the dance floor?"

Kaitlyn transitions from a seductive prowess to Satan in all of two seconds. She pushes away from me, then apologizes to Hadleigh before she cuts in.

She stabs her finger into his chest. "Don't make me knee you in the dick because so help me God, I will take you down," she threatens loud enough for Hadleigh and me to hear.

Knox laughs loudly, which only pisses her off even more.

"Okay, okay, that's enough brotherly and sisterly love for tonight," I say, yanking Kaitlyn away before she causes a scene.

She's a seething mess.

"You good?" I ask, noticing the color drain from her face.

"I think I'm gonna be sick," she admits, so I lead her to the ladies' room. She goes inside, and after five minutes, I go in and check on her. Kaitlyn's bent over the toilet, dry heaving.

I stand behind her, pulling her hair to the side and rubbing her back. "This a good time to say I told you so?"

"Shut up," she groans, and I bite back a laugh.

Once I'm certain she's done for the time being, I ask if she's ready to go. She won't make it through the rest of the evening.

She nods, and I help her to her feet, then make sure she's stable before leading her out the door. Instead of going through the reception area, I walk toward the back exit and hope we can escape without her having to chat with everyone.

I know she'll hate missing Kane and Ivy's send-off and will regret not seeing all those dicks on her brother's truck, but if she stays any longer, she'll be puking on the dance floor.

With my arm firmly wrapped around her waist, I steady her as we walk around the building. Carrying her would've been easier, but Kaitlyn's too proud to let that happen, so I tightened my grip to prevent her from tripping over her feet.

As soon as I reach the passenger door, I dig my keys from my pocket, unlock the truck, and help her inside.

"You okay?" I ask once she's buckled.

She nods with her eyes closed and head tilted back. "For now."

Once I'm in, I start the drive back to the ranch. Kaitlyn leans her cheek against the cool window. "I need air. I might…"

"Don't you dare blow chunks in my truck," I warn, pulling off onto the side of the road. When she struggles to open the door, I rush around to the other side and help her out.

Seconds later, round two begins, and I hold back her hair once again. After a few moments, she takes a deep breath and wipes her mouth with the back of her hand. "Okay, I'm fine now. Let's go back to the reception."

"Kate…" I warn, knowing that would be a horrible idea. "I think the night is over."

Her shoulders slump in defeat. "Fine, Mr. Party Pooper."

Once we're both back inside the truck, we continue our journey. I roll down the window for her because the fresh air seems to help. The gravel road to my house gets bumpy, so I take it as slow as possible to keep her comfortable. She leans her head back on the seat and closes her eyes.

"How much longer?"

"Five minutes."

"I swear it feels like we drove to Mordor."

I chuckle. "You're such a nerd."

Her eyes pop open. "And you're a nerd for knowing *The Lord of the Rings* reference."

"Touché."

After I park, I help her up the porch stairs. It's times like this that I'm grateful I moved out of the ranch hand quarters. When the stud operation opened and I was asked to help run it with the twins, I knew I wanted to spend the rest of my life in Eldorado. I was given the opportunity to lease a slice of land and build a house on-site. My place is much bigger than what I currently need, but I know I'll need the space if I ever have a family.

Two weeks after the property agreement was signed, they poured the foundation for the barndominium, and I've been living in it ever since it was completed.

Kaitlyn immediately kicks off her high heels and struts to the breakfast bar. She nearly falls while trying to sit on one of the tall stools but manages to steady herself. With a sly grin, she looks at me. "I'd like some of that, please."

She points at the small bottle of Fireball that she left here after movie night last week.

Instead of giving her what she wants, I pour her a glass of water, then set it down in front of her. She flashes a death glare. "Oh, come on. I even said *please*!"

"Blowing chunks twice in an hour wasn't enough for you?" I arch a brow.

She rolls her eyes, then takes a sip.

"You need to hydrate because you've still gotta get up in the morning and feed your horses. I already know you're gonna feel like utter shit when six o'clock rolls around. Mixing booze is the worst thing you could do."

The frown on her face has me laughing.

"Nah, once I throw up, I'm good."

"I've heard that one before. Two New Year's Eves ago and guess what?"

Kaitlyn eyes me as she takes another gulp of water. "I felt like ass the next day."

"Yep. I know you well enough to know when you need to be cut off."

She chugs the rest of the water and sets the empty cup on the counter.

"Time to get some sleep. You can have my king-sized bed if

you want, and I'll take the spare room." It's just a twin mattress, but I'll manage for a night.

"Perfect," she slurs with a smile. As she stumbles her way down the hall, I grab a cleaning bucket from under the sink.

When I walk into my room, Kaitlyn's struggling with the zipper on her dress. She moves her blond hair off her neck and looks at me with a heated gaze. Silently, I step forward and slowly unzip it. The fabric slides from her body, and when she turns to face me, she gives me the perfect view of her silky black lingerie. Her breasts are falling out of her bra, and I inhale deeply to keep myself from saying anything embarrassing.

"I wasn't kidding about what I said at the wedding. I know you—"

"We shouldn't talk about this when you're shit-faced. Do you want one of my T-shirts to sleep in?"

She looks disappointed as she shakes her head and saunters over to the bed. Kaitlyn folds the quilt down and climbs under the sheets. Her head falls against the pillow as she pats the vacant space next to her. "Join me."

I stare at her for a moment, contemplating doing that very thing. A million different scenarios flash through my mind, and the thought of having her warm body pressed against mine all night is tempting as hell. But I don't allow myself to go there. Instead, I lock my jaw in place and move the bucket closer.

"Good night, Kate. That's just in case ya need it."

She flashes a mischievous smile as I turn and walk out of the room before I do something stupid like take her up on her drunken offer. As I make my way toward the living room, Kaitlyn yells, "I know you want to! I could see it in your eyes."

She couldn't be more right.

CHAPTER THREE

KAITLYN

I WAKE up to Payton's firm palm on my shoulder. It takes a few seconds before my eyes adjust, but I immediately smell coffee.

"Mornin'," he says in his gruff tone. I sit up and realize I'm in my bra and panties, so I quickly lift the sheet to cover myself. When he hands me the cup, I inhale the scent of freshly roasted beans.

"Mornin'. What time is it?"

"Just after six."

My head throbs as soon as I adjust my position. "Shit. I drank too much."

He chuckles darkly. "That's the understatement of the century. How do ya feel?"

"Like someone punched me in the back of the skull and then threw me in front of a tractor. Please tell me I didn't embarrass myself." I suck in a deep breath, hoping I can look my parents in the face later.

"Nah, I got you outta there before you made a complete and utter ass outta yourself."

"Thank God. I probably wouldn't have ever lived it down.

My brothers don't tend to forget shit very easily." I take a small sip of the coffee, wishing the caffeine would jolt me awake.

"Well…" He lingers, then stands. "Guess I'll let you get dressed."

"I'm not puttin' that back on." I point at the heap of silk lying on the floor.

Payton chuckles as he walks to his dresser. He slides open the bottom drawer and pulls out some clothes.

"Here ya go." He tosses them on the mattress.

"The last time I wore this shirt, I spilled beer all over me." I laugh at the memory as Payton walks out. I find it sweet that he has my old clothes in a drawer. I put it on along with a pair of old shorts, then make my way to the bathroom.

When I return to his bedroom, I bend over to grab my dress off the floor, and the world feels like it shifts on its axis. "Shit," I whisper-hiss, realizing just how terrible my day will be. Then again, just like Dad always says, for every action, there's a reaction. I fully set myself up for this disaster when I was double-fisting glasses of wine last night, but at the time, it helped me cope.

Once I've grabbed my shit, I pick up my mug and go into the living room.

"Hungry?"

I throw my dress on the back of the couch, then move toward the kitchen. "Depends. Whatcha got?"

He opens the cabinet and pulls out a box of strawberry Pop-Tarts. "This is about it."

"I'm gonna have to pass. Processed food is the last thing I should eat after a night of drinkin'."

Payton smirks, then pulls a to-go box from the microwave. "Just kiddin'. I stopped by the B&B and picked you up some biscuits and gravy with triple sausage patties. After your bender, you need carbs."

"See, this is why I love you."

He smirks. "And I'll even help you feed your horses too. I got up early and took care of my tasks so I'd have time."

"Don't know what I did in a past life to deserve you as a best friend, but I'm glad I have you."

He hands me a fork, and I happily take it.

"Not that I need rescuing, but you always have my back when I need it the most," I admit, digging in.

"You'd do it for me."

"Very true." I let out a moan as I finish one side of the biscuit that's still warm. Maize's cooking hits the spot, and I'm already feeling like a new human. "This is delicious."

"I know. I had a plate or two before coming back."

As I eat every bite of the food, Payton places my dress and heels in a bag. I clean up my mess, then he gives me a pair of his oversized flip-flops to wear when he drives me home to change. No way am I going to the stables dressed like I'm doing a drunken walk of shame.

When he turns into the long driveway, I notice my dad's truck is gone, which means my parents are either at the training facility or eating at the B&B. Though it wouldn't matter if they were home or not because I come and go as I please, even if Dad still jokes about grounding me. It's been nice living with them because they live close to the training facility and only ten minutes from Payton.

Payton parks, then follows me inside my house.

The house is pitch black except for a small lamp that's warmly glowing in the living room. On days like this, I wish I could just crawl into bed and sleep until the afternoon, but that's just not reality when working on a ranch.

I push open my bedroom door and allow Payton inside. After grabbing some jeans, a T-shirt, and my boots, I make my way to the bathroom to change and brush my wild, tangled hair. Even though I'm sluggish, and my head is killing me, I somehow manage to look presentable. I grab some water and medicine for my hangover.

When I step into my room to ask Payton if he's ready, I see him standing by my desk. He's holding a piece of paper in his hand.

"What's all this?" He turns to face me, his lips turned into a frown.

I move closer because I have so much scattered around that I'm not sure what he's referring to. As soon as I see the header on the page, I smirk. He's found my sperm bank printouts.

"Just searching for my future baby daddy."

He raises a curious brow.

"I've wanted a family for as long as I can remember. I've watched all my cousins and brothers fall in love and start their families. I know it's cliché as fuck, but I can't help feeling like my life is passing me by with no real purpose." I've never said those words out loud to anyone.

"Kate," he says softly.

I think about my failed attempts at relationships and how tired I am of waiting for Mr. Right. "You know dating hasn't worked out for me, Payton. And I get it. I'm not girlfriend material, but I can't let that stop me from getting what I want. It took me a long time to decide on this, and I like to call it my new and improved plan A. I'm convinced that if I don't take matters into my own hands, I'll never get the chance to be a mom. I'm not getting any younger."

I swallow hard, realizing I've said too much, something he should be used to by now.

Wanting to shift the conversation away from my inability to find a man, I take the pages, clear my throat, then read the first one out loud. "Age thirty. Blond hair. Blue eyes. Athletic build. Engineer. Enjoys fishing and getting his hands dirty." I smirk at him. "Doesn't this sound like the perfect guy? He's my age, intelligent, patient enough to fish, and a hard worker."

Payton's crystal-blue eyes peer into mine, and I have to look away before the intensity burns my skin.

"I don't understand how this works," he finally speaks up.

"There are donor websites where women can search for specific characteristics. Just think of it like a *build-a-baby*. You get detailed descriptions and even sound clips of their voices sometimes. I seriously listened to them for hours one night while polishing off some Fireball. Their slogan should be, *get pregnant with no strings attached*." I laugh, and Payton smiles, but I think it's just to appease me. It's obvious he's tense by his clenched jaw.

"I think I'm at a loss for words."

"That's okay. I don't need you to say anything. It's basically like what you guys do for the stud farm, but for humans. The goods are frozen and shipped straight to my door within two business days." I glance at the pages again, then scatter them on my desk. "I've tried to narrow it down and study their baby pictures. They don't show current photos for privacy reasons, so I've been using my imagination."

I grab one of the pages. "See, here's one."

He looks at the photo of a two-year-old and then back at me. "Sounds like you have enough options to find the perfect match that checks all your boxes."

"I hope so. At least the options are endless, but it's a big decision. Someone can look great on paper but be a psycho in real life."

His face cracks into a soft smile. "That's true."

After I reorganize the stack, I turn to Payton. "But anyway, ya ready to go? I swear those horses know when I'm late."

"Sure."

As I turn to lock up, my parents drive up.

"Well, look what the cat dragged in," Dad says with a chuckle. "Surprised you're even standin' after last night."

"Doesn't surprise me. You are your father's daughter," Mom teases.

I nod and turn my attention to my father. "Exactly, this is actually your fault. I got your stubborn Bishop genes that don't give two shits about consequences."

He holds up his hand to give me a high five, and Mom shakes her head.

"Good mornin', Payton." My parents greet him in unison.

"Mornin'."

"Y'all hungry? We just had biscuits and gravy at the B&B, and it was really good today." Dad pats his stomach.

"We already ate," I tell them as we make our way toward Payton's truck. "Going to go feed. I'll be back later."

Dad wraps his arm around mom's shoulders, then flashes me a wink. "Take your time."

Once we arrive, I walk past each stall and say hello to each horse by name.

Payton chuckles behind me as we move toward the storeroom where the feed is stored. "You're like a Disney Princess."

"What? How so?"

"Good morning, pumpkin. Good morning, pecan pie. Hello, Cinnabon. And it's like they anxiously await your arrival."

I playfully smack his chest. "You know that's not their names. This ain't the goat farm."

My cousin Ethan runs that part of the ranch, and they're all named after desserts.

"My horses have sophisticated show names like Widowmaker and Sergeant Rogue," I say smugly. "And they're treated like royalty."

"Just like their trainer."

Payton sets out buckets, then grabs the alfalfa bales and distributes them while I portion out the food. They eat a balanced diet so they can perform at a high level.

After they're fed, Payton and I wait around for them to finish.

Since it's a no-training day, I want to put them in the pastures to graze. When we finally leave the barn, the bright sun pokes at this headache I've been trying to ignore since I woke up. I can't wait to get home, close my curtains, and go back to bed.

"Damn." Payton groans, blocking the sun from his eyes as we walk toward his truck.

"Seriously. Not looking forward to the summer months, considering it's already this hot."

"Oh yeah. It's gonna suck," Payton agrees as we head back to my house.

"Breeding season," we say in unison.

Since a mare's heat cycle is late April to August, the chaos has just started for them. Next week is when the real fun begins. Soon, their stables will be full, and they'll rotate in and out for months. My brothers created one of the most successful breeding operations in the state. I honestly don't think they would've been able to pull it off so successfully without Payton's help.

Though we're mindlessly chatting, I can tell weird energy floats between us. When I open my mouth to ask, he talks at the same time.

"Sorry, go ahead."

"No, you start first," I urge.

He glances at me before putting his eyes back on the road. "I was just gonna ask if you're serious about using a sperm donor."

"Yes. It might be my only option. Hey, since you have so much experience helping horses get pregnant, maybe you can help me out when the special sauce comes in the mail?"

He chuckles. "We do have a one-hundred-percent rate of conception."

I smirk but am nervous about the process and scared it won't work. "I hope I have the same stats. Do you think it's a bad idea?"

"It's your body and your choice, Kate. I'll support whatever you want to do because I just want you to be happy."

He pulls up to my house, and before I get out, I turn to him. "One day, you're going to make someone really happy."

Payton grips the steering wheel. "I could say the same about you."

"Thanks for helping me today and last night. I owe ya one."

"Any time."

I wave before getting out of the truck, and when I get into my room, my mind is still reeling.

When it comes to finding a partner, I'm doomed, but at least he still has a chance to find love. And I hope he does.

CHAPTER FOUR

PAYTON

IT'S BEEN a few days since I found out about Kaitlyn's plan to find a sperm donor, and if I'm being honest, it hasn't set well with me. I know women do this all the time, and I will support anyone's personal choices, but I can't imagine her being pregnant by some stranger she's never met. By how much research she's done, it's obvious she's more focused on getting pregnant than ever before. I meant what I said and will offer my support to her in whatever capacity she needs. I just want her to make the right choice for her, whatever that may be.

"You still watchin' Netflix with my sister tonight?" Kane asks while rounding the corner in the barn.

"Yep, that's the plan." I drop a few bales of hay from the top loft.

On Wednesdays, we usually catch up on our favorite show unless we're both so tired we can't stay awake long enough to finish an episode. I offered to make cheeseburgers for dinner tonight because Kaitlyn mentioned craving them.

"I think Mr. Patrick's pullin' up right now," Kane announces as I climb down the ladder.

"I got it." I remove my gloves and shove them into my back pocket.

"Send him to the office once you get 'er unloaded."

"Will do." We've waited two hours for this horse to arrive. The owner called and said he was running late, which threw off our schedule. Instead of being idle, I've been trying to get ready for the evening feedings.

I move the hay out of the main entryway just as a dually diesel truck with a gooseneck trailer comes barreling down the road. The guy gets out and apologizes at least three times. I actually feel bad for him because he looks stressed.

"Had a blowout, then had to get the trailer tire changed, and roadside service took their sweet time. I woulda changed it myself, but my spare was flat too."

"It's not a big deal." I offer a smile and introduce myself before sending him to Kane's office.

After he walks away, I carefully back the horse out of the trailer. The sequestered studs run to the edge of their pastures to check out the new lady in town. I lead her to the freshly cleaned stall that will be hers for the next month, then take several pictures. I search for wounds and scarring, really anything that could be an issue just so we aren't held responsible. She looks great, though, and seems gentle.

I poke my head into the office and let Kane know I've finished boarding her before completing my final tasks. As I reorganized the feed room for tomorrow, I can't stop thinking about Kaitlyn.

What she said at the wedding as we danced has played on repeat in my mind. After learning about her future plans, I wonder if she was serious about wanting me to knock her up or if she was just tugging my balls. I don't always know because drunk Kaitlyn is just as honest as sober Kaitlyn. I'm beginning to wonder if there's more truth behind her jokes, and now I'm questioning everything.

I'm not sure if she remembers anything from that night, but I won't be able to think about anything else until I confront her. There's been a lot on my mind lately, and I'm trying to work up the courage to just put it out there.

Where do I even begin?

"Shit," I whisper under my breath, not knowing why I'm so damn nervous.

After I finish my duties, I tell Kane I'm heading out. Knox took a half day to help with the kids, so we've been busting ass and running the place without him. I don't mind, though. It's respectable that the twins can run a successful business and still make time for their families, but I'm not surprised because all the Bishops are the same.

On the way home, I listen to country music to clear my mind. But the lyrics are a little too close to home, so I turn it off. I don't see her truck when I park in my driveway, so I quickly go inside and shower. As I'm drying off, my phone buzzes on the bathroom counter, and I read the text.

Kaitlyn: Heading over now.

Payton: See ya soon.

She's all of ten minutes away, so I put on some clothes and fire up the flat top grill on my back porch. I pound the hamburger meat into hefty-sized patties. By the time she arrives, they're cooking but barely brown.

"Mmm, smells good." She looks over my shoulder.

I chuckle, turning my head toward her and catching a hint of her flowery shampoo.

"They'll be a few minutes."

"I was talkin' about you," she taunts, then walks around to sit in the patio chair.

"I smelled like horse shit and sweat twenty minutes ago."

"Some ladies like that."

"I heard about a ranch hand selling his dirty, worked-in socks on the internet. Got like two-hundred bucks for them."

"Damn, I should look into that. Or selling my panties. Bet I'd make enough to build my own house." She chuckles, staring into the distance as the sun begins to set. Splashes of purples and pinks fill the sky as a cool spring breeze brushes against our skin. "This view should be illegal."

I look at her, with her legs propped up on the table, thinking the same thing. I swallow hard and get back to reality. "It's why I chose to build here. Love gettin' up in the mornin' and coming out on the porch. I've seen a few deer grazing and rabbits."

Kaitlyn grins. "And you called me the Disney Princess."

I laugh. "You are. But I'm lucky to have this place." I think about where I'd be if I hadn't moved to Eldorado. This ranch saved me from a future full of mistakes.

She keeps her focus on the rolling hills in the distance. "I think every person who's ever set foot on Circle B is lucky. Not a day passes when I don't appreciate where I came from. While it's hard work growing up and workin' on a ranch, it's a privilege. Couldn't imagine being raised in a city or living in a small apartment."

"I can relate to that."

"I think it's why I'm so determined to get pregnant. I want to share all of this. Teach a child of my own about ranch life. When I'm gone, I want my legacy to live on through my kids. And their kids. Kinda like Grandma. I strive to be just like her."

Considering she brought it up, I feel like this is my chance to ask the question that's been burning in my mind all day. "Were you serious about what you said at the wedding?" I meet her eyes when she faces me.

"I don't know. What'd I say? I was inebriated, and words just roll off my tongue when I drink way too much. In fact, I had to do some mighty fine apologizin' to Knox over how I acted."

"Yeah, you were being a dick toward him, but he usually deserves it."

I add double cheese to the meat and let it melt before removing them. While the patties rest, I throw some Texas toast on the flat top.

"So ya gonna tell me what I said or pussyfoot around?" she blurts out.

I clear my throat, keeping my gaze on the grill. "If my memory recalls, you wanted me to pull your hair, fuck you raw, then knock you up."

She bursts into a roar of laughter. "Oh yeah, I totally remember saying that."

"Did you mean it?" I flip the bread, then glance back at her.

With a tilted head and a sexy smirk, she nods. "Oh, I was dead serious. But since you didn't jump for joy at the idea, I figured you didn't want to hurt my feelings. So a sperm donor will do."

The thought of her wanting me to do those things has me growing hard. Though I try to ignore those feelings, my heart says yes, but my head says no.

I grab the plate of burgers and toast, then she gets up to help. Once we're inside, I pull some baked beans from the microwave, and we make our plates.

"Can we eat outside?" she asks.

"Absolutely." I bring everything to the table, and we take a seat. She sits so close that her knee touches mine.

"What's on your mind?" she finally asks when silence brews between us. There's a little mayo on the corner of her mouth, and I lean over to wipe it off.

"I don't know how to even start this conversation, so I'm just gonna say it. Instead of choosing some random guy based on his baby photo and family history, let me help you."

Kaitlyn stops chewing, and her brows rise.

"I know it's a wild idea, but hear me out. I'm thirty-four and have always wanted kids too. I'm not asking you to marry me or even be in a relationship, nothing like that. I live on the ranch and can help raise a baby with you so you won't have to do it alone. And I check all your boxes—blue eyes, blond hair, smart, good lookin', intelligent, and healthy. I'm literally what you're lookin' for on those pages."

She blushes. "You definitely do. So…you'd just offer me your sperm to insert instead?"

"I was actually thinkin' the old-fashioned way…by having sex."

She gulps. "Oh."

"Of course, it'd just be transactional until you were pregnant." I fidget nervously as I wait for her response. Even saying it aloud sounds crazy, but I can't imagine having a baby with anyone else.

"So we'd remain friends and co-parent? Rotating weekends and all that?"

"I haven't figured out all the details yet, but I'd be there whenever you needed me. You could even move in, so neither of us had to share custody. Roommates who share the responsibilities. I built this big house for when I had a family. I have four bedrooms and two bathrooms for just me, so there's plenty of space. You'd have your own room, and we could set up a nursery in one of the others. Either way, you wouldn't have to do it alone, and we'd both get what we want in the end."

She swallows hard as if the food is stuck in her throat. Finally, she blinks. "Wow…that's a lot to process, but it does make sense. We get along great as friends, so I'm sure we'd co-parent just as well. Not to mention, I'd love to move out of my parents' house and have space for a baby. I wouldn't want this to ruin the dynamic of our friendship because you're literally the only person I've got. If we did this…there'd need to be rules and boundaries so things don't get messy or complicated."

"Of course. Ruining our friendship is one of my biggest fears, but doing this together as friends would be amazing. Though I never got along with my stepdad, I loved my real dad. All I'm asking is for you to think about it before you overnight a gallon of sperm to your house."

She chuckles at my exaggeration. "Okay. I'll think about it."

Her heartbeat ticks in her neck, and I wonder if our attraction is mutual. Fucking up our friendship is the last thing I want, and it's why I've always been so damn scared of making a move. Since I've been burned in the past, I refuse to make the same mistake twice.

We finish eating as the sun sets, and then we head inside.

"Dinner was amazing. I swear that was the best cheeseburger I've ever had."

"Yeah, it was good and juicy," I gloat. "I'm sorry, but Maize is missing out by not serving burgers."

Kaitlyn snorts as she rinses the dishes. "She's a food snob. Always has been, always will be."

"If I had her skills, I'd be too."

After she puts the plates and forks in the dishwasher, we go sit in the living room to start our show. We fall into our routine like I didn't just offer to knock her up.

"So I have a question," Kaitlyn asks once it ends, though neither of us paid close attention.

"Okay, shoot." I turn toward her, wrapping my arm over the couch.

"What's one thing you've always wanted? Like for me, it's to have a family and raise babies. It's all I've ever thought about since I was a kid. I want five children, just like my grandparents have. It seems like the perfect number."

"You really wanna know?"

"Of course."

I scratch my cheek. "Well, I've always wanted to start a horse rescue. I love working at the stud farm, but I'm more passionate about helping animals that need a second chance. Maybe it's because I can relate, but it's important to me to help the ones that can't speak for themselves. So many horses have been abandoned because of age or injury, or they're neglected and abused. It makes me so fucking sad and angry. I wish I could do more to make a difference. The local rescues are completely overwhelmed, and many don't want to deal with large animals."

Kaitlyn places her warm hand on top of mine. "This could be a reality, Payton. Let me help you do this."

I shrug. "I wish. The start-up costs alone would be out of my reach. Not to mention, I'm already working full-time hours at the stud farm. I'd need some extra ranch hands, a barn with nice stalls, and a pretty large piece of land for pastures."

"If my idiot brother can start up his own operation, there's no reason you can't do a horse rescue. Do you have any sort of business plan written up? Or ideas fleshed out?"

"Not really. I did some research a few years ago after I read this sad article about this rehabilitated horse that had to be shipped all over because the rescues had been so inundated. I don't know where to start with creating a nonprofit organization, but I'm sure I could figure it out if I was given the opportunity."

"Making this a reality seems doable to me."

I search her face. "Wait, are you serious?"

"Of course! My family's passionate about rescuing animals and expanding the ranch. I think they'd be interested."

I smile wide. "A new facility in the state would be so damn helpful."

"I love the idea! I'm kinda mad I didn't think of it myself." She snickers. "If you can get the business details together, we can present the plan to my dad for his approval. Then he could bring it to everyone else."

I lean over and pull Kaitlyn into my arms. "You have no idea how much I appreciate you."

She grins wide as we pull apart. "I love that we're both passionate about horses. My parents are gonna love this. I just know it. Don't be surprised if they're volunteering their asses off after they retire."

"That would be a dream come true." I beam. I can't explain the happiness that washes over me. If she agrees to my baby proposition, then I'd have everything I've ever dreamed of.

Kaitlyn stretches and yawns as she stands, giving me a small peek of her bare stomach. She leads the way to the front door, and then I walk her to her truck.

"Thanks so much for dinner and a movie. And the great conversation."

"You're welcome. *Please* think about what I said earlier," I nearly beg. I don't want to keep imagining her having some random man's baby.

"I will. It's gonna take a day or two to wrap my head around it, but I won't make any drastic decisions before talking to you first."

I wrap my arms around her, pulling her close and enveloping her in my warmth.

"When you can, get some details together for the rescue so my dad and uncles can review it. The sooner we get approval, the sooner we can get it started," she tells me as unwanted space forms between us.

"I will."

Kaitlyn gets in her truck and backs out of the driveway. I watch her taillights disappear in the distance, then look up at the twinkling stars and hope like hell she understands how important this is to me. She's been my best friend for years, and if it's a baby she wants, I want to be the one who gives that to her.

I can live with being just friends if I never have to live without her.

CHAPTER FIVE

KAITLYN

AFTER CHATTING with Payton a few days ago, I haven't stopped thinking about his offer. He nearly *begged* me not to pick a sperm donor and let him be the one to get me pregnant. The longer I think about it, the crazier it sounds.

However, it'd mean having a partner to help and our kid growing up with both parents involved. Not to mention, Payton would have the opportunity to be a dad.

This proposition has its perks, but the whole *sleeping with my best friend and sticking to our rules* will be hard. I've never had a one-night stand, so I've never had to deal with the awkward aftermath.

What if I can't even look at him after we do it?

What if I don't end up getting pregnant, and we slept together for nothing?

What if he changes his mind after we have sex for the first time?

My mind floods with doubts and possibilities, keeping me preoccupied while I'm supposed to be working. Instead of risking my life and getting kicked by Malice, I quickly remove the gear, then put him in a stall. Once he's settled, I head to the B&B for lunch.

"Hey, Uncle John!" I greet as I poke my head into the office.

"Hey, kiddo. How's it goin'?"

"Just fine. You workin' hard or hardly workin'?" I tease, eyeing his feet propped up on the desk as he sits back in a chair.

"Little bit of both, actually." He smirks. "Waitin' on Mila so we can run some errands."

"Aw...how sweet. Like an old couple day date."

His gaze wanders over my shoulder, and my back straightens when I hear a throat clearing.

"Who ya callin' old?" Mila stands next to me with her arms crossed.

"Did I say *old*? Oh no, you misheard me. I meant *older*. As in, just a little older than me." I swallow hard, then add, "And wiser!"

John snorts at my failed attempt to cover my ass. I stand with my wrists casually crossed in front of me.

"Uh-huh." Mila's brows rise. "Older, wiser, and going deaf, right?"

"Oh, c'mon, y'all know I was just givin' y'all a hard time. "Fifties are the new thirties."

"In that case, I'm still a teenager!" Maize's voice makes me jump. She walks up behind me, laughing at my expression. "They makin' ya sweat?"

"Nah. Your parents don't scare me."

"They shouldn't. They're softies." Maize cracks up.

"Don't be tellin' people that. I have a reputation to protect." Uncle John stands, goes to Mila, then pulls her in for a side hug. "Ain't that right?"

"Mm-hmm," she responds, dragging him closer before smacking her lips to his.

"Y'all are gonna make me lose my appetite." I groan at their cute PDA.

"Welcome to my life." Maize sighs.

"Y'all are welcome to leave," John states.

"Don't worry, I am." I turn and head toward the dining room. Maize catches up with me, and I notice she's not wearing her chef jacket. "You not workin' today?"

"Half day. Told my staff to take over for a few hours so I could spend the afternoon with Gavin and the kids. But I'm starvin', so I'll stay and eat with you if ya want."

"Sounds good. What's on the menu?" I ask.

"Cajun chicken and sausage gumbo with rice and potato salad."

"Mmm...sounds and smells delicious."

"And of course peach cobbler."

I grab a bowl, then add rice and pour the gumbo on top. Maize and I chat while we eat.

"Somethin' on your mind?" she asks after I bite into my cornbread.

"No, why?"

"You've barely eaten your gumbo, and I know it's your favorite. My life consists of third-grade girl drama so spill the tea."

I glance down, realizing she's right. Sighing, I look around to make sure no one's within earshot.

"You can't tell anyone."

She zips her lips and flicks away the imaginary key. "To the grave."

Lowering my eyes, I inhale softly before blurting out, "It's...Payton."

"You two finally hook up or somethin'?"

"No, not exactly, but he offered to."

Her face scrunches. "*Offered to*? Like a *if we aren't married by thirty, let's get hitched* kind of offer?"

I snort, shaking my head. "Not exactly. I told him I was gonna order sperm online and basically baste myself with it to get pregnant. He offered to knock me up instead."

Maize nearly spews out her sweet tea but quickly covers her mouth and chokes it down.

I hand her a napkin. "Jesus, Maze. You okay?"

She dabs her mouth and chin. "I wasn't ready for that and almost regret askin' now. I know you've joked about going the donor route, but I didn't know you were serious."

Shrugging, I take a bite of my gumbo and smile at how good it tastes. "I'm tired of waitin'. I want a baby. If I wait for this mysterious *Mr. Right*, I'll never have one."

"Okay, I understand wanting to have a baby. So how did Payton randomly get involved?"

I recap his finding the donor pages and our conversation on Wednesday.

"You're messin' with me," she deadpans.

"Nope. And even better, he wants to be a dad," I confirm, still worried about how this will play out. "To be fair, I drunkenly told him at the wedding reception to fuck me raw and knock me up. So his volunteering to get me pregnant isn't completely out of the blue. But I never thought he'd actually be interested."

"So...you'd just do the deed until you're knocked up, then what?"

"We'd co-parent, I guess. We'd be roommates raising a baby."

She stares at me. "Excuse my language, but that's the stupidest fuckin' thing I've *ever* heard." Her voice is just above a whisper, but her harsh tone could be heard across state lines. "At that point, why wouldn't y'all just date? Or hell, get married. Lord knows y'all are perfect for each other."

I roll my eyes. "Because we're *just* friends."

I've said those words at least a hundred times over the years.

"So you'd be friends who'd just...*fuck*?"

"With one goal in mind. Hopefully, I'll get pregnant right away without any added weirdness. A week of baby-making sex and then we can move on like it didn't happen."

Her facial expression tells me I'm crazy, and hell, maybe I am, but I want what I want.

"Kaitlyn, have you ever looked at Payton? Like, *really* looked?"

"Yes, and...?"

"I may be a married woman, but I can recognize a good-lookin' man when I see one. He's a muscular, tall, tattooed god...and those are just his physical features. Payton worships the ground you walk on, and while you deny it, we all see it. He's also genuine and hardworking, which makes him even sexier. Hell, I'm startin' to wonder if I should leave my husband for him." She snickers, then continues, "Payton's literally everything you've ever wanted, and you're just going to use him to make a baby, then just be like *thanks for the sperm*!" she whispers in a high-pitched voice meant to mock me.

"*He's* the one who offered," I remind her between gritted teeth.

"And you think you'll be able to bang Mr. Sex on Legs without catchin' feelings?"

"Well, we'd set ground rules to ensure we stayed within the boundaries of friendship."

She snort-laughs. "The ones you'll be crossing as soon as you kiss."

"Then we won't kiss," I quickly retort. "Actually, that's a good idea. No kissin' and absolutely no catchin' feelings."

"That's not how it works..." She points her spoon at me. "Let me ask you this. How do you feel about Payton? How do you see him as of right now?"

I adjust in my seat as I inhale. "I don't know. I had a sex dream about him once, but I was also drunk and dreamed about sexy blue aliens on the same night, so I figured it didn't mean anything. He's always just been one of my best friends. We shit talk, watch our shows, eat and hang out, and there's never been anything more to it than that."

Minus when I nearly begged him to admit he wanted to sleep with me during my drunken night at the wedding reception.

"Why have I never heard about this sex dream?" she quips, and I roll my eyes.

"About the blue aliens?" I taunt, and she snorts.

"You might not wanna hear this, but he's been holding back when it comes to you. No one can figure out why, though."

"I guess I never thought about it because crossin' those lines meant I'd potentially lose him if things didn't work out. And with my dating track record, it's too much of a risk."

"And you don't think rollin' around between the sheets to make a baby isn't a risk?"

"Oh, it is. But going into it with rules gives our friendship a better chance at survival. Maybe then things won't turn out badly." *At least I hope.*

"Well, I don't know about that. It's hard to control how you feel, even with boundaries. However, you should have tons of crazy sex before you get pregnant because babies take over your life."

"Oh, like you and Gavin aren't bangin' like rabbits."

"Of course we are, but it's nothing like when we were newlyweds. Instead of sneakin' around so no one knew we were dating, now we're hidin' from the kids and doing it in the closet. That's part of life, though. You get older and grow your family, and then your priorities shift. So before you tie yourself down, have some fun."

"I'm ready to be a mom, though," I reiterate. "The sex is just a steppin'-stone to get there."

She tilts her head at me, unamused. "Alright, so what happens after? What're you gonna tell people? What will Grandma say? And everyone else who asks where your husband is?"

I know she's not being judgmental but rather preparing me because our family is traditional in nature. It *is* unusual to purposely get pregnant by a *friend* with no intentions of pursuing a romantic relationship. Not all of my cousins got married first, but my situation is different, and I'll be bombarded with questions.

"It's my life, and I make my own decisions without anyone's permission. If worse comes to worst, I'll tell them we got drunk and hooked up. Not like my parents and grandma don't beg for more Bishop babies or anything. Once they get over the initial shock, they'll be excited."

Maize leans back in her chair. "I don't know, Kate. Maybe it'd be easier to just fake date, and then you can say you broke up but are gonna raise the baby together."

"I don't wanna lie more than I have to. They'll get over it, or maybe they won't, but it's my choice. They can either be happy and supportive, or they'll miss out."

She releases a heavy breath. "I hope you know what you're doing. I don't want you to get hurt, and even though I don't know Payton that well, I don't want him to get hurt either. He's worked at the ranch a long time, and it'd be sad to see him leave because you broke his heart."

I lean forward and lower my voice. "If he wanted more, don't you think he would've told me by now?"

She shrugs, then sips her iced tea. "Might be a reason he hasn't, but you two crossing the line will change things. Your friendship will *never* be the same."

"I know that, but we'll always be close, especially while co-parenting. If I agree to this, I'll make sure all our cards are put on the table first. That way, we both know the expectations and outcome."

"God, you make it sound like a business deal."

"That's kinda what it'd be," I confirm. "No different than me buying sperm online and agreeing to their terms and conditions."

"But he isn't just a jar of sperm. He's your best friend, and he's going to rail you six ways to Sunday to get his little soldiers inside you."

I choke-laugh as I cover my mouth, not wanting to spew the lemonade I just sipped. "That was cruel. You knew I was takin' a drink."

"Better get used to liquids squirting out of you. Especially if you intend to breastfeed."

"I know that's not what you meant, you dirty little ho."

Maize grins like a little she-devil as we continue eating our lunch. I've dreamed about getting pregnant for so long that it feels surreal for it to be a possibility.

"You look like you've made a decision," Maize says after we've finished dessert.

I smile wide because she's right. "I have."

After lunch, I go back to the stables and finish the rest of my training sessions for the day, although my mind is elsewhere. Once I'm home and in a better headspace, I take a shower, then text Payton.

Kaitlyn: Can we talk tonight?

He responds almost immediately.

Payton: Yeah, I'll be done in about an hour. Meet me then?

Kaitlyn: I'll be there.

Butterflies invade my stomach as I think about how our conversation will go.

How I'm going to tell him.

How he'll react.

How *everything* will change.

CHAPTER SIX

PAYTON

I'm SWEATING as I walk into my house after work.

And not from busting my ass in the heat.

From the moment Kaitlyn texted me, I haven't been able to stop thinking about what she'll say.

Hell, the thought of her having my baby has consumed me the past few days.

I know asking her what I did was impulsive, but to be fair, she mentioned it first. If Kaitlyn wants a baby, why not have mine and give me a family too?

After my dad died, my childhood took a turn for the worse. My mother met Stanley, and we never traveled and explored new things once he came into the picture. I'll make sure I'm nothing like him.

I can't wait to show my children everything Texas has to offer, especially on the ranch. They'll grow up with animals like I did, but they'll be surrounded by constant love.

Once I've showered and dressed, I grab a beer and chug half of it before taking a breath. Next, I pull out Kaitlyn's Fireball.

She'll either change my life or break my heart.

Either way, I'll respect her decision.

I hear her truck roaring as she turns into the driveway. Moments later, she walks in and calls out, "Hello?"

"In the kitchen," I shout.

As soon as she enters, she eyes the bottle of amber liquid. "Oh good, I can't be sober for this conversation."

Instead of grabbing a glass, she unscrews the cap and chugs it.

When her eyes meet mine, I arch a brow. "You okay?"

She takes another swig before responding. "Yeah, I just needed something in my system."

I smirk with amusement. "Wanna go to the living room and chat?"

"Sure, I'm bringing the Fireball, though."

Nervously, I follow her to the couch. My gut feeling tells me she's going to say *thanks, but no thanks,* and I wouldn't even blame her. It's a big deal and not something just casually mentioned in passing. Bringing sex into our friendship *would* change everything.

Still, I'm holding on to hope.

"I've thought a lot about what you asked," she begins as I wipe my sweaty palms down my jeans.

Before continuing, she takes another shot but coughs and makes a face.

"Kate, just tell me," I prompt. "It's okay if you say—"

"Yes," she blurts out.

I grab the bottle and take a drink. Did she really just say *yes?*

"I'm gonna need you to repeat that," I say once I come up for air.

"I'm agreeing to your proposition."

My brows rise in shock.

"With conditions," she adds. "We're crossing big lines, so we need to have some ground rules."

"I agree," I tell her, my breaths finally steady.

She readjusts on the couch to face me. "This should be kept

strictly transactional so neither of us gets hurt. I want us to do everything we can to prevent feelings from entering the picture so it's less complicated."

As soon as those words leave her mouth, a dagger stabs me in the heart.

Years ago, I came to the conclusion that my feelings for her were one-sided, but I was hoping to be wrong. If Kaitlyn felt anything, she wouldn't be so hell-bent on making sure we stay *just friends*.

But I'll live with it.

I suck up my pride and nod in agreement.

"That means no kissing on the mouth," she confirms. "No cutesy romantic pet names. Sex *only* during ovulation week. Absolutely no dirty talk."

"Oh, come on. You had me until that last one," I tease.

She rolls her eyes with a grin. "If I can fall in love with a fictional character who says *good girl*, there's no way I can hear it in real life and not get attached."

Leaning back on the sofa, I sigh. "I'll do my best, but no promises. You can't restrict *everything* I do in bed. Otherwise, I won't be able to give you what you need, so just be vocal about what you want while we're doing it. I'll keep my lips off yours and avoid the cutesy names, but the rest comes instinctively."

Now she's the one to raise her brows. "Alright. Fair enough, but keep it vanilla."

I snort. "Yeah, sure, okay."

Kaitlyn grabs a throw pillow and chucks it at my head, laughing. "I'm serious!"

I catch it and groan. "Next, you'll tell me no foreplay."

"Actually, I do need that. It helps get me in the mood."

Thank God.

"Even if most of the guys I've been with have sucked at it."

I try to hide my jealousy, but knowing she's not had many

good sexual experiences makes me want to give her multiple orgasms.

"You won't have to worry about that with me," I tell her confidently.

She swallows hard, and I notice the way her nipples peak through her shirt.

"I still want you to have a decent time and make you feel good. So let's just agree to always be open and honest. I'll never do anything you don't want, okay?"

She bites down on her lower lip before responding, "Yeah, I can do that."

"Good. Anything else, then?"

"Yeah, you'll need to be on-call during my ovulation cycle. That means when I say it's time, you'll drop everything and meet me. I plan to track it, so I'll know two days before it happens, but the key is to do it before ovulating so the sperm is there to meet the egg."

I scratch my cheek, holding back a grin because I do this for a living with horses. "Alright."

"I also think we should put a timeline in place. If I don't get pregnant by the holidays, I'm picking a sperm donor and going that route. That way, we can say we tried, but we're not forced to keep this up. Basically, I want results, or I'm changing gears."

That gives me about six to seven months to knock her up.

"Fair enough," I say, although I hate the thought of that.

"I'm sorry if that sounds selfish, but it's not cheap to do artificial insemination, and that's what it'd be considered when a doctor injects sperm inside me."

"I understand, Kate. I think my swimmers will get the job done." I flash her a wink.

"I hope so, or I'm writing one scathing review."

I chuckle. "Alright, so what now?"

"Now I'm going to actively track my ovulation, and you're going to withhold from jerking off every day."

"*Seriously?*"

"Yes! Women have a small fertilization window each month, so save all your sperm for me."

"Does that mean you're quittin' caffeine then?"

She shoots me a murderous glare, and I chuckle.

"So...during this window, sex every day?"

"Oh, *multiple* times a day," she confirms. "Each time I lose an egg, my ability to get pregnant decreases. Eventually, my ovaries will stop doing that, so time is of the essence."

"You're gonna psych yourself out if you don't relax and stop stressin' over it."

"Easy for you to say." She blows out a breath as her head falls back on her shoulders. "I'm just anxious now that we're going to actively try. It's blowing my mind a little."

"Really? Because it's blowing my mind *a lot*."

She snorts. "Just wait until we have to tell my family."

"Speaking of that—"

"We had a drunken one-night stand," she says. "And decided to co-parent as friends."

"Your father is gonna murder me—or worse, chop off my nuts."

She shrugs. "They'll get over it. Either that or you'll get a free vasectomy."

I narrow my eyes at her, unamused.

Then I work up the courage to ask another big question. "So if we're really pursuing this, perhaps you should go ahead and move in with me? When you get pregnant, I'll take care of you. That way, it won't be suspicious when we have to sneak around during your ovulation week, and our drunken hookup story is more believable. We'd be able to co-parent under the same roof and not worry about custody schedules."

Though I brought it up the first time we discussed this, I want her to know I was serious about it.

"You'd really want to live with me?"

"Of course...kinda weird you aren't already, considering how much you're here, but now's the perfect time."

"Yeah, that'd be so much easier than trying to make room for a baby at my parents' and juggling him or her back and forth. And bonus, it finally gets me out of my childhood bedroom," she says with an unamused laugh.

"Yeah, I agree. We can take turns on night duty. Plus, it kinda gets lonely coming home to an empty house."

Kaitlyn nearly leaps into my lap when she wraps her arms around me. "Thank you, Payton."

"I should be the one thanking you." I hug her tighter.

"Can I move in now?" she pulls back and asks.

I laugh at her eagerness. "Yeah, whenever you want."

"Perfect. I'll start packing right away and break it to my parents. It'll allow us to get to know each other even better."

I reposition myself closer to her on the couch. "You don't think we know everything about one another after almost a decade of friendship?"

"There are some things I don't know..." She hesitates before continuing, "Mostly stuff about your past and life before you moved to Eldorado."

Oh, *that*.

"There's not much to discuss." I shrug. It's not something I like thinking about, nonetheless, talking about it. "Anyway, you hungry? I haven't made dinner yet."

"Yeah, I could eat! Have any pasta?"

I get to my feet. "You know I always do for you."

As we eat, I catch Kaitlyn up with what I've been researching for the horse rescue. I appreciate how excited she is about it.

"I can help you put a business plan together. When Knox was trying to write everything out for the stud operation, I helped him a little."

"That would be great. I've called a few horse rescues down south and got some great insight. I made a lot of notes, went to websites they suggested, and already started printing out the forms we'll need. Having you look it over to make sure it's presentable and has all of the information your dad and uncles need would be helpful."

"I'm more than happy to go through what you've got. I'd like to chat with my dad about it before June, but I don't want you to rush either. Is that enough time?"

"That's in a few weeks and totally doable," I admit. The smile on my face feels permanent.

After we've cleared our plates, Kaitlyn helps me clean up. As I wash the dishes, she dries and puts them away.

"Would you be opposed to some...redecorating?" she asks once we're done.

"Not at all. It's gonna be your house too." I wipe my hands on a towel before hanging it to dry.

"Okay, I'm gonna remember you said that." She smirks.

"Am I gonna regret sayin' that?"

Her mischievous grin tells me everything I need to know. *Yes, I am.*

"We'll see," she sing-songs.

"As long as you don't make it look like an eighteen-year-old's dorm room, I won't care."

She leans against the counter, crossing her arms. "How do you know what a dorm room looks like?"

"I haven't had many relationships, Kate, but I'm not a virgin."

"Alright, so what's your magic number?"

"My what?"

"Ya know, your body count. The notches on your bedpost. The panties you've kept as souvenirs."

I raise a brow, amused by her ability to blurt out whatever comes to mind. "I think it's time to call it a night, don't you?"

"Payton Jamison!" she barks when I attempt to lead her out of the kitchen. "You aren't dodging this question!"

I'm not afraid of what she'll think, but I don't want to know *her* number, and if I say mine, she'll share hers.

"It's gettin' late, and we've both gotta get up early for work," I explain as I walk toward the front door.

She finally follows me, then narrows her eyes when we face each other. "Don't worry, you'll tell me eventually. I'll get it outta ya," she warns as she puts her shoes on.

"Why do you wanna know so badly anyway?" I fold my arms over my chest.

"You're my future baby daddy. Don't you think we should share those kinds of things?"

"No. I don't need to know your number."

"Don't worry, it's not *that* impressive," she mumbles.

Thank God is what I want to say, but I keep my mouth shut. Relationships are one thing we've never talked much about in our years of being friends. We're close but not *share bedroom stories* close.

I flick on the porch light, then walk her to her truck.

Before I can open her door, she wraps her arms around me.

"Thank you for everything. You're the only person in the world I'd trust to do this with."

Instinctively, I inhale the scent of her shampoo mixed with whatever perfume she's wearing. "I'll do whatever it takes to give you what you want...maybe twice."

She pulls back in shock. "*Twice*? Someone's cocky."

"Hey, the little rascal might want a sibling someday."

She nearly chokes on her saliva. "Let's work on making the first one, then we'll talk."

I chuckle, then open her door. "Fair enough. Drive safe, okay?"

She hops in and fishes for her keys before buckling. "I will. If you wake up and change your mind about me moving in, text me before I tell my parents."

"I won't, Kate. Even if you're a drunken pain in my ass at times, I still think rooming with you will be fun."

"When I'm eight months pregnant and pissed that nothing in my closet fits, I'm gonna remember your words. No groaning about how annoying I'm being."

Laughing, I shrug. "If you're tryin' to scare me, it won't work."

She snaps her fingers. "You have a pregnancy fetish, don't you? I should've known."

Rolling my eyes, I shut her truck door, but she quickly lowers the window. "If we're sharing secrets, I kinda have a praise kink. Earlier, I wasn't kidding about the good girl comment."

When my mouth falls open, she laughs, then reverses.

"Good night, BD!" she shouts as I walk backward toward my house.

She laughs at my confused facial expression.

"Baby daddy!" she explains.

"So that makes you my pain in the ass BM?"

"Hey!" she scowls.

"We'll work on it."

She scoffs. "Night!"

As I watch her drive away, I think about how our lives are about to change. We'll be living together, having sex, navigating pregnancy, and raising a baby.

While I'm excited about the future, I'm also nervous as hell.

Kaitlyn's the only woman I can imagine settling down with, but she doesn't want that. I'll follow her rules, keep my feelings tucked deep inside, and cross my fingers we don't get hurt along the way.

CHAPTER SEVEN

KAITLYN

Kaitlyn: Guess what?

Maize: Do I even wanna know?

I SMIRK at her *thinking face* emoji. She's the only one I can talk to about this, so whether she wants to hear it or not, I'm giving her details.

Kaitlyn: Of course you do. You live for hot steaming tea!

Maize: You got me there...okay, what is it?

Kaitlyn: I accepted Payton's offer and am finally moving out of my parents' house!

Maize: OMG...what did they say?

Kaitlyn: I haven't exactly told them yet.

Maize: When are you moving in with him?

Kaitlyn: Saturday...

Maize: Kaitlyn Rose! That's in 2 days!

I laugh because I can hear her scolding tone in my head. It's been five days since Payton suggested it, and I would've told her sooner, but I've been swamped at work. Plus, I was still processing everything.

Kaitlyn: Relax! I'm telling them tonight. It'll be fine.

Maize: Call me and put me on speakerphone so I can hear them yell at you.

Kaitlyn: Very funny. No sex stories for you now!

Maize: Yeah right, liar! You're the one who shares way too much. I'm expecting diagrams, drawings, and videos at this point.

Dammit, she's right.

Maize: And if that's the case, please give me a warning so I don't expose my eight-year-old girls to sex education earlier than they need it.

I snort.

Kaitlyn: Fair enough. Although, I'm surprised they haven't walked in on you and Gavin by now.

Maize: Oh, I've always been paranoid about that. I lock the door, then move the nightstand in front of it just in case one of them figures out how to unlock it. I'm not about to scar them the way I was!

Unable to control my laughter, I recall the stories she's told me about accidentally catching her parents in the act.

Just as I'm getting ready to take my break, I get another text.

Payton: Do you have time to join me for lunch? I warmed up leftovers from last night.

As we do every Wednesday, Payton made us dinner, and we watched our shows together. He made a delicious tomato basil penne pasta dish that was to die for.

Kaitlyn: Hell yeah! On my way.

I don't waste any time and drive there as fast as I can.

As soon as I walk through the door, I smell the food, and my stomach growls. I set my bag down and find Payton in the kitchen.

"Hey there."

"Hey, just in time. Food's ready."

"Perfect. I'm starvin'."

He hands me my plate, and we sit next to each other at the table.

"What's in there?" he asks, pointing at my mini backpack.

"Oh, I brought my ovulation kit and TTC journal. Wanted to do a test on my break and see if a second line appears." I dig it out and show him.

He arches a brow and continues chewing as he looks through my stuff. "What's TTC?"

"It stands for trying to conceive. I've been reading forums like crazy, and most recommended tracking your ovulation with these strips. I was gonna wait until I started my period to track, but I figured I'd waited long enough. I ordered the kit a few days ago so I can start testing my urine three times a day."

His eyes widen as he stares down at it. "Three times?"

"Yep, because hCG levels, which is basically a pregnancy hormone the body naturally produces, will rise the closer I am to ovulation. So I gotta check as frequently as possible so we don't miss the window. It's crucial. As soon as the test line is as dark or darker than the control line, I'll have one to three days until ovulation. Hopefully, we won't have to do this for very long," I state with an encouraging smile.

"Imagine if we had to do this for the mares three times a day and track their cycles." He looks at me with amazement.

"Considering y'all have a one-hundred-percent success rate, you wouldn't need to, but if you did, you should make Knox do it," I say, and we laugh.

"He'd be the one to fuck it up, and our customers would be pissed."

I flip through a few of the pages of my journal and show him how I plan to track my days and times. Though I think I'm past this month's ovulation window, it doesn't hurt to check, especially since I'm not on any birth control and my cycles can be sporadic.

"Isn't this the journal Kane made you?" he asks, inspecting the leather cover.

I snicker. "Yep, finally putting it to good use."

"I gotta admit, tracking all that sounds intimidating."

"It's not too bad. I'm actually having fun learning about it," I admit because I love researching the process.

While we finish our lunch, I share more information I found on the TTC forums. Some couples have been trying for years, and my heart breaks for them when it doesn't work out. I hope that's not the case with me, but I'm not naïve enough to think I'm the exception. Most of the women in my family haven't had issues, but my aunt Courtney and uncle Drew did years ago. It's why they did IVF and ended up with triplets. I can only imagine how ecstatic they were, but I'd be content with just one.

"I think this was even better than the first time," I say as I swallow my last forkful of basil pasta.

"It really was. Had more time to marinate," he confirms.

He takes my plate, and I follow him to the sink. "I'm gonna tell my parents tonight."

"Finally, Kate." He chuckles while loading the dishwasher.

"I know, I've just been nervous, but I shouldn't be. I've lived at home long enough." I breathe out. "As much as I'll miss them, I'm excited to be your roommate!"

"Me too. Besides the baby-making times, not much will change, considering how often you're here anyway."

"Yes, but now I'll have my own room. I've been thinking more about all the redecorating I'm gonna do."

"Just remember, no dorm room-inspired vibes."

My head falls back as I laugh. "Don't worry, I'm way past that phase. But maybe some nicer blinds, a few framed photos, and a couple of fluffy rugs. You also need a handmade quilt hangin' off the back of your couch. Why hasn't that happened yet?"

He shrugs. "Because you haven't moved in yet. Guess you're right, though. It's finally time to gussy up the man cave."

My heart hammers in my chest at how sweet and warm he always is to me, but especially now.

We chat for a few more minutes before we have to go back to work.

"Text or call me later after you chat with your folks, okay?"

"I will," I say over my shoulder when I reach my truck. "If you don't hear from me, they've murdered me."

"Hey, Mom!" I greet her in the kitchen after showering away the day's sweat. "Where's Dad?"

"On his way home now," she replies. "I have a seafood dish in the oven. Are you hungry?"

"Sure, can I help set the table?"

She nods with a smile, and I focus on the task. My nerves are on fire as I overthink what I'm going to tell them.

"Is that shrimp I smell?" my dad asks when he walks through the door. Mom and I laugh as the pounding of his boots grows closer.

"It is. I made my buttery-baked shrimp with garlic-lemon sauce and roasted Brussels sprouts," she tells him once he enters.

He wraps his arms around her and slides his lips across hers, ignoring my presence completely. My parents have always been affectionate, no matter who's around. While I think it's sweet as hell, it's a constant reminder that I'm alone.

"I'll be ready in a few, gonna clean up," he says, then smiles at me. "Hey, kiddo. How was your day?"

"Just fine."

Once he returns from a quick shower, Mom pulls the skillet out and brings it to the middle of the table. We say grace, then dig in.

After a few minutes of eating, I decide it's now or never. With each bite I take, the more nauseous I feel.

"So there's something I need to tell y'all..." I shove a piece of shrimp into my mouth and stall.

"Who is he?" my dad demands in his husky *you're in trouble* tone. You'd think I was sixteen and about to tell them I got hitched to a complete stranger or something. Not a thirty-year-old woman still living at home.

"What are you talkin' about?" I wrinkle my nose.

"Jackson, let her talk." Mom nudges him. "Go ahead, sweetie."

"You know I love you both, but it's time that I move out," I blurt, sounding more assertive than I intended. "Payton's offered me one of his spare rooms, so I'm moving in with him this weekend."

"*This* weekend?" my mom squeals. "Why so sudden?"

"You're gonna live with a *boy*?" Dad arches a brow.

I shrug. "Can't be any worse than livin' with a female roommate who brings a different guy home every weekend."

"That's true," Mom admits. "I've had plenty of friends like that."

Dad glares at her, triggering a memory, I'm sure.

"Anyway, there's really no rush, but I'm too excited to wait. Plus, I basically live there already, so it'll almost be exactly the same. You'll still see me every day at work, and I'll come visit, I promise."

"Yeah, that's what your brothers said, and then they got married and had babies." Mom smiles. "Though I'm not opposed to that."

I groan. "Yes, I know."

"Are you and Payton sleepin' together?"

"*Dad!*" I shout.

At the same time, Mom yells, "*Jackson!*"

"What? I'm not stupid. I know what being *roommates* implies."

My heart beats harder as I try to keep it together. I hate lying, but I'm not confessing what we're really doing.

"We're *just* friends," I confirm for what feels like the thousandth time.

Dad and Mom share a look, and I know what they're thinking. They were childhood friends before getting together, but my situation is different. Payton and I don't have a history, and we've never experienced jealousy. I've done nothing but encourage him to give a chance to all the women who've flocked to him over the years. Bottom line: we're friends who are making a baby...hopefully.

"This is a bad idea," Dad says. "You should stay home and save your money."

"I've saved plenty of money over the last decade." I groan. "Also no one wants to date an old maid sleeping ten feet away from her parents."

"Jackson, she has a point. She probably wants to be on her own and have some privacy."

He snarls, stabbing a Brussels sprout with his fork. "Fine, but I'm giving Payton a little talkin'-to."

I roll my eyes with a smile, then pat his shoulder. "Sure, Dad. Go ahead."

"How do you think your brothers are gonna react to you livin' there?" Mom asks.

"Oh, I'm sure they'll give us shit just like everyone else, but oh well."

By the time we get to dessert, Dad has calmed his uncertainty and even asks about helping me move.

"Sure, the more, the merrier. Shouldn't take too long, though. I've already packed half of my room, and the rest is just furniture."

Mom smiles at me as she takes our empty plates from the table. "I can help you with the rest tonight."

"Thanks, Mom. There's actually one more thing I wanted to talk to y'all about."

My stomach twists as I prepare to share the news of Payton's horse rescue idea.

"There's also *another* reason we want to live together. We want to start a new venture on the ranch, and being roommates will help us plan it better."

Dad lifts a brow, looks at Mom, then back at me. "So what is it?"

I explain everything Payton and I have discussed so far and how we've been working on the business plan since last week. They listen to every word I say, and even though I don't have the research we've done in front of me, I've memorized most of it.

"Well?" I ask nervously once I'm done, wishing my heart wasn't racing so hard.

Mom's smiling wide as Dad processes it.

"I love it, kiddo. That's an amazin' and selfless idea. Plus, I can't think of two better people to run it."

Saturday morning finally arrives, and I work faster than I ever have to get my tasks done. Mom spent the past two nights helping me pack, and although I could tell she was sad, she wore a smile and told me how happy she was for me. On the other hand, Dad kept walking past my doorway and grunting.

"You're his baby girl," Mom reminded me as she added another folded pair of jeans onto the stack. "Mine too. You were always the perfect mixture of us. I'd put you in a pretty church dress, and minutes later, you'd be out in the yard runnin' around and tryin' to keep up

with your brothers. When I'd ask you who told ya you could go play in the dirt, you always smiled up at your daddy."

I laughed, remembering many times playing outside in my nicest clothes during my youth. Mama wanted a girly girl, but instead, she got a tomboy who wrestled with her twin brothers more than she played with dolls.

"We're gonna miss you, so you better find time to visit, okay?" Mom said as she taped up the final box.

"Of course. I'll be less than ten minutes away and will see y'all at the training facility every day." I smirked at how they acted like I was moving across the state.

Last night, before bed, I kissed my dad on the cheek and reminded him how much I loved him. He held me so tight that I could barely breathe. We've always been close, and they're the reason I love horses as much as I do, but it's time I branch out on my own.

"Ready, kiddo?" Dad startles me as memories of my final night at home surface. He wraps his arm around me and pulls me in for a hug as I stare into my now empty bedroom.

"It somehow looks so much smaller in here," I say.

"Big enough for my new man cave, though."

"Dad!" I gawk, and he bellows a laugh.

My brothers' old rooms were being used for storage until the first grandchild arrived, and then they became a nursery and a playroom. Mom continuously reminds Kane and me that she has plenty of room for more babies to visit.

"Just giving ya a hard time. You know your mom won't let me touch it."

Moments later, Payton arrives and greets everyone. Butterflies surface in my stomach when our eyes meet, though I don't know why. We see each other a lot, but today's much different.

Today, we officially become roommates who are trying for a baby.

CHAPTER EIGHT

PAYTON

It doesn't take long to move Kaitlyn in. Her dad and I set up her bed, nightstand, dresser, and bookcase while she sorts her clothes. She spends another hour organizing her bathroom. While we wait, Jackson mentions the horse rescue and how excited he is for us. Kaitlyn told me last night how he reacted, but hearing it from his mouth confirms this is *really* happening. Knowing how the Bishops work, they'll want to get started as soon as possible. When someone pitches a new venture for the ranch, and they approve it, they make it happen right away, which I'm looking forward to.

Once we say goodbye to her parents, Kaitlyn and I head into the kitchen.

"Any dinner ideas for your first night here?" I ask, opening the fridge.

"I'm really craving pizza," she tells me. "With mushrooms, pepperoni, and—"

"And extra cheese," I finish her sentence, smirking. "Yes, I know. That's why I always have dough on hand."

She helps collect the ingredients as we chat. Once the oven is heated and the pizza is piled high with her favorite toppings, I place it inside and set the timer.

"So I know you don't talk about your family often, but will you tell them about the baby?" she asks while sipping on her sweet tea.

I blow out a breath and nod. "I haven't decided yet."

Once the pizza is ready, I cut it into slices, and we eat on the couch. I share more details about my mom and how she met my stepdad. After my dad passed, my mom was so depressed and already had low self-esteem that when Stan entered the picture, she was eager to do whatever he wanted. But regardless of our strained relationship, I think my mom deserves to *eventually* know. Maybe not right away.

"Do you think she'd be excited?" Kaitlyn asks.

I scratch my cheek, wondering how I'd even tell her. "Yeah, I think so."

Being that I'm an only child, I'm her only chance of having grandkids.

"I was lookin' up some birthing plans. We should probably have one."

"Like what? Go to the hospital and push out the baby?" I tease and am rewarded with a hard punch to my shoulder. Kaitlyn hits like she has a personal vendetta against you, even if she's messing around. With brothers like Knox and Kane, I understand why.

"Ha ha, you're funny. There's actually a lot more to it than that. A birthing plan lets the doctor and nurses know your wishes in the event a major decision needs to be made. Do I want pain meds? What if I need an emergency C-section? What if I bleed out? What if there are complications in surgery? What if the baby's breech?"

"Jesus Christ," I mutter. My heart leaps into my throat at all the possibilities.

"Childbirth isn't always safe, Payton. If you have to choose between the baby and me, you pick the baby's life."

"Absolutely not, Kate." My deep voice harshly rushes out.

"Yes, that's *my* decision. In some cases, there isn't time to save both. I read an article about a woman who was eight months pregnant and got into a car accident. She was bleeding out and begged them to save her baby first. They promised her husband they'd do their best to take care of them both, but it was too late. They only had a few minutes to make a decision, and it was the woman's final plea that made them deliver the baby. She ended up passing away." Kaitlyn wipes away a tear, and we sit in silence for a while.

"Wow," I finally breathe out.

"I know. Anything could happen, and I want us to be prepared."

How am I supposed to raise our baby alone if something happens to her? And then see Kaitlyn's sweet face in our child every day? I can't do that.

"Kate..." I want to argue but based on the look in her eyes, it'd be a losing battle.

"For me, okay?" She leans over and tenderly presses her hand over mine. "If it comes down to it, you do that for me. You be that baby's daddy, and you give them everything."

I hate that we're having this conversation, but I swallow hard and force myself to nod. If that's what she needs from me, then I'll do it. Kate's always been passionate and strong-willed, and there's no talking her out of something once she's made up her mind.

"Aside from that, there are other things such as who will be in the delivery room and other prenatal concerns," she adds, then grabs another slice of pizza. "But we have time to get it documented. It's just something I wanted to mention so we can start thinkin' about it."

"You mean panickin'..." I mutter, losing my appetite.

"You worried about me, huh?" she taunts with a cocked brow. "You know you can't get rid of me that easily. Plus, I should be the one worried about you. Out in the pastures, using heavy equipment, and being around horses who want to do nothing but fuck. You could get injured or killed at any time."

"Probably why Knox made me sign a contract that they can't be sued if anything happens," I say with a chuckle, though I'm being serious.

Kaitlyn gawks at me and shakes her head. "That's because guys are stupid. Y'all out there acting like ya have nine lives with thousand-pound animals."

"Your brothers certainly do."

"Speaking of them, just wait until they hear about us livin' together." She readjusts on the couch, tucking her legs under her, looking just as at home as she always has. Being in her presence has always put me in a better mood, but now that she's permanently staying, I'm happier than ever.

"I'm already anticipating it," I tell her honestly. "Their shit-talking will be even worse when I knock you up."

Kaitlyn and I spent Saturday night on the couch talking and hanging out. Then she woke up early on Sunday to feed the horses, but I had the day off. While we typically grab breakfast from the B&B on the weekends, we avoided people and stayed home. She read me her list of favorite baby names from her journal and some theme ideas she had for the nursery. Though

I've never thought much about any of this stuff before, I love talking about it and planning with her.

That night, she told me she got her period and was now tracking a full cycle. She warned me she'll be ovulating in about ten to fourteen days.

Just that thought had me sweating through my T-shirt.

By the time Monday morning rolls around, I have a knot in my stomach. Everyone must know she's moved in by now, and it's only a matter of time before I start getting shit for it. For years, they've ridden my ass about my secret crush that I pretend doesn't exist, but this isn't the same. In a matter of months, we could be announcing a pregnancy.

"Hey, you okay?" I answer the phone when I see Kaitlyn's name on the screen.

"Yeah, fine. Headin' to the B&B for a late breakfast. Wanna meet me there? Figured we could get the gossip out of the way."

I chuckle. "Sure, I can be there in fifteen."

"Perfect. See ya soon."

Since I skipped breakfast and have been dealing with grumpy-ass horses all morning, I'm extra hungry and ready for a break. I hop in my truck and drive down to the pasture where Kane and Knox are working.

"Headin' to the B&B. Be back in a half hour."

"Sweet, I'll come with ya," Kane says.

"Me too." Knox follows, and they jump in my truck, uninvited.

"So when were you gonna tell us you shacked up with our sister?" Knox blurts out a minute later.

"Yeah, when are y'all gettin' married?" Kane smacks me on the shoulder. "We've helped out with our fair share of weddings 'round here, so we can help plan it if ya want."

I snort at the idea of the twins helpin' me organize anything.

Shaking my head, I turn onto the gravel road that leads to the B&B. "We're just friends and roommates."

"You're feedin' lies to two guys who were once *just friends* with a girl, so stop your bullshittin'."

"Believe whatever ya want, but I'm tellin' the truth. I fell for someone I worked with years ago and swore off datin' coworkers after she broke my heart. It made everything awkward as fuck, and I don't need that in my life again."

"Oh, so instead, you have her move in so y'all can play house. Makes perfect sense," Knox muses.

Locking my jaw, I resist the urge to tell him to shut the hell up because he has no clue what's really going on.

Considering my underlying feelings for Kaitlyn, I know what I'm doing is stupid, but I couldn't let her get away.

We can be friends who share a child while also keeping it platonic.

At least that's what I'm telling myself.

As soon as we walk into the B&B, I see Kaitlyn chatting with Maize, Hadleigh, and Harper. Knox grabs his wife and pulls her in for an inappropriate kiss with tongue and all. I wish I could do the same with Kaitlyn.

"Hey, Payton," Maize greets with a warm smile. She's the only one who knows our master plan, but I act indifferently and simply nod before greeting her.

I grab a plate and fill it full, then wait for Kaitlyn so we can sit together. Her brothers sit across from us while Maize chats with the other girls next to her.

"So you finally moved out of Mom and Dad's, huh?" Knox doesn't waste a minute before he starts teasing his sister. "You two gonna admit being together now?"

Kaitlyn shoots him a death glare. "Why don't you mind your own damn business?"

"As your big brothers, you are our business," Kane offers. "We thought you'd live at home until you got married."

"Which at this rate...you'll be fifty," Knox bellows.

Kaitlyn kicks him with her boot underneath the table.

He loudly hisses. "That was my fuckin' shin."

I enjoy watching her get even with them when they push her too far.

"How do you expect me to take dating seriously if I have to tell guys I still live at home?" she fires back. The thought of her bringing someone home has me stabbing a piece of sausage with my fork.

"Pretty sure they're not gonna like you livin' with another man, either," Kane interjects.

Kaitlyn rolls her eyes. "You two look like y'all have been bathin' in horse shit all day and still managed to find wives, so I'd say my chances are about the same."

We haven't talked about the possibility of one of us dating other people after the baby, but I have no desire to be with anyone other than Kaitlyn, and she's not interested. I came to terms with that fact a long-ass time ago.

Kaitlyn: GET YOUR ASS HOME NOW! IT'S O-TIME!!!!

I swallow down the lump in my throat as I re-read her text. *Holy shit, this is really happening.*

I've been on high alert ever since she told me her cycle started. Over the past couple of weeks, we've formed a nice routine.

We briefly see each other in the mornings while getting ready for work and making coffee. Sometimes we meet at the B&B for brunch, and then once we're home, we eat dinner together and hang out. Now that the paperwork and permits have been filed for the horse rescue, it's been the center of our conversations. Jackson's already got the blueprints for the stables being drawn, too, so they can start building soon. We still watch our shows every Wednesday, but now we've started two new series on Mondays and Thursdays.

I look back down at my phone and send her a response.

Payton: On my way.

After I've replied, I try to think of an excuse to send Knox for my abrupt departure. He's on the other side of the barn, so I get in my truck before texting him.

Payton: Running home real quick to get some meds for a headache.

Knox: Hurry back, or I'm putting you on double shit duty.

I grunt, locking my phone instead of telling him to fuck off. Like that bastard has any room to talk. He's left for hours at a time to meet Hadleigh. Pressing down on the gas, I rush home as fast as I can.

As soon as I walk into the house, I find Kaitlyn in the kitchen chugging back vodka.

"Are you okay?" I grab the bottle, screwing the top on.

"I'm too anxious to do this sober," she admits.

"Kate, we can wait till tonight if you..."

"No! I don't want to waste any time or miss my window. It's just been a while for me, and the last guy who was down there made a comment about my thighs being too thick, so I haven't felt super—"

"Are you fuckin' kidding me?" I nearly throw the bottle across the room. She's never talked about anyone she's been with, but hearing she wasn't treated right has my nostrils flaring. *Unacceptable.*

"What're you doing?" She startles when I grab her hand and lead her toward her room.

"I'm about to show you how a real man appreciates a woman."

"Payton!" she squeals when I pick her up and toss her on the bed.

"Get naked, Kate. We're on a time crunch here," I tell her, ripping off my shirt, then undoing my jeans. Next, I kick off my boots and remove the rest of my clothes while she does the same.

If it were up to me, I'd strip her bare and kiss every inch of her smooth skin. I'd take my sweet time licking and sucking her nipples and clit.

"Lie back," I demand.

When she does, I cup underneath her legs and drag her ass to the edge. The sight of her bare pussy makes me hard as a rock. Kaitlyn's curves and soft belly have me aching to get inside her.

"Jesus!" She fists the blanket, arching her back. "Maybe don't manhandle me the first time? I might've drunk a little too much."

I hold back a chuckle. Leave it to her to get tipsy beforehand.

"Spread your legs."

As soon as she does, I slide my hands up her thick, beautiful thighs and bring my mouth between them.

"Payton, what are you—?" The words die on her lips as I suck her clit between mine. "*Holy shit.*"

A gasp releases from her as she lifts her hips like a good girl. It's taking every bit of willpower I have not to tell her as much, knowing how much she likes it. I dig my fingers into her skin, craving all of her. Kaitlyn moans, and her heavy panting tells me she's close. It didn't take long to nearly push her off the ledge.

Releasing one of her legs, I thrust a finger deep inside her pussy. She's wet and ready, quickly coating my hand with her juices. I swipe my tongue along her slit, tasting her sweetness. As soon as I add a second finger, Kaitlyn moans in pleasure, her hips bucking as I lap over her again.

I wanna taste her come and am not slowing down until she explodes all over my face.

Breaking away for a quick moment, I keep my pace finger-fucking her. "Give me one, Kate. I'm not stoppin' until you do."

"Damn, it's so intense," she murmurs between rapid breaths.

"I can tell you're close," I coax her before diving back in, switching between flicking and sucking her clit.

She flails against me, forcing me to hold her down as I suck harder and pump faster. Kaitlyn squeals and pants as her body tightens, finally releasing a long, breathy moan. I watch her mouth morph into a perfect O. Watching her orgasm is a memory I'll never forget.

"*Oh my God.*"

My tongue slides up her slit, capturing everything.

Oh my God is right.

She tastes even better than I imagined.

I finally release my hold and rise above her.

"You good?" I ask around a chuckle as she struggles to catch her breath.

"I've never...from that...holy shit."

Arching a brow, I rest my palm flat against the bed next to her head.

"What kind of douchebags were you with, Kate?"

"Now's not the time to criticize my lack of quality bedmates, okay?"

I grab my cock and stroke it a few times. "If you found that mind-blowing, I'm about to rock your world, baby."

"No pet names," she reminds me.

"Not even baby?"

"No. That's too cutesy."

I groan, getting restless and needing inside her.

"Move up, Little Devil."

"Not that either," she scolds, inching her way to the middle of the bed.

"That's not cutesy," I argue, lining my dick between her thighs.

"No, but it sounds like something you'd call a girlfriend," she clarifies.

"How 'bout you shut the hell up and let me knock you up now?" I watch the blush creep up her neck and face.

Without another word, I slide inside her perfect pussy and nearly pass out at how tight she feels.

"Fuck," we both mutter in unison.

Her head falls back as I pull out, then thrust back in again. I squeeze her hips, seeking her G-spot so we can add another orgasm, and watch her tits bounce with every move.

Kaitlyn wraps a thigh around my waist, pulling me closer and tempting me with her lips. I wish I could kiss the fuck out of her, but I'm following the rules, so I sink in deeper and bury my face in her neck instead.

"Am I allowed to tell you how good it feels?" I murmur in her ear. "Because getting lost in you is incredible."

"It's *so* good," she agrees. "I'm close again."

"Yes, come on my cock, Kate. I can't wait to see your pregnant belly."

I've never had a breeding kink, but now I can't think of anything else I'd rather do than fill her up with my come. Imagining her round stomach growing with my baby inside makes me harder than I've ever been in my life.

"Fuck, *I-I*..."

She screams while digging her nails in my back. Unable to resist, I suck on her neck and kiss along her jaw.

"Thatta girl," I praise as she rides out her release, sitting up so I can watch her expression.

Feeling her squeeze and climax on my cock is something I could definitely get used to. And most likely, *addicted* to.

"I'm about to come, Kate." I thrust harder, chasing the high that's right on the verge.

Moments later, my entire body stiffens, and I explode like the fireworks finale on the Fourth of July.

"Shit, that was a lot." My eyes widen as I pull out and look between us. "I'll grab a towel. Hold on."

"Okay..." she responds out of breath.

I can't believe that just happened.

Kaitlyn and I had sex.

I just fucked my best friend.

Once we're cleaned and dressed, I check my phone and see three text messages from Knox and two missed calls from Kane.

"Shit, your brothers are probably on their way to find me." I shove my phone into my pocket. "Sorry, I've gotta run."

"Don't be. We'll do it again later." She says the words so casually as if we're talking about going on a hike.

Except the view of her shuddering beneath me was worth every ounce of sweat.

I chuckle. "You just want me for my sperm."

She rolls her eyes with a smirk. Her blond hair is a complete *just been fucked* mess. She looks in the mirror and quickly combs her fingers through it.

"I should get back to work too. My parents are gonna wonder what's taking me so long to change." She explains she already had before I arrived because one of the horses really did get her dirty.

"Alright, I'll see ya tonight, then." I pull her into a side hug, hoping like hell things won't be awkward now. Though I don't suspect they will be. Kaitlyn's never been the type to be weird around me. Even when she got her period while we were out riding trails, it didn't faze her at all. I expected her to be embarrassed, but she wasn't.

Nothing rattles her, and that's one of the many qualities I love about her. She doesn't apologize for things she has no control over but will be the first to say sorry if she's wronged you.

"Okay, I should be home around six to shower and eat before our dance show starts at seven!"

I chuckle at her excitement. Even though I'm not a huge fan of watching reality competitions, I enjoy every second of watching it with her.

I never thought I'd say this, but this past week might make my dick fall off. Kaitlyn's stamina gives me a run for my money. I've never had complaints about my bedroom skills, but she's ready for another round within minutes of us finishing.

And having sex with her is better than I ever could've expected.

Though I'm constantly reminding myself of the rules, I enjoy being with her. I'm undeniably setting myself up for heartbreak, but giving her this chance to be a mom is more important. When this is over, I'll move my focus to being there for her every step of the way.

Kaitlyn's my best friend, and losing her would destroy me more than my ex ever did. I eventually got over Edna, but I'd never get over Kaitlyn.

I'd die before I could.

Last night was our final time trying for the month, and now we play the waiting game.

In a couple of weeks, we'll find out if our lives will be changed forever.

And even if she's not pregnant, I'll never be the same after witnessing the way she looks when she comes.

The way she writhes under my touch.

The way she begs for more—*harder, faster, rougher.*

There's no doubt in my mind that Kaitlyn will be my undoing, and I welcome it.

CHAPTER NINE

KAITLYN

TWO WEEKS LATER

A COUPLE OF WEEKS AGO, I shaved, moisturized, and exfoliated nearly every inch of my body in preparation for a week of nonstop marathon sex.

In bed, on the couch, bent over the kitchen counter, and even in the shower.

Not gonna lie, that last one was super hot.

He barged in on me like a damn caveman, lifted me, and fucked me against the wall as hot water poured over us.

It was like a movie or a porno. *A hot as fuck one.*

My pussy still clenches anytime I think about it.

Payton damn sure knows what he's doing and how to pleasure a woman. My nerves got the best of me before our first time, but a couple of shots of vodka and Payton's tongue between my legs helped settle me. After that, it became second nature, falling into a rhythm of sweaty skin and breathy moans.

But now I'm pacing in my bathroom, waiting for a pregnancy test to tell me if I am or not. I'm due for my period any day, but since it's irregular, it just might be late.

I still haven't wrapped my mind around what being pregnant entails. I've watched my cousins and their wives experience pregnancy and having babies. Each time, I'd feel a pang of jealousy and sadness that it wasn't me instead. While I was always happy for them, I wondered when it'd be my turn.

The timer on Payton's phone goes off, and we meet each other's gaze, neither wanting to look.

"Are you gonna check it?" he asks when I don't move.

"I'm too scared," I admit. My bottom lip trembles as I move to pick it up.

Payton stands behind me, cupping my shoulders. Holding my breath, I turn it around and find one pink line staring back at me.

Negative.

"Maybe it's a false negative," Payton offers, but my gut tells me otherwise. "Take a couple more just to be sure."

So I do.

I bought them in bulk and dip two more sticks in the pee cup. We wait another few minutes in tense silence.

Stupidly, I get my hopes up, so when I see two more negatives, I chuck them in the trash and walk out.

"Kate," Payton calls as he follows me to the kitchen. "Don't be discouraged. We'll keep tryin'."

I say nothing as I dig around for the vodka. If I'm not pregnant, I might as well drown my sorrows with booze. When I find it, I untwist the cap, then drink straight from the bottle.

"Kate!" Payton grabs my jaw and makes me look up at him. "It's still too soon to know for sure. No drinkin'."

He steals it from my grip and screws the top back on.

"I really thought I'd be pregnant," I whisper sadly, almost feeling foolish for assuming it'd happen so quickly.

He pulls me into his arms, and I cling to his warm embrace. His hard chest muscles press into me, and memories of his sculpted, naked body against mine flood my thoughts. Every inch of him is perfection. I've always thought so, but getting to touch him while inside me is an entirely different experience.

"You will," he promises, pressing a kiss to my temple. "If I have to fuck you every day for a month to make sure of it, I will."

I laugh into his shirt. "Sorry for the hardship."

He pulls back and shoots me a wink. "It'd be my honor."

That evening, we fall into our Monday night routine. Payton brought home baked chicken from the B&B, one of Maize's specialties, and then we settled on the couch.

"So I thought of a cool boy name," he tells me as we bring our dishes into the kitchen.

"What's that?"

"Ezekiel."

I arch a brow. "I can't even spell that."

He snorts. "He probably wouldn't be able to either, then."

"It's a cute name. Do you have any ideas for a girl?"

"I thought of Kaylee the other day. Sounded like a cute little princess name."

Smiling wide, I nod. "It does. Kaylee Jamison. Has a nice ring to it."

"What about a middle name?" he asks, rinsing our plates, then placing them in the dishwasher.

"It might be weird."

"Weirder than Ezekiel?"

I burst out laughing. "No, nothing beats that. But I've seen a rise in mother's maiden names being used as the middle name. And since we aren't getting married or anything, it could be a way to represent both of us without giving a hyphenated last name."

"So Kaylee Bishop Jamison?" he confirms.

"Yeah. Does that sound too strange?"

"No, I love that, actually." He leans against the counter with his ankles and arms crossed.

Talking about our plans puts me in a better mood, and my spirits are slightly higher.

Unfortunately, that feeling lasts all of twelve seconds because I get a text from Kane.

Kane: Since you weren't at the B&B earlier to hear the news, we didn't want you to miss it!

Then I see the selfie of him and Ivy holding up a positive pregnancy test.

Jealousy fuels my veins, and before I can think better of it, I throw my phone and storm out of the kitchen toward my room.

"What the fuck?" Payton follows me, and when I don't give him an explanation, he grabs my elbow and spins me around. "What just happened?"

I hate myself for crying and being upset over something so exciting for my brother. But I can't help it.

"Ivy's pregnant."

Payton rubs over his trimmed jawline, then scrubs a hand through his hair. "Kate, I—"

"I'm acting selfish, I know, and I really am happy for them." I blow out a frustrated breath, trying to gather my thoughts. "Someone else in the family is pregnant *again,* and it's not me."

"I don't know what to say besides I'm sorry. You can be excited for them and disappointed that you aren't at the same time. That's completely valid, Kate."

My shoulders slump, and I frown. "I should respond before he thinks I'm ignoring them."

He follows me into the kitchen, and I grab my phone off the floor.

"Wow, not a scratch or dent," I say, impressed.

"Thank God you had an indestructible case on it."

"It needs one when working around horses all day."

He watches as my fingers fly over the screen, congratulating

Kane and Ivy and telling them how excited I am for another niece or nephew.

Maybe it's good timing. If I get pregnant soon, at least our kids will be close in age.

The following night, I come home after a long, hot day at work and hear soft spa music drifting from my bedroom. As soon as I walk in, I'm hit with a strong lavender scent and see candles burning along my dresser.

What in the world?

"Oh, good. You're home. Get naked," Payton says from behind me.

I turn and blink up at him, wondering if he's drunk.

"Are you tryin' to seduce me?"

"Considering I'm still tryin' to recover from a couple of weeks ago, you don't gotta worry about that. However, you're getting a massage. They can be good for fertility, plus you need to relax. Being too tense and stressed can affect your ability to conceive."

Since when did he become the expert?

"And you know this how?"

"I took a massage course a long time ago when I wanted to move out of my mom's house. Before I got my license, I saw the Circle B Ranch job listing and decided to move here instead."

I can't imagine how different my world would be if he hadn't.

"So *you're* giving me the massage?" My brows shoot up to my hairline. Although this man has seen every inch of my body, that's different from him rubbing oil all over it.

"Would you prefer someone else? Weird Willie or Serious George maybe?"

I playfully smack his chest. Both of them are cattle herders and are my dad's age. George got his nickname because he never laughs at anything. Trust me, we've tried to crack him for years. He responds in grunts and growls.

On the other hand, Weird Willie is super friendly and laughs at everything. But his nickname comes from the inappropriate jokes he tells that no one understands.

"Alright, let me rinse off first. I'm a sticky, sweaty mess."

He smirks, holding back laughter as if the words for a dirty comment are on the tip of his tongue. I roll my eyes and head to the bathroom. Deciding I don't want him touching my prickly legs, I quickly shave and slather on moisturizer. Then I throw my hair into a messy bun and put on a robe.

Payton's sitting on a stool next to the bed when I come out. When he spots me, he stands and pulls back the sheet.

"Ready?"

"Can you spin around while I get into position?"

The corner of his lips tilts up as he silently turns away. Even though he's already seen me naked, this feels more intimate.

I drop the robe and climb under the sheet. "What position do you want me in?"

"Start facedown," he replies.

Quickly, I adjust myself. "Okay, I'm ready."

I turn my head to the side and watch as he grabs the sheet and lowers it just above my ass. A man has never massaged me before. The last time I got a professional one was years ago. Even then, it was a woman.

Payton pumps lotion into his palms, then cups his hands over his mouth. "Just makin' sure it's not too cold," he tells me. "They might feel a little rough from workin', though."

Then he slowly rubs over my back, and I die at the tender way he moves.

Even with his calluses, it feels amazing. I try to hold back my moans, but my uneven breathing gives me away. "You have the biggest, strongest, most gentle hands I've ever felt. How the hell are you single?"

He smirks but keeps his focus on my back and shoulders.

I close my eyes as he moves down each arm, meticulously rubbing over every inch. He takes his time, and it nearly puts me to sleep.

Once he's finished with my upper body, Payton slides the bottom half of the sheet up, then places it between my thighs. Again, he goes slow and carefully rubs lotion into each leg and foot. Next, he digs his knuckles and thumbs into my glutes, and I nearly scream at the intense pleasure. But I hold it back because, knowing me, it'd sound erotic.

"Okay, I'm finished with your back side. You can flip over now."

"I 'bout nearly passed out that felt so good," I admit, pulling the sheet up to my neck.

"That was the longest I've ever heard you stay quiet."

"Ha ha." I grin and wait for him to continue.

Payton lowers the sheet just above my breasts, and my breath hitches when he tucks it underneath me. His touches shouldn't be sensual, but his fingers set my skin on fire.

"You do this well," I tell him as he digs his thumb over a knot. "A girl could get used to this."

"This one's on the house, but the next one will cost ya," he teases.

My eyes fly open. "Agreeing to carryin' your baby isn't enough?"

He grins. "Fair enough."

His gaze wanders down to my hard nipples. I wish I knew

what he was thinking as he focuses on my neck and shoulders. Closing my eyes, I try to relax and enjoy this.

Payton adjusts his position, then slides his large hand across the tops of my breasts. His fingers dip between them but never inappropriately, though a part of me wishes he would.

"How many other women have you massaged?" I ask without looking at him.

"Including you? One."

"Just me? Really?"

"Yep."

My stomach flips with butterflies, though it shouldn't. Payton's just trying to help me feel better after getting a negative test. And this definitely has put me in a better mood.

"Not even for your ex?"

"No, she was too busy fucking my best friend."

"*What*?" I had no idea that was why they broke up. "What kind of person would cheat on you? And with your so-called friend? Wow. I hope you punched him out."

He stays silent, and I worry I said something I shouldn't have. When I meet his eyes, he's already staring at me.

"I wanted to. But it wouldn't have changed anything. Found out later she was pregnant."

"Payton, why have you never told me this?"

"Wanted to forget it." He moves his hands up my neck and sensually rolls his thumb over and over. "I stuck around and waited for the paternity test results. It wasn't mine."

A deep ache in my heart is only a fraction of what he must've felt. Even if she'd been cheating, he wanted a family, and she yanked it out from under him.

"I'm so sorry."

He shrugs, narrowing his eyes on my lips. "Trust me, it worked out the way it was meant to."

"Still...what they did to you was shitty."

"Karma came back around. After they got married, he knocked up another girl."

"Jesus. Does no one believe in commitment anymore? This is why I gave up on dating a long time ago."

A part of me always wondered why he didn't date much because he's the full package.

Payton moves his fingers over my scalp, massaging my head and giving me a hairgasm. I swear, the man has magic hands.

"When you get pregnant, I'll massage lotion over your belly. It's supposed to help with dry and itchy skin," he tells me once he's finished.

"*If* I get pregnant," I correct.

"No, *when*. Keep the faith." He shoots me a wink.

"I'm tryin'."

"How do you feel now?"

"Like I'm floating on a cloud and never want to come down."

He grins, readjusting the sheet for me. "Good. I'll let you change, then I'll come back and clean up. But take your time. I'll get you some water too. Helps release the toxins from your body."

"Thank you. I really appreciate you doing this for me."

"You should know by now that I'd do just about anything for you, Kate."

"Motherfucker!" I yell when I see blood.

My period would be late and playing games with me.

Even though I had a negative test a few days ago, I was holding on to hope that it was too early to test and I could maybe still be pregnant.

Now I know I'm not.

The mindfuck my head has gone through isn't something I was prepared for, and it's only been a month.

Once I'm done in the bathroom, I text Payton to let him know we'll be trying again in ten to fourteen days. Which means I'll be taking more ovulation tests as soon as my period's over.

Not that having sex with Payton is a chore—it's the opposite, actually—but the reality that I might not be able to get pregnant consumes me.

If we can't, I'll have to see a specialist or get tests done, and then I might get news I don't want to hear.

Payton: Guess I better think of some better excuses before Knox fires my ass.

I chuckle, knowing he's trying to make me laugh.

Kaitlyn: Just tell him you have explosive diarrhea. He can't fire you for that!

Payton: I'd rather not. He'd find a way to harass me about it.

Kaitlyn: Guess we'll have to meet somewhere closer for a quickie, then!

Payton: As long as you can keep it down.

He sends a winky face, and my cheeks heat. I can't help it. He hits just in the right spot over and over, sending me over the edge every damn time. The man has skills.

After my lunch break, I head back to the training facility and chat with my parents. I'm working with Malice still, who's been extra stubborn and salty lately. Perhaps she's mirroring her mood to match mine.

When I get to my desk, there's a box with my name on it. My dad likes to play little pranks on me, so I'm wary about whether I should open it or not.

Curiosity gets the best of me, and I rip off the tape, cautiously opening it in case a flying snake shoots out at me. Instead, I see a bottle of prenatal vitamins.

There's a Post-it note attached.

I read these are good to take while conceiving and searched for the best brand and flavor. Take two a day after breakfast. And drink lots of water! Don't need my pain in the ass BM getting dehydrated.

His sweet and thoughtful gesture has me grinning like a fool, even while calling me names. Since I usually grab breakfast at the B&B or eat a snack a couple of hours later, having these here will remind me to take them. As long as I can keep them hidden for a while. Knowing he wants this baby as much as I do makes it even more special.

Kaitlyn: Thanks for the vitamins...if I don't get pregnant, we're suing.

Payton: I don't think it works that way. But you're welcome.

Kaitlyn: Meet at the B&B for dinner?

He wasn't able to break away for lunch, so I went home and warmed up some leftovers. I don't think either of us will be up for cooking tonight since we need to go grocery shopping.

Payton: Sure will, around 6.

Kaitlyn: Okay, see ya then, BD!

Since I just ate, I open the bottle and take out two of the gummies. They actually do taste decent.

Kaitlyn: Payton and I are coming for dinner tonight. Will you still be working?

Maize: Yeah, one of my cooks called in sick so I'm pulling a double.

Kaitlyn: Oh, that sucks. I'm sorry. What's on the menu?

Maize: I had a feeling you were gonna ask.

I smirk because she knows me too well.

Maize: Buttermilk fried chicken, homemade mac 'n cheese, and banana pudding.

Kaitlyn: Oh my God, I'm already drooling.

Maize: Save it for your man.

Kaitlyn: Ha! Joke's on you, I don't have one.

Maize: Mm-hmm. Pretty disappointed I never got a sex update, by the way.

We've been at the B&B plenty since then, but it wasn't something I could talk about with Payton around. Plus, we're so busy with work and finalizing paperwork for the horse rescue, that I don't always remember to text back.

> **Kaitlyn: That's because I was in a sex coma. Got a negative test, though. So we'll be trying again in a week or two.**

> **Maize: Sorry it was negative, but I'm sure all the banging will cheer you up. I just know that man knows how to fuck.**

Jesus Christ, she's going to put the dirty thoughts of him back in my head for the rest of the day.

> **Kaitlyn: The man definitely does...**

> **Maize: How many times did you guys do it?**

> **Kaitlyn: Like two or three times a day for a week.**

> **Maize: It's not unheard of to take a few months, sometimes more. I know you want this badly, but be patient, and hell, enjoy the amazing sex.**

Oh don't worry, I am.

CHAPTER TEN

PAYTON

TEN DAYS LATER

Just as I wake up, I roll over and spread my hand across the cold spot on the bed next to me. It's been too long since another body has warmed it. Kaitlyn comes to mind, and my cock begs to be stroked. Wanting to save my sperm for her, I push the thoughts away and wait for my boner to disappear.

When I finally get up, I go straight to the bathroom and then head to the kitchen. Kaitlyn's got a bag of whole coffee beans and the grinder on the counter. She's fiddling with it, still dressed in a thin T-shirt and bright white panties. I purposely make a noise so I don't startle her, and she turns to face me as I enter the kitchen. It's been nearly a month since Kaitlyn moved in, and I can hardly imagine her not living here forever.

Her eyes land on the chubby in my joggers, and her plump lips turn up into a smirk. That's when I notice her nipples poking through the slinky fabric like pebbles.

"Well good mornin'," she taunts, placing a hand on her hip. I keep my inappropriate thoughts to myself and silently repeat the rules.

"Mornin'. You need some help?"

Kaitlyn bites on her bottom lip. "Yeah, but let's start with this coffee bean grinder. How the hell do you turn it on?"

Just a few short steps and I'm pressing down on the reservoir of beans, which makes the blade spin.

"I see," she says, moving forward to finish the job. She pulls the top off and looks at the fresh grounds. "Oh my God, it smells so good."

"You're gonna get bougie once you start grindin' your own beans," I warn as she pulls two mugs from the cabinet and starts a pot of gourmet coffee.

"I grew up drinkin' the same as Mom and Dad grew up drinkin'—Folgers."

I smile and think about the jingle on the commercial. "In my opinion, it's the official ranch coffee. It's either that or Seaport, and the latter will make hair grow on your balls. It's strong, the stuff sailors drink."

Kaitlyn bursts into laughter. "Actually, it sounds pretty good."

"It's an acquired taste, not my favorite. My mom likes it, though."

"She must have hairy testicles like a caveman, then," she says. I softly chuckle, realizing how much I miss my mother. That's the last thing I wanted to think about today, though.

After it's brewed, Kaitlyn hands my mug over, and I take a sip.

"It's good. You want some eggs?" I offer.

"Nah, I'm gonna stop by the B&B. Maize pulled out some deer sausage and fried it up. Not missin' that."

"Been a while since I've had that. I won't be able to stop by until later. Gotta take care of some shit at the office first thing," I tell her. Her eyes are locked on my lips, and I'm oddly aware of how she studies the different parts of my body. Or maybe she's always done that, and I tried hard not to notice before.

She frowns. "Can't you just tell my brothers to go fuck themselves and then come eat with me?"

Chuckling, I shake my head. "You know for a fact they'd flip their shit. Plus, they're already stressed enough because of how busy we've been. That'd just be cruel."

"I guess."

"What about lunch? You have plans?" I ask.

"Not at the moment. Unless you're askin'."

"Of course I am," I say, checking the time.

She watches me finish my coffee as she adds creamer to hers. "I gotta run." I set my mug down once I've emptied it.

"Have a good day, BD."

"It won't be until lunch," I tease with a wink, and she playfully shoos me away.

After I'm dressed, I grab my keys to leave, and Kaitlyn follows me. She's wearing her riding pants that hug her ass like they were painted on. It doesn't help that they're nude. Makes me wonder how many ranch hands will stare at her today. Better only be me.

"See ya later," I say with a wave.

"Bye!" she says as she pulls her blond hair up into a ponytail.

On my way to work, I stop by the horse rescue to see how much progress has been made since the construction started. Fifteen acres were designated for the nonprofit. The foundation for the large eighteen-stall barn has been poured. The steel support beams were delivered yesterday. When I talked to the construction company, they said it'd be completed in three to four weeks, so we're planning a dedication and grand opening right after the Fourth of July. I'm still pinching myself that this is my life. But the Bishops play hard, so the fact that everything is getting built so fast doesn't surprise me. Also, it helps that the construction company's owner is a friend of the family.

As I finally make my way to the stud facility, I suck in a deep breath and try to push the dirty thoughts of Kaitlyn out of my head. Right now, I need to get my shit together because her brothers aren't nearly as stupid as they sometimes act. They've been pushing Kaitlyn and me pretty hard lately—trying to get the truth out of us—but we haven't slipped.

When I enter the barn, Knox sloshes toward me because he's soaking wet. The fucking sun isn't even awake yet, and he's already found trouble. Typical.

"What happened?" I try to piece together every scenario that could've caused this.

He sucks in a frustrated breath while holding the bridge of his nose. "I tripped on the water hose and landed face-first in the trough I was fillin' up."

I try not to laugh, but it bursts out of me in a roar. As I struggle to breathe, Kane walks up and joins in on poking the bear.

"Fuck y'all. Both of you."

We're bent over, sucking in air as he storms off.

"I'm going home, ya bastards. I'll be back." Knox angrily holds up his middle finger until he's out of sight.

"God," Kane wheezes. "He's so damn clumsy sometimes. I really needed that laugh."

"I'm just pissed I didn't get to witness it. It would've been priceless."

Kane's eyes widen, and realization hits us at the same time—the cameras. I follow him to the office, where he logs into the computer and goes straight to the storage with all the recordings. Once he finds the clip, he presses the button. We watch as Knox clumsily dives into the gigantic tub. He screams obscenities and kicks the hard plastic once he pulls himself out.

"I'm saving this for a rainy day." Kane taps his temple. "Or maybe I'll text this to the family and blow everyone's phones up this morning. Hmm. Decisions."

"Remind me never to piss ya Bishops off."

"Maybe I should let a coin decide?" He pulls a quarter from the top drawer of the desk.

I shake my head and laugh because we both know he'll send it either way. "I don't want to have any part in this."

He flips, catches, and shows me it's on tails.

"Guess I'm sending it," he calls out.

"You never called a side."

"Exactly." Kane sends the forty-second clip to his phone, then attaches the video to a text message. "Should I send it to Hadleigh?"

I lift a brow. "How fast do you want him to find out?"

"You're right. She's not getting a copy yet."

It takes him a minute to find the *family and close friend* group chat we helped set up for the older people. Making a show out of it, he counts down. "Three. Two. One. *Blast off.*"

As soon as it says delivered under his message, I swear I hear every single Bishop laugh at once. I pull out my phone, reading the message Kane attached to it.

Kane: Let's see how long it takes for Knox to realize you all know. Don't tell him or Hadleigh. Have a nice day!

Messages start flying in one by one.

Grandma Bishop: The Lord works in mysterious ways, and laughter is the best medicine.

Kaitlyn: OMFG. He's an IDIOT!

Alex: Someone needs a flashlight. Also, no workman's comp.

Kiera: My poor baby. Y'all be nice.

Jackson sends a laugh-crying emoji.

Jackson: I'm never letting him live this down.

Then Riley, Diesel, Ethan, and so many more numbers all have something to say.

Ivy: For a second, I thought it was you, baby. Glad it wasn't!

She sends a zipped-lip emoji. I swear, they're perfect for one another.

Kane proudly grins as he reads through them.

"I have a feeling your brother is gonna lose his mind when he finds out what you did."

"Oh, they won't tell him for a while, but they'll give him hints about it. Then he'll question them, but they'll never admit it. Hadleigh will find out first, though. Guaranteed. Oh, and before I forget..." He presses the delete key on the keyboard. "So if he gets suspicious and checks the video for it later, he'll think there's zero evidence."

"Smart," I admit. "But I guess if I had a brother like Knox, I'd have figured out all the tricks too."

He stands, and we make our way to the feed room to start our day. After the horses are taken care of and moved to their pastures, I busy myself organizing all of our supplies. We onboard another mare, then the two of us go over the schedule. Knox finally returns, looking freshly showered and dressed.

"Hey, lifejacket," Kane mocks.

Knox flips him the middle finger. "I'll be in my office if you need me."

When we hear the door close, Kane whispers, "He's going to check the cameras."

"How much you wanna bet his mood changes when he sees there isn't any evidence of it?"

"Not a bet I'd take in a million years." He laughs, and we go back to what we were discussing. After fifteen minutes, Knox walks over with a renewed pep in his step.

I give Kane a look, and he gives me a knowing nod but keeps his expression muted.

Knox clears his throat, his cockiness returning. "I'm gonna be makin' the confirmation calls for next week. If there are any cancellations, I'll probably start on the waitlist so we can get those breeding slots filled."

"Sounds good," Kane tells him. "I'm probably gonna go eat in about five minutes, then we can take turns."

"Fine with me," I tell him, then make my way over to the ranch hand truck so I can pick up supplies to build a few more shade shelters for the horses. It's good to have a variety of coverage from the sun, especially since it's been so damn hot lately.

On the way to the supply shed that has all of our tools, wooden posts, and cloth for the roof, I can't help but laugh at Knox. When I park, I text Kaitlyn.

Payton: How many times have you watched the video?

Kaitlyn: My mind has replayed it a thousand times. My parents have been snickering all morning. That was gold.

Payton: Your other brother's idea.

Kaitlyn: See, I'm not the only one who's a savage. You sure you wanna make babies with me?

Payton: Absolutely.

No catching feelings.

I shove my phone into my pocket, then load up everything I need. It takes me about thirty minutes, and when I pull back up to the facility, they're unloading a new horse. I take over for Kane as he handles the client.

Right after I get the new mare settled, my phone buzzes in my pocket again.

Kaitlyn: GET YOUR ASS HOME RIGHT NOW!

I try to understand if this is an emergency, and as I'm typing my response, she sends another message.

Kaitlyn: I GOT A POSITIVE O TEST!

I check the time, and it's not even eight yet. There's no way I can break away.

Payton: I can meet you at the house in an hour when it's my turn to eat at the B&B.

Kaitlyn: Works for me! I'll be naked and waiting.

My heart rate increases thinking about it. I've never wanted Kane to rush while he eats until today. I try to keep myself busy and struggle to keep the thoughts of fucking Kaitlyn raw out of my head. While I'm overly aware of how her body reacts to mine, I try to remember that this is purely transactional. That's it.

Forty-five minutes pass, and when Kane pulls up and parks his truck, I'm already climbing into mine.

"I'll be back in an hour," I tell him after I roll down the window.

He gives me a cautious look. "Going to screw my sister this early?"

I brush him off, forcing out a chuckle that sounds a lot like denial, but I wonder if he somehow knows what's going on. Or maybe he's just fucking with me like usual. When I arrive at my house, her truck is already there. Stepping out, I take my belt off, and Kaitlyn shouts from her room when I walk inside. I kick off my boots, then make my way toward her.

When I finally reach the doorway, Kaitlyn's waiting for me in a bra and panties set that makes my cock hard.

"Ready?" She smirks, then slides off her panties.

"I'm ready to fuck that smirk right off your face."

I cross the room and bend her over the bed. With her perfect ass in the air, I want nothing more than to run my tongue down her slit and taste her pussy.

I lower my jeans and boxer briefs, then stroke myself a few times between her folds.

"Fuck me," she demands. I slam every single inch inside her, and Kaitlyn lets out a groan as she fists the comforter.

Digging my thumbs into her hips, I hold her waist as I pound into her. Grunts release from my throat as her tight pussy squeezes my dick.

"Yes, thatta girl," I whisper, and the sound of my voice has her crying out.

When Kaitlyn reaches down to rub her clit, I encourage her with a smack to the ass. The vibrations from her hand movements as she viciously massages herself feel so fucking good. As Kaitlyn desperately searches for her release, I pump faster to find her magic spot. I love the rhythm our bodies make as we search for the ledge.

Her moans are magical, like the sound of wind chimes blowing in a summer wind, and I can't get enough of her like this. When her body tenses, I don't think I can last much longer.

"Go as deep as you can when you come," she commands as her muscles convulse beneath me. She whimpers, pushing against me and creating more friction as we fuck like animals.

We're both chasing the high, though I have to remind myself that this means nothing. A minute later, my eyes slam shut, and I force myself as deep as I can while emptying every drop inside her.

"God yes," she moans with ragged breaths, her hair a tangled mess as she rolls over. I laugh when she lifts her legs straight in the air.

"What're ya doin'?"

She turns her head and looks at my cock. "That thing is ridiculously talented."

"Don't change the subject." I push at her feet, which are still lifted above her head. She even points her toes for good measure.

"This is supposed to help guide your sperm to my egg. I'm just helping gravity do its job."

"My boys know where to go. I gave them a pep talk." I pull up my boxer briefs, giving my cock time to chill out before I dress. My eyes avoid looking at Kaitlyn from the neck down. Otherwise, he'll be ready for round two at any moment. And we're on a time limit.

"I wish there was a GPS inside my vagina to help them since the others got lost. On a serious note, I've read some pretty weird things people do, and they swear it helps." She wiggles, then holds her hips up higher.

"And how long are you plannin' to do that for?" I finally zip up my jeans and readjust myself.

"At this point, if they said holding a handstand for five hours after sex would guarantee I get pregnant, I'd do it."

I sit on the edge of the bed and turn my body so we can still see each other.

"We'll shoot for round two tonight after we eat dinner. Maybe a round three if you're up for it," she offers with a smirk.

"If I'm up for it?" I scoff. "I can fuck you ten times before work tomorrow. There's no such thing as over-insemination as far as I'm concerned. Following your lead."

"Did you learn that at your fancy stud farm?"

"Actually, yes. It's been *very* educational."

She grins wide as I stand. Before walking away, I take a mental snapshot of her naked body splashed across the bed.

She meets my eyes. "You better grab something to eat, or they'll know you lied about taking your lunch break." Of course she knows I didn't tell her brothers that I was leaving to fuck her brains out.

"You're right. I gotta stay five steps ahead of 'em." I walk down the hallway in search of my boots.

"I'm going to bang you so much during this cycle that your dick's gonna fall off," she shouts from her room.

"Don't get too cocky, *Bishop*." I slip on my boots.

She laughs, and I love the sound of it. A real one, not the sarcastic act she plays with everyone else.

"Have a good rest of your day," I say, grabbing a shitty protein bar but feeling on top of the world.

"You too. I'm serious about tonight!" she calls out, and I hear the springs of her mattress flex just as I walk out the door.

Kaitlyn's everything I want and need, but the one person I can never have.

CHAPTER ELEVEN

KAITLYN

TWO WEEKS LATER

"Son of a bitch!" When I see the negative pregnancy test, I literally want to break it into pieces, but I rein in my frustration and toss it in the trash. Just to be safe, I take two more.

Both. Fucking. Negative.

Considering how many times we've had sex this past month, I was certain I'd see a plus sign.

I sit with my face in my hands and try to push away all the destructive thoughts that fill my head. Then I remind myself to be patient, even if every other Bishop woman has been a fertile Myrtle. I was hoping Payton had super sperm, and I'd be pregnant with blue-eyed, blond hair quadruplets.

After I've gotten dressed and stretched, I make coffee. Once I've drained my first mug, I text him the bad news.

Payton: Don't worry, I'm not stopping until you're knocked up.

I chuckle at his eagerness, though I'm still disappointed.

Kaitlyn: Thanks, but hopefully sooner rather than later.

Patience isn't my strong suit. I'm not great at hiding my feelings, and my parents will be the first ones to call me out since they spend the most time with me during the day. I grab my keys and stop by the B&B to eat breakfast before work.

As soon as I walk into the buffet area, I look around and am thankful I've beaten the crowd. I fill a plateful of French toast and sausage links. As soon as I sit at a table, I see Maize coming out of the kitchen carrying more fruit. She sees me, then makes a beeline toward my table and sits.

"How's the food?" she blurts just as I start chewing. Lifting her hand, she snaps for me to hurry and swallow. Maybe I'm not the only impatient Bishop woman in the family.

I gulp it down. "Great, as always."

Maize tilts her head, studying my face. "What's up with you today?"

I let out a huff and lean forward like we're teenagers sharing secrets. Uncle John has been known to sneak up on us and listen to our conversations before. "I'm frustrated. Another negative test," I tell her.

"That happens, Kate."

"I know, but I'm worried I could have fertility issues like Aunt Courtney. What if I've waited too long to start this process, and now it's too late? What if Payton is shooting blanks, and he can't have kids? My mind is all over the place, and while I knew this wouldn't be easy, I thought I'd have a better chance than being struck by lightning."

She shakes her head. "Get it together before anyone suspects something. Stressin' about it won't help you either."

I blow out a breath. "You're right. I'll try."

A few ranch hands walk in, and Maize gives me a sweet look before lowering her voice. "Maybe more sex is the answer. Start before you get a positive ovulation test and do it three times a day if you have to."

"That's...not a bad idea."

"Of course it isn't because I only have good ones." She smirks before heading back into the kitchen.

After eating, I put up my dishes and head to the training facility.

Today, I'm saying goodbye to Widowmaker since our time together is officially over. His owner, Susan, has been super impressed each time I've updated her on Widowmaker's progress. I'm certain that horse will win some competitions in the near future. It's also a little serendipitous for me to send him home because we bond during our sessions.

He was a good horse—a scaredy-cat but he listened to commands.

As soon as I arrive at work, Mom reminds me that Susan's on her way.

"Do you need any help?" she asks me just as Dad walks over.

"Don't ask me. Can't stand that devil woman."

Mom playfully slaps him. "She's a nice lady."

Dad and I make eye contact, but I refuse to get pulled into this argument. They all know how I feel about her. Honestly, Widowmaker was easier to handle than Susan Henderson.

"Gavin's gonna grab him when she arrives. We've got it," I tell them.

Twenty minutes later, Mrs. Henderson pulls up with her luxurious horse trailer that has the horse's photo airbrushed on both sides. A bit obnoxious for my taste, but I'm also not surprised.

"How's my big boy doin'?" she asks. Her jewelry, belt, and the jewels on her boots rattle with each step she takes.

"He's great," I say, just as Gavin leads him over. Somehow he makes her horse look like a pony. "I think you're gonna be impressed with his progress."

She smiles wide. "I knew you'd get it done, Kaitlyn. I'm willing to say you're better at this than your parents."

I know she means it as a compliment, so I keep my smile planted. "Oh, thank you, but I don't know about that. My mom is the best around. She taught me everything. Well, and my dad, too."

"So how much do I owe you?"

I lead her to my office to sign the release and document her final payment.

Without hesitation, she writes a check, signs the paperwork, and then she's out the door.

"You good?" Gavin asks me as we make our way back to the barn.

"Yeah, but I'm gonna miss that cranky horse. I get too attached." I frown, and he chuckles.

"Nothin' wrong with that. Just means you're actually a big ole softy and like to act scary so people fear ya," he teases.

I swat at him but miss because he's one of the only ranch hands who isn't intimidated by me. Then again, he married Maize, and her attitude is worse than mine.

"I'm telling your wife to withhold lovin' for a week if you spill my secret."

He chuckles. "I'd like to see ya try."

"Make it a month!"

Gavin shakes his head and goes back to what he was doing before I asked for his help.

For the rest of the morning, I stay busy doing work in the saddle and don't get a free moment to think while switching out horses.

By the time lunch rolls around, I don't have an appetite, but Mom brought leftovers, and I couldn't say no to her spaghetti and homemade meatballs.

While eating in my office, I read several articles and forums about fertility issues. Several blogs mention cleaning up my diet.

I've already tried a handful of ridiculous things and cut back on my caffeine. Then I find one that lists a number of things the male partner can do.

Maybe Maize has the right idea after all.

Kaitlyn: Hey BD! We're gonna have to fuck more often.

I know he's busy as hell, so I'm shocked when he immediately replies.

Payton: More than twice a day like we were?

Kaitlyn: Yes, it's obviously not enough. So as soon as my period's over, we're starting again. Getting way ahead of my ovulation might secure your little swimmers are in there when I do ovulate.

Payton: Okay.

Kaitlyn: Also, I'm really gonna need you to stop wearing the briefs and switch to straight old-fashioned boxers.

Payton: Uhh.

Kaitlyn: I already ordered them for you.

Payton: And what's that gonna do?

Kaitlyn: Be less restricting and give you super sperm.

Kaitlyn: Oh and you gotta eat Brazilian nuts until I'm knocked up. Allegedly, they help your little swimmers' mobility and increase testosterone.

Payton: It's only been five or six weeks, Kate.

Kaitlyn: Right, but each day is another one closer to my 31st birthday!

Payton: Are you still meeting me at the horse rescue at 1?

I notice the abrupt change in subject, but I'm happy for the reminder. I'm supposed to meet him in about fifteen minutes so we can make sure everything's on track to get done in a couple of weeks.

Kaitlyn: Yep, that's the plan.

Payton: Awesome! Your brothers are around, and they have wandering eyes anytime I get on my phone. See ya in a few.

Kaitlyn: Sounds good.

Instead of locking my phone, I make a list of things I haven't tried yet, like eating the core of a pineapple when I'm ovulating or using a magic menstrual cup to keep the sperm inside longer after sex. One article talked about placing egg whites in my hoo-ha, but that's where I'm drawing the line.

As soon as my mom walks in and stands next to my desk, I lock my phone and finish eating.

"How was it?" she asks, grabbing a bottle of water from my mini fridge.

"The best. Always love your cookin'. Kinda miss it," I admit.

She smiles. "I miss you being home too. It's taken some adjustin'. That's for sure."

"I'm just down the road," I remind her.

"Oh, I know. I was just spoiled havin' all the kids around, and now that the house is empty, it's a daily reminder that we're all gettin' a little older and that my babies are grown up."

"I'm sure Dad's enjoyin' the quiet, though."

She nods. "He walks around naked ninety-nine percent of the time now. So if you come over, ring the doorbell first."

"Oh God, the visual I just got." I shiver, hoping I keep my food down after that.

Mom's phone buzzes, and she walks off with a quick wave as she answers. I rinse out the plastic container, then check the time, knowing I need to leave now.

As soon as I arrive, I meet Payton inside the nearly finished structure.

"Wow, it's so huge," I say, walking around the space. Right now, it's just an empty building, but it's progressing.

"I can't wait to see it once the stables and offices are built," I say, visualizing where it will all go.

Payton turns around, and he's smiling so wide it's contagious. I move forward, and he wraps his arm around me. "This would've never happened without you."

A blush creeps up my cheeks as his fingers slide against my bare skin. I place my arm around the backside of his waist as we look around in awe.

"All you, Payton. I wouldn't want to go on this journey with anyone else."

He slightly squeezes me. "I couldn't agree more."

CHAPTER TWELVE

PAYTON

ONE WEEK LATER

As I WALK AWAY from the water trough, I try to adjust the loose-fitting boxers I'm wearing today. Nothing like having my balls tap against my leg with every step I take. Kaitlyn's lucky she's my best friend because these are uncomfortable as fuck.

"You're still walkin' funny," Knox mocks as soon as I enter the barn.

"Shut the hell up," I mutter, adjusting the material in my jeans. I'm not sure I'll ever get used to wearing them. I know I'm not the only one who's making sacrifices. Kaitlyn's been eating like an athlete now by adding more vegetables and protein to her diet. She's just as strict with herself as she is with me, which I respect.

After mucking out the stalls and leading several horse couples to their free-roam pastures, I take my lunch break. I grab my bag from the fridge, then warm up my large bowl of lima beans with chunks of bacon.

Another one of Kaitlyn's *ideas*.

Kane looks at me over his shoulder. "What is that gross smell?"

"Just some legumes."

His face wrinkles. "Smells like dog food. Did Maize cook that?"

Laughter escapes me. "No, but I'll be sure to give your sister your compliments."

"Jesus, Payton. You don't have to eat that shit when she's not around. She'll never know."

The microwave beeps, and I stir the beans, then put it back in for twenty more seconds.

"Smells like a punishment."

"It's actually pretty good," I admit.

He barks out a laugh. "Doubt that." Once he grabs what he needs, he leaves.

I sit at the small table we've got set up in the break room. I take the lid off the spinach salad and set the giant bag of Brazilian nuts on the table.

Once I've finished half of my beans, Knox walks in. "What stinks?"

I roll my eyes. "Shut up."

"Smells like baby shit." He stands over me and glances in my bowl. "Looks like it too."

"You'd know," I quip.

Reaching forward, he takes several nuts out of the bag and pops them in his mouth. "Damn. These are so good."

"I wouldn't eat too many of those," I warn.

"You've got the supersize bag. Don't be greedy." He takes a few more, then shouts over his shoulder. "Kane! He brought those weird nuts again!"

Seconds later, Kane crowds the table and fills up his palm.

"Dude. These things aren't cheap," I explain, snatching the bag out of his hand.

"They're delicious, though. I'm gonna tell Hadleigh to buy

me some," Knox says, throwing one in the air, then catching it in his mouth.

All I can do is shake my head as they finally leave me alone. They already have super sperm.

Just as I take my last bite, my phone buzzes in my pocket, and I immediately grin when I see her name.

Kaitlyn: It's time to bang, BD ;)

I send her a teasing reply.

Payton: Might need to check my schedule.

Kaitlyn: Don't you dare play with me!

With a knowing smirk, I think about being inside her again. Fuck, I'm already growing hard. My body shouldn't respond like this when this is just about making a baby and nothing more.

Payton: Who said I was playing?

Kaitlyn: You're gonna pay for that.

Payton: Lucky me.

Kaitlyn: Not sure I'd be lookin' forward to what I have in store for you.

Payton: Does it involve rope?

I must not flirt, I say on repeat in my mind, but clearly, my heart isn't listening.

Kaitlyn: It can. Or handcuffs.

Now she's teasing *me*.

Payton: Throw in some candle wax and you've got yourself a deal.

Kaitlyn's text bubble pops up and disappears.

Kaitlyn: I've been called Kinky Kaitlyn before...so be careful what you wish for. Not sure you could handle that side of me.

I can't help but imagine her biting the corner of her lip as she responds, swiping her blond hair away from her face. Even though she wears it in a ponytail while she's working, little strands always fall out. I find myself longing to tuck them behind her ears.

Kaitlyn Bishop is a firecracker, and I'm attracted to her scorching flame. Kaitlyn isn't afraid to tell me what she wants, but her body tells me everything she holds back.

Fuck, fuck, fuck. When I stand, my cock is at full attention, and it's so goddamn hard it feels like it's gonna snap off. These damn boxers aren't doing shit to conceal it.

"Next horse just arrived," Knox shouts from the thoroughfare.

Closing my eyes, I suck in a deep breath, but when my phone vibrates, I brace myself for what she's sent.

A picture of her from behind. *Wearing a thong.* One sentence accompanies the picture.

Kaitlyn: Get your best swimmers ready.

If her tight cunt was here right now, I'd shove myself so goddamn deep inside her and roughly pull her hair to show her what happens when you taunt the beast. I crave hearing her breathy pants and moaning my name as she takes me all in. Fuck, her seduction techniques are working.

I shove the dirty dishes into my lunch bag, then adjust my cock.

Payton: You're gonna pay for that. Horse just arrived, so I can't ditch. But I'll be there as soon as I can.

Kaitlyn: Well, shit. I'm gonna have to get back to the stables. Rain check? I expect more than one time then to make it up to me.

Payton: You've got yourself a deal.

I lock my phone and shove it in my pocket, begging my boner to disappear. I grab the lead rope hanging by the door on my way to meet the customer outside.

As soon as she hops out of her truck, she roams her eyes up and down my body, then licks her ruby lips like I'm hot chocolate on a cold day. Her mouth curves into a devious smile, and I politely greet her with a nod.

"Howdy. Is this Gypsy Moon?"

"Sure is," she drawls, eye-fucking every inch of my body. *Jesus fucking Christ.*

She opens the trailer door and out backs a beautiful gray Appaloosa with black and white spots.

Moments later, Knox comes out, and luckily, every bit of her attention focuses on him. Until she sees the gold wedding band on his left hand.

"Ma'am, if you could follow me, we'll get your paperwork taken care of," Knox tells her as I take the horse.

She glances at me over her shoulder, but I ignore it as I lead Gypsy Moon into her stall. As soon as she goes into Knox's office, she giggles, and it's obvious she's a flirt, even with married men.

I check the horse's hooves, teeth, and walk around her hind quarters to make sure she has no scratches or scars. She's in perfect, healthy condition, and I appreciate how unbothered she is by my presence.

Once I've completed my checklist, I let Knox know she's settled and good to go. I'm tempted to text Kaitlyn and tell her to meet me at the house, but I know her schedule has been hectic as hell lately. Instead, I head out to the pastures to check the fences. It's busy work or, rather, a way for me to avoid everyone inside.

An hour passes and when I return to the barn, Knox hands me a sticky note. I look at it and see a phone number written down.

"What's this?" I ask.

"Gypsy Moon's owner. She asked if you were single. I mean, unless you want to finally admit you're datin' my sister." He crosses his arms over his chest. He's grinning like a fool, so I know it's a trap.

"I'm not datin' your sister," I confirm.

He lifts his brow as if he doesn't believe me. "So you're just fuckin' her, then?"

"Don't talk about your sister like that. It's not my responsibility to prove shit to you, and I really don't give a shit whether you believe me." I bark out, ignoring his last question.

"I don't want this." I hold up the note, but he holds up his palms as if he's not touching it either, so I begrudgingly shove it in my pocket to trash later.

Kane walks up with my Brazilian nuts in his hand, and I quickly snatch them away. "Get your own damn nuts."

They both burst into laughter, but the jokes on them because they have no idea what these things do. Good thing Ivy's already pregnant.

The rest of the day passes by quickly, but I'm counting down the minutes until I can leave. On the way home, I get a burst of energy, remembering what I'm planning tonight. When I walk in the door and find Kaitlyn in the kitchen, she's pulling food out of a to-go bag.

"Mm, smells good," I say, removing my hat and scrubbing a hand through my hair.

"Maize made chicken fried steaks, macaroni and cheese, and Southern green beans. Oh, and I got us a slab of cornbread. I know I've been strict lately with the carbs, but I couldn't say no to this."

"Don't blame ya." I empty my pockets, then sit on the stool next to her at the breakfast bar. After she plates our food, we dig in.

"What's this?" she asks, grabbing the crumpled note next to my keys.

"Some chick's number who dropped off her mare today."

"Are you gonna call her?"

Her tone shifts as if she's worried. "No."

"Was she cute?"

"She was pretty. Not my type, though."

"*Pretty* isn't your type?" she muses.

"What's this really about?" I furrow my brow.

Kaitlyn breaks off a piece of cornbread. "Nothin', but if you wanted to date—"

"I don't," I quickly say before she can finish. "Pretty sure no woman would be okay with their man tryin' to knock up his best friend. Not a real conversation starter."

She snorts. "Fair point. But if you wanted to, I was just lettin' you know you don't have to avoid it on my account."

My jaw ticks, but I don't continue the conversation. Now wouldn't be the time to tell her I have no interest in dating other women because she's the only person I could see myself having a future with. I'm still surprised she can't see how enamored I am with her.

"Both your brothers said your beans stink," I say with a chuckle.

"Yeah, well that's Grandma's recipe. You think they'd dare tell her that?"

"She'd serve their heads on a platter at Christmas." I laugh, then take a huge bite of the buttery cornbread.

"Exactly."

She continues to chat about her busy-as-hell day. After we clear our plates, I clean up, then smell myself. "I'm gonna jump in the shower."

She looks down at her smartwatch, then I meet her heated gaze. "Make it snappy. I've been waitin' for you all day."

I shake my head. "Why are all you Bishops so damn demanding?"

She shrugs. "Runs in the family."

"The truest words I've ever heard. Gimme about fifteen minutes," I tell her, then make my way down the hallway.

"Make it ten!" she shouts, and I chuckle.

The steaming hot stream cascades down my back, and as it runs down my sore muscles, I sigh with how amazing it feels. Between work and getting ready for the rescue to officially open, I've been exhausted but in a good way.

Just as I'm rinsing the shampoo out of my hair, I hear the bathroom door creak open. Seconds later, a naked Kaitlyn slides in next to me.

I lift an eyebrow, utterly confused. "What're ya doin'?"

"If I'm gonna get pregnant as soon as possible, we should use all our free time." She bites the corner of her lip and takes a step forward, placing her hands on my chest. My cock is already at full attention and poking her in the stomach.

It was only a few weeks ago when I barged in while she was taking a shower, so I'm not even mad about it. Sex with her anywhere is hot as hell but in close quarters like this, it's even better.

Kaitlyn reaches down between her legs and plays with her clit. A small whimper releases from her and I'd be goddamned if

I didn't crumble to dust right then and there. When she inserts a finger inside, then places it in her mouth to taste herself, I can't take it any longer.

"My body is always ready for you," she admits

"Turn around," I demand.

She does and carefully steadies herself with her palms against the wall and arches her back. I stroke my erection and slide it down her ass crack before slamming inside her wet pussy. A loud gasp escapes her as I pull out, then thrust back in.

Taking a risk, I lean in and whisper against her ear, "That's my good girl. Your tight cunt feels amazin'."

Her breathing immediately rushes out in heavy pants, and I know she enjoys the dirty talk.

Reaching around her waist, I rub circles on her clit. She's so goddamn greedy, and I want to give her everything I have.

"Fuck," she hisses, pushing back against me as if she can't get enough. "Rules."

I hold in my laughter. Go figure, she'd try to scold me.

"God, Kate," I groan as she squeezes my dick.

"I need to come," she begs, but somehow demands me at the same time. I pull out, and she looks over her shoulder with a glare as if I wronged her. Carefully, I turn her around and drop to my knees, then lift her thigh over my shoulder. Not waiting another second, I devour her sweet cunt the way she's always deserved. Sneaking a glance up, I watch as she looks at me, and the moment feels too intimate. Kaitlyn sinks into me and tugs my hair as she writhes against me. My gaze gravitates toward her plump breasts and nipples that are at full attention. I want to take one into my mouth and nip it with my teeth, but I opt for a light twist while I flick and suck her needy clit.

Her hips buck as I tongue fuck her beautiful, bare pussy. I lap up all of her arousal and tease her with my tongue the way she likes—fast and forceful, then so damn slow it's agonizing. Her orgasm builds, and when she throws her head, I know she's close. As she tenses and shakes, I grab a handful of her breast with one hand and press a finger in her puckered ass with the other. She gasps, forcefully running her fingers through my hair, then comes all over my face.

I eat her cunt like it's my last meal. She tastes better than a sugary-sweet snow cone on a hot summer day.

When I stand to meet her heated gaze, I say, "I don't get on my knees for just anyone." I flash her a wink, proudly licking my lips and wishing I could kiss her.

Kaitlyn looks up at me with sultry bedroom eyes, and I place my hands against the wall, caging her in. I beg her with my eyes to tell me what she's thinking, but we're in a trance. One I never want to escape.

Kaitlyn's chest rises and falls as the magnetic tug pulls our mouths closer. If she wants me to kiss her as badly as I need to, she has to be the one to cross this line.

Something dangerous brews between us—an avalanche that neither of us will be able to stop once it starts. When her eyes flutter closed, I cup her cheek and rub my thumb over her mouth. My willpower is holding on by a thread, dangling in our faces as we struggle to hang on. By some goddamn miracle, I take a step back and recompose myself so we can continue and finish.

Kaitlyn looks down at my hard cock, then turns around and bends over for me again.

"Break me," she says over her shoulder with her blond hair stuck to her wet body.

Digging my thumbs into her hips, she eagerly spreads her legs and gives me plenty of room to thrust in deep with one swift movement. She groans as I slam into her, over and over. Heat rushes through me, and emotions I shouldn't be feeling gather in my heart.

When I forcefully slap her round ass, she begs for more.

Sounds of our bodies slapping together echo throughout the bathroom.

"Payton," she cries out my name—which drives me absolutely wild—as I continue my pace. "I'm so close again. Don't stop."

"Say please, and I won't," I taunt, desperate to hear her say it. *Beg* for it.

"God, please! I'm—"

The words sit on the tip of her tongue as her body convulses and teeters over the edge. I continue my pace, pumping inside her and chasing ecstasy. As she tightens around my cock, the build takes over, and the explosion rocks through me. Kaitlyn sinks deeper, taking all of my come. Once I've spilled everything inside her, she squeezes her legs together and leans against the wall.

"That felt..." She struggles to catch her breath.

I study her expression as neither of us wants to admit we nearly lost control. Whatever is brewing between us is undeniable, but I'm too scared to risk it by making the first move.

"Hopefully, like we finally made a baby," I add with a forced grin, and she softly chuckles.

"I hope so."

"We'll find out soon," I say, moving to the side so she can get some of the warmth from the stream.

"I hate to break it to you, but that was only round one. Better prepare for another later." She smirks, then steps out of the shower and grabs a towel.

"I'll be ready," I tell her.

When she walks out, and the bathroom door closes, I stand under the water and try to calm my racing heart.

How the hell am I gonna survive this?

CHAPTER THIRTEEN

KAITLYN

AFTER MY MORNING lesson with Starstruck, I hop off the saddle, brush him, then send him into the pasture to graze. I have an hour before I start working my next horse, but I also need to eat. Before making my way to the B&B, Dad stops me in my tracks.

"Kaitlyn!" he shouts from his office.

I huff, then turn around and walk back toward him.

"Yes?" I ask, looking at my smartwatch, hoping he catches the hint that I'm pressed for time.

"This came," he says, grabbing an envelope and handing it to me.

Confused, I take it and pull the piece of paper from the neatly cut slit at the top. I read the first few lines and realize this is the official paperwork for the rescue. There's an official seal from the state of Texas declaring the sanctuary as an official nonprofit. Of course we'd applied electronically and were approved, but holding the certificate in my hand makes it more real.

"Thought you could hang it in the office in the new barn," Dad suggests with a proud grin.

"Yes, wow." I look down at it in awe. "It's really happening."

"Considering the stables are nearly done, I'd say there's no doubt about that," he teases.

I tap the envelope against the palm of my opposite hand. "Thanks for this."

"Proud of you, sweetheart."

Now I'm the one cheesing.

"Grab me some apple pie from the B&B, will ya?" he calls out as I walk out.

"Yeah, okay!" I shake my head.

I quickly stop by the rescue to see how the progress with the barn is coming along. We have a little over two weeks before the grand opening. Once I'm out of my truck, I take a quick walk through the barn for some photos. I hold up the envelope in front of the entrance, then snap a picture for Payton.

Kaitlyn: All we need is a frame!

Payton: I'm on it. We'll have our first rescue before we know it.

Kaitlyn: I'm getting a little nervous! A giddy nervous, though.

Payton: Me too. Feels surreal.

I smile at his message before heading to the B&B. Instead of piling my plate full of carbs, I make a grilled chicken salad with a side of fresh strawberries.

Just as I take my first bite, Maize walks up and stares at me. "What are you doin'?"

"What's it look like?" I swallow down the lettuce.

"It looks like you're eatin' like a rabbit." She plops down in front of me.

"I'm just tryin' to stay healthy."

She meets my gaze. "So how's the baby-makin' goin'?"

"Not great." I take a bite of chicken and angrily chew. "I'm frustrated as fuck."

"Let me reword that. How's the sex?" she mocks, stealing a strawberry.

I sigh. "Good. Oh my God. So fuckin' good. It makes it worth it. I mean yeah, I want a baby, but I can't say I'm not enjoying myself trying to make one."

Maize narrows her eyes at me. "But you're still *just friends*?" She lifts her fingers and quotes her final words.

"How're the girls and Mav doin'?" I ask. Between her and Gavin's busy work schedule, I don't know how they keep up with three kids.

"Don't try changing the subject. The kids are rowdy and keeping us busy as usual. Now answer my question."

"Yes, we're friends, roommates, and future co-parents." Sighing, I try to ignore the fact that he called me *good girl* in the shower yesterday or that I've been fantasizing about it every minute since. I cross my legs underneath the table, the movement causing friction between my thighs.

"Whatever you say," she sing-songs as she goes to the buffet, then returns. "You look like you could use this," she tells me, sliding a piece of apple pie across the table.

"Oh, my dad wanted a piece. Thanks for the reminder."

She shakes her head and makes her way back to the kitchen. I quickly finish eating, sneak a bite of the crust and filling, then shove it in a to-go box.

When I return to the training facility, I hand it over to Dad. Five seconds later, he's complaining in his doorway about it being half-eaten.

"I had to make sure it tasted good and wasn't poisonous." I grin.

He narrows his eyes.

Mom walks up. "Oh, let me check too."

"Just a little." Dad lifts the top for Mom, who then snags a huge bite and pops it in her mouth.

"Oh yeah, it's good enough for you, honey."

Dad slams the lid down. "A buncha pie thieves."

"What's yours is mine," she taunts.

"I'm tempted to ask Maize to make me a whole one," he says, walking away with his sad half-eaten slice.

Mom walks over and gives me a high five.

"I needed that laugh," I admit.

"Me too," she says.

I head to the tack room and grab my riding helmet. Rolling Thunder and I will be practicing walking pirouettes. It's a turning movement that must be executed flawlessly in dressage. The rhythm of their walk is crucial during competition.

After I have the saddle and bridle on him, we get to work in the arena. My outside worries and fears melt away when I'm training. Only when I'm not riding can I be reminded of what I don't have.

An hour passes, and I notice Zach running through the arena. I want to scold him to slow down so he doesn't spook the horse, but it's too late. Immediately, the agitation and bucking start. Though I'm used to it, I'm still annoyed because I've told my little cousin a million times not to do that. But he's only eleven and tends to forget sometimes.

Once the Arabian settles, I hop off and lead him out so I can remove all of the gear. As soon as we step into the equipment stall, I snap the two lead ropes on the halter to hold him in place.

Zach eagerly follows me like a shadow while talking my ear off. I swear his dad gave him a bucket of sugar to eat for lunch.

"Do you remember the rule about no running in the practice area when I'm training?" I ask, keeping my tone level when he finally takes a breath long enough to listen. He's been talking a million miles per minute about some new video game I have zero concept of.

"Whoops. I forgot." He shrugs like it's no big deal.

"I could've fallen off with all that hollerin' you were doin'." I shoot him a stern look.

"Nah, you're too good at ridin'. You're like the best on the ranch. No, in Texas! Everyone knows that."

I brush my shoulder off and give him a wink. If he wants to boost my ego, I won't stop him.

"I mean you're not wrong, but that still doesn't mean you don't need to follow the rules. Even the best fall and get hurt, Zach. Just gotta be aware and not make any sudden movements, loud noises, or anything like that when hooves are on the dirt. Got it?"

"Okay, got it. I just wanted you to know I'm already here and workin'," he states. "Do you remember what today is?"

"Well, I know it's not your birthday because you just turned eleven last week." I purse my lips as if I'm thinking hard about it.

He laughs when I remove the saddle and put it up.

"It's payday!"

"Are you sure?" I'm messing with him, but it's too easy at his age.

He nods frantically. "Yes!"

"Did you hang the hay nets in the first few stalls?" I adjust my ponytail.

"Yep. I even cleaned some of them. I'm gonna finish doin' that, then feed them so I can be home before dark."

"Good idea. Once I'm done here, I'll come find you." I take the bridle out of the horse's mouth, then grab a brush and start at the top of his back down to his hind quarters.

Zach smiles wide. "Awesome! I've got some things to buy."

I look at him over my shoulder, narrowing my eyes at what an eleven-year-old would need to buy. "Like what?"

"My friend's birthday is coming up after July Fourth, and I want to get her somethin'," he explains.

"Ohh...your *girlfriend*?"

"No, gross!" His face wrinkles, and he reminds me so much of Riley it's scary. "She's *just* my friend who's a girl!"

"Whatever you say," I sing-song as he storms away. I chuckle to myself, realizing I act the same way when people call me out. Riling him up is much more fun than being on the receiving end of it.

After everything is put up, I check the time, then go to my office and grab the cash I set aside for Zach. Ever since he's been on summer break, the kid has worked his butt off without me having to micromanage his every move. He works harder than some of the adult ranch hands. Without him, I wouldn't have had nearly as much time to finalize things for the horse rescue.

I've been keeping up with construction and ordering all the supplies we need. Some of the ranch hands have helped build the corral and finish adding locks and doors to the stalls.

When I meet up with him, sweat drips from his forehead. Working in the late-June heat is miserable for everyone, including the horses.

He sets down the shovel and looks up at me.

"Ready?" I ask, and he holds up his palm. When I went to the bank, I got mostly fives, tens, and a couple of twenties so he has a variety.

I count out two-hundred dollars, and his eyes light up at how thick the stack is.

"Oh wait. Can I borrow a hundred?" I ask with a smirk.

"Sure," he says, handing me half of what I've given him.

Laughing, I shake my head. "I was just jokin'. You're too sweet.".

"I think you overpaid me, though," he tells me, flipping through it.

"No, I didn't. You earned that. Consider it a bonus. But don't spend it all in one place for your girlfriend."

He shoves it in his pocket, pride radiating off him. "She's a friend who's a girl!"

"What's her name again? Lilac? Lily? Layla?"

"Lilia!" he corrects with an eye roll. "And she wants fairy lights and a vanity mirror for her room. Think I'll have enough money?"

I chuckle. "Yes, you'll have plenty. Make sure to also get her a sweet birthday card with a handwritten note. Chicks dig that."

"Ugh." He smacks a hand on his forehead.

Laughing, I watch as he gets back to what he was doing.

"You still gonna have time to feed the horses before dark?" I ask when I check the time.

"Yes, ma'am. And I've memorized the checklist," he explains. "But I'll mark off each box once I'm done."

I wrote out how much food each horse gets so he could keep track on his own. It's been a good way to teach him about responsibility and proper horse care.

Even though he's only eleven, the kid pays attention to detail better than my dumb-ass brothers. He's my buddy, and one of the reasons I can't wait to have my own little ones running around. Showing them all about ranch life and caring for horses is something I hope we can bond over once they're older.

As I leave Zach to his tasks, I grab my keys from my office and tell my parents I'm heading out.

"Dinner tonight at seven," Mom says. She's been reminding me for over a week that she's cooking for the family tonight.

"Ya know I never pass up free food. I'll be there!"

"And what about Payton?" she inquires, but I see something more behind her eyes. Maybe it's an insinuation, but I can't pinpoint it.

I sigh. "He'll be there, too."

Once I'm in my truck, I drive to the B&B real quick, then I go home and shower.

When I'm ready, I message Payton in case he needs a reminder about tonight.

Payton: I didn't forget.

Kaitlyn: Good, cause I think my mom would've been sad if you weren't.

Payton: What can I say? Your parents love me.

I smile because he's right. They've always adored him and have treated him like he's one of their own.

After I'm dressed, I'm tempted to pour myself a glass of wine, but instead, I opt for a large glass of orange juice. I randomly read that vitamin C can help a person conceive. I'd drink a truckload if it'd guarantee a positive pregnancy test.

As soon as Payton walks in, his warm smile fills the room.

"Hey," he greets as his gaze wanders over me. "You look nice."

"Thanks."

"Smell nice too." He grins. "I'm gonna quickly shower."

"I'll be waitin'," I tell him, tempted to join him to get my mind off things. But I know it wouldn't be a good idea after the way things got heated between us the last time. Though I'd never admit it aloud, I wanted Payton to kiss me and let me taste myself on him. The lines were nearly crossed, and I selfishly wanted him to be the one to cross them first.

I wish I could read Payton's mind, but at the same time, I'm too scared to know what he's thinking.

Payton enters the room in clean clothes and smelling like body wash. "Ready?"

"Yep." I stand, grabbing the dessert dish covered in foil.

"What's that?" he asks.

"I asked Maize for a favor."

He lifts the top. "Mm. Apple pie."

"Dad's favorite." I grin. "Kinda owe him after Mom and I ate half of his slice today."

"I'm sure he'll appreciate that."

Payton puts on his baseball cap, then leads me to his truck. When he opens the passenger door for me, he lightly places his hand on the small of my back. It's a gesture he's done a million times before, but now, it feels different. Intimate. Something a boyfriend would do.

When we pull up to my parents' house, I grow nervous, and Payton notices.

"You okay?" he asks as he kills the engine.

"What if they see through us? Our plan?"

He smirks. "It won't be any different than the shit they always give us."

"That's true," I say, relaxing my shoulders.

We get out of the truck, and I suck in a deep breath before we enter my parents' house.

"What's that?" Mom asks with Hendrix and Hannah on her lap. They're climbing on her like a jungle gym.

"It's for Dad and *only Dad*," I confirm.

Mom laughs because she knows what we did earlier.

Knox yanks the foil off the top, and his jaw drops. "Apple pie?"

"That's mine!" Dad stands and grabs it from my hands. Wrapping his free arm around me, he kisses the top of my head. "This is why you're my favorite kid."

"Suck-up." Kane rolls his eyes at the same time as Knox makes a face at me.

Hadleigh and I make small talk while Mom pulls a lasagna out of the oven along with two loaves of garlic bread. The hearty aromas have my mouth watering. It's been a while since I've had her homemade recipe.

"You look really good, Kaitlyn," Hadleigh says, eyeing me up and down. "I love that top on you."

"Thank you. It's a newer one." And it shows off my boobs

nicely, which wasn't on purpose, but I was able to buy a smaller size, and now it's accentuating my chest.

"Okay, dinner's ready, y'all," Mom announces, and we all find our seats.

"Time for the blessing 'cause I'm starvin'," Dad says once it quiets down.

We bow our heads as he says grace, and then we immediately dig in.

"This is so good, Mom," I tell her. "I'm gonna have a food baby later."

Ivy snickers, and Kane gives her a look before clearing his throat. "Do you wanna tell them, sweetheart?"

"Sure." She swallows hard as we all wait. "So we had our ultrasound, and it turns out we're having twins!"

The room bursts into chatter as a whirlwind of emotions nearly knocks the breath out of me. Of course, Payton notices, and he gently squeezes my thigh. I force a smile, not wanting to make this exciting moment about myself.

"Congratulations," I say. "I'm so happy to be getting two more nieces or nephews!"

"Or one of each," Hadleigh gushes, wrapping her arms around Ivy. The rest of us join in celebratory hugs.

"You're gonna have your hands full," Mom teases. "But don't worry, we'll help as much as we can."

Everyone is smiling, but right now, I feel like crying.

I'm excited for them and hate the feeling of jealousy that burns inside me. Kane and Ivy deserve this just as much as anyone else who wants a baby, but constantly watching everyone around me get pregnant is just a reminder that it might not be in the cards for me.

Although Mom has fudge sundaes, Dad shares his apple pie with us. After we finish eating, Payton stretches with a yawn, glancing over at me. If I didn't know any better, I'd think he was trying to give us an out to leave early. He's the only one who knows I'm having an internal meltdown.

Once we help put the dishes away and the kitchen is cleaned, we say our goodbyes. We thank my mom for a delicious dinner, then I tell my brother and Ivy congratulations again and punch Knox in the shoulder before walking out.

As soon as the warm summer air hits my cheeks, a few tears slip down my face. I hurry and wipe them away, but Payton catches me.

I'm angry with myself for feeling envious. I'm mad at my body and how unfair all of this feels.

Once we're in Payton's truck, he cranks it, then meets my eyes.

"Just because you don't have what you want right now doesn't mean you'll never have it," he reminds me, just as he has several times before.

Frowning, I nod. "I know. Patience isn't my strong suit."

He places his hand on top of mine as we back out of the driveway and make our way home. "No, but you're strong and resilient, Kate."

"I wish I was stronger. This might actually break me," I admit, my voice cracking.

He pulls onto the main road and takes his time driving.

"There was a point in my life when I thought I was broken, too. But the reality is, we have both lived through a hundred percent of our worst days."

"That's true. Never thought of it that way."

"I planned a future with my ex, hoping to start a family with my wife, and even after she tore it apart, I know now that just because I didn't get it with her doesn't mean I won't ever have it. But for years, I thought that was my reality. *Years.* I was hell-bent on accepting it, too."

I stay quiet, allowing the rumble of the engine to soothe me as I listen.

"What changed?" I ask.

"My life and everything that I'd known had fallen apart in a matter of weeks. I dreamed about coming home every evening to my wife and kids, and growing old together. Talkin' about our days over dinner and spending the evening relaxing or playing. I craved the consistency and family atmosphere. It was something I never really had after my dad died."

I glance at him, hearing the crack in his voice.

"Yes, I know I don't have those things now either," he clarifies as if he's reading my mind. "And maybe I don't have a wife, Kate, and perhaps I never will. But I have you. That makes me just as happy."

His words have my face splitting in half. "You'll always have me." I can't imagine my life without him in it, and even if we don't have a baby together, I hope nothing changes between us.

"And you'll always have me, too."

A million different sentences build in my head, but not a word comes out when I open my mouth. After he parks and we walk inside the house, his words play on repeat in my mind.

"What're you thinkin'?" He plops down next to me on the couch, and we're so close that I can feel the warmth of his body.

"Nothin'," I lie, though I'm wondering how things would change between us when he does want to start dating and putting himself out there. The last thing I'd ever want to do is get in his way or hurt his chances of having a partner. Any woman would be lucky to have him as a husband.

Payton turns and tucks loose strands of hair behind my ear. His intense gaze burns my skin, but I welcome it. I swallow hard, studying his mouth, wanting to feel his scruff trail along my face and thighs. Being with him right now isn't a want. It's a goddamn need, a burning desire rooted so deeply that if I don't have him, I might lose my mind.

He licks his lips as I hold his gaze, and we hold a silent conversation. Then he stands, takes my hand, and leads me to his bedroom. Payton slowly brushes my hair over one shoulder and carefully undresses me as if he wants to memorize every bare inch.

I lie back on the bed as he removes his shirt, giving me the perfect view of his washboard abs. As we watch each other, he kicks off his boots and strips down.

I widen my legs as he kneels on the bed, climbing over me and settling between my thighs. Though we've been fucking like rebellious teenagers, it feels different this time when he intimately slides between my folds. I gasp, sucking in air as he fills me deep and full. His slow rhythm and calculated movements are intentional as he traces around the shell of my ear with his tongue. With each thrust, my heart thumps harder.

I've read that when you have sex with someone you have feelings for, your body releases a hormone that helps the chances of getting pregnant. I can't help but wonder if that's what we've been missing—*intimacy.*

It's something we both need and crave. A connection we could never have with anyone else.

Payton groans and hisses as he pumps harder, slamming into my G-spot over and over. I get lost in the sensations as they build toward the peak. His expression is unreadable as I scratch my nails down his back. The sound that releases from the back of his throat is rough and animalistic.

Wanting to ride him, I gesture for us to switch positions. As soon as I straddle his legs, I slowly slide down his thick cock, and we moan together. He reaches up to my breast and pinches a nipple, encouraging me to arch into him. Then I grab his wrists and force them over his head. As I lean down, our mouths are mere centimeters apart, and our breathing is unsteady when I rotate my hips. I don't know what comes over me, but I want nothing more than to crash my lips to his.

Once I release his wrists, he grabs a fistful of my hair, and I imagine his tongue inside my mouth. He smacks my backside as

I focus on my breathing and not crossing the lines. He palms my ass cheek, squeezing it in his hand and grinding us faster together. The sensations are almost too much, too intimate, too everything.

This feels like more—more than just making a baby, more than just friends, more than being roommates.

An undeniable emotion is attached to every touch as goose bumps trail over my body. While I have a million thoughts running through my mind, I don't give a shit about anything other than losing myself right now.

When I sit up, Payton reaches between us and thumbs my clit. It shoots fireworks up my spine and has me gasping for air as I moan louder and drop to his chest.

"Fuck, Kate." His groan deepens as I nibble on his ear, and then I lightly bite down his neck. His strong hands steady my hips as his thumbs dig into my skin, helping to create more friction as our bodies slap together.

"I'm...Oh my God." I can hardly get the words out as I ride out my release. Long and powerful, it's never felt this good before. The orgasm has me in a chokehold as I squeeze my eyes and moan his name.

"Thatta girl. Just like that."

Payton continues our rhythm, fucking me hard and fast just the way I love.

"So goddamn good, baby," he hisses.

I don't have the heart or desire to scold him for that slipup. A few moments later, he spills inside me, grunting out his release. I love watching his expression as his face tightens, then quickly relaxes as ecstasy takes over.

When our gazes meet, all that can be heard is our rapid breathing and my pounding heart. Neither of us wants to acknowledge the intensity in the air. Quickly, I roll over onto my back and lift my legs to the ceiling, not wanting to waste a drop of him.

We stare at the ceiling, neither of us speaking as we come down from the high. That felt different, and I know he thinks the same. Even if I can't read his mind, I've memorized his mannerisms. Payton won't say or do anything out of respect for our boundaries, but I know I can't fall in love with my best friend.

That's the worst thing I could do.

CHAPTER FOURTEEN

PAYTON

TWO WEEKS LATER

THIS YEAR'S July Fourth celebration was bigger than ever, with a longer firework show. Rose made it very clear that she wanted to go all out, and fortunately, her sons did not disappoint.

With the construction of the horse rescue facility finally complete, we've been getting ready for the grand opening that's in two days. The only thing left is finishing up the fences, which we're doing today.

As I walk through the barn, I look at how well laid out it is. We designed the facility exactly the way we wanted, but it's similar to the stud operation floor plan. There are two offices, a storage and tack room, a loft for hay, and eighteen stalls. It's wild to have such a big place, and although I hope we're never at full capacity, we have the ability to take more if needed.

It's all hands on deck to get the fence done. It feels like the old days when I first started working for the Bishops. Like one big-ass ranch hand reunion with Riley, Diesel, Gavin, Grayson, Ethan, Knox, and Kane. They help dig and set posts, then run barbed wire for the fences to get it done as soon as possible.

"So your dumb ass is the one I need to thank for having to work so damn much?" Diesel asks with a smirk as Riley laughs. They've been coming over after their shifts and staying till nearly dusk all week.

"I guess you could say that." I roughly pat his shoulder. "Nothin' like some charity work to prove you've still got a heart."

He grunts. "Kinda had to when Rowan threatened my balls."

"It was this or triple bath duty." Gavin snorts.

"I'd take that over all night potty training duty. The twins don't wake up on their own to go to the bathroom yet." Grayson grunts.

"So all your wives threatened ya, huh?" I bark out a laugh.

Each one of them nods. "Kaitlyn made sure of it, I suppose. She knows how to get what she wants."

"Speakin' of Kaitlyn…" Ethan drawls. "When are you gonna admit you two have been sneakin' around?"

My heart races as my jaw locks in place.

"He won't admit anything," Kane speaks up. "Trust me. I've tried. The dude ain't budgin' with his denial but still thinks we believe him."

"Might as well just put a fuckin' ring on her finger at this point. Y'all are already livin' together and screwin'. Next thing I know, you'll be announcing she's knocked up," Knox blurts out, and I've never felt the need to punch him as much as I do right now.

I adjust my hat to take some attention away from my face as I load all the supplies we'll need in the back of a ranch hand truck. They finally decide to pitch in after I've packed half of it.

Once that's done, we continue to the next step. It's been a while since I've done something as physical as building a fence, even though we use the digger to set the posts. Riley and Diesel hand-mix concrete as Gavin and Ethan add tension to the wire. It's one of the most important steps in the process.

The fifteen acres of land that the Bishops allotted for us will be more than enough for all the good we want to do. Seeing everything fall into place has me looking forward to the future.

After one of the largest sections of the fence is complete, I see Kaitlyn's truck in the distance. She parks on the side of the road, then steps out wearing her tan riding pants, high boots, and a shirt that hugs her in all the right places. Her blond hair is in a side braid, and it takes every bit of willpower I have not to gawk because she's so damn gorgeous.

Quickly, I look away so her brothers don't start shit again. If they catch me staring, their mouths will run wild and piss her off. They're already warmed up from earlier.

I try to act indifferent and pull my attention away even when she comes over next to me, but I can't resist wrapping an arm around her shoulders and pulling her against my chest.

She looks up at me with a giddy smile. "Doin' some amazin' work out here! I'm so excited about the dedication. I was on my way to Grandma's but wanted to stop and check in to see how y'all were doin'. Apparently, she's going to call the local newspaper and see if they'll come take some pictures and do a full write-up. Oh, and I have Elle and Connor on board to help us since we might be gettin' our first horse on Friday."

I release my hold on her but stay close. "Wow, that's great news. We're gonna need all the help we can get. I spoke with the game warden, and he's gonna call me back tomorrow so we can prepare for his arrival."

"Perfect." Kaitlyn beams and opens her mouth to say something else, but her brothers walk up and steal her attention away. When I turn to keep working, Ethan comes over, and when I look at him, he's glaring.

"What?"

"I thought it was bullshit and a joke to piss you off, but now I have no damn doubt about it. You're in love with her."

"You don't know what you're talkin' about. We're just friends, always have been."

"Really? You don't think I recognized the same look I used to give Harper when we were just friends. Out of every person here, I actually know what it's like to be in love with my best friend and be too chickenshit to admit it."

I've been here for so long that I almost forgot that Ethan married his best friend, Harper, after they pretended to be engaged.

"It's not the same," I growl.

"How so?" he challenges.

"It's just not," I snap, not giving him any further details. "Trust me."

They were pretending to have feelings publicly while actually having them. There's no make-believe, fake relationship going on between Kaitlyn and me. Just a bunch of rules and purely transactional sex exchanges. Ethan would never understand that.

"Mm-hmm," he says, but I know he doesn't believe me. Luckily, he drops it and walks away.

Before Kaitlyn leaves, she says goodbye to everyone, and I try to fade into the background before anyone else can call me out on my bullshit lies. When she's out of sight, I can finally breathe again, even if Ethan's watching me like a hawk.

Now that she's out of her ovulation window, we haven't been having sex, but I find myself craving it and needing more of her. Once she's pregnant, all of this has to stop. The intimacy ends, and we go back to the way things were before we fucked.

Once the sun sets and we're stuck working by flashlights, I decide to call it a night.

"Meet y'all back here at the same time tomorrow afternoon. We should be able to finish it before the deadline."

A round of thank fucks echoes as we all grab our tools and go our separate ways. My body's sore from all the pushing and pulling I did, and I was already tired from working a full shift beforehand. However, in the end, I know the difference we'll make will be more than worth it. That's what keeps me going when I'm about to fall over from exhaustion.

When I get home, I kick off my boots, then throw my hat on the table. Kaitlyn's pulling dishes from the cabinet, standing on her tiptoes to reach the bigger plates at the top. I move beside her and help, pressing my body into hers as I pull them down.

"Thanks," she mutters, smiling when she spins around. She's freshly showered and smells like honeysuckle. It makes me want to lick her all over.

Our proximity is all I can think about, but I make no attempt to move. After the day I've had, I just want to get lost in her. But she's the first to speak up. "Are you hungry? I made dinner."

"You cooked?" I ask, taking a much-needed step back and looking at the pan filled with steaks, roasted potatoes, and green beans.

"Yeah, I thought you could use a good meal after how hard you worked today. Plus, Grandma forced me to take a bunch of the steaks she got from the butcher. Couldn't deny that woman even if I wanted to."

"They smell and look amazing. Thank you," I graciously tell her.

"Want to watch the new superhero show?" she asks, handing me a fork and knife. It's a series with lots of action.

"Yeah, didn't the latest season just come out?"

"Yes, it did, and if I don't get to binge it immediately, I might actually die."

I snort at her dramatics. "Fine by me."

We take our plates to the couch, but before I sit, I quickly change into clean clothes and wash up. When I return, she's got the remote in her hand and the first episode cued up. I sit next to her, and our bodies practically melt into one another as we eat.

"This steak is incredible," I tell her, cutting another huge bite and popping it into my mouth.

"Want to know my secret?" she asks with a smirk.

I nod.

"Butter. Lots of it," she gloats. "And seasoning, of course."

"Best steak I've ever had," I tell her truthfully. "Could eat this for the rest of my life and never get sick of it. Just like you." I blurt out that last part before I can stop myself.

She gulps as we stare at each other. We never talked about the last time we had sex or how close we've gotten to crossing the lines. The sexual tension streaming between us is almost unbearable. I wonder if she feels it too or if I'm just imagining it because I want to haul her into me and kiss those plump lips I can't stop craving.

After we finish eating, half of the episode is still left. Kaitlyn pauses it as I take our plates to the sink, then return to the couch with two sodas.

I lean back, and when she does the same, I open my arm to let her rest against me. This is nothing out of the ordinary, but still, it feels different. I trace circles on the outside of her arm, and the goose bumps that cover her skin each time I touch her return.

"Oh my goodness," she says during a gory scene in the show. "I can't believe I just witnessed that."

I'm actually shocked too. "Same. That was... a lot."

We can't pull our eyes away from the TV. Its unpredictability is one of the things we love most about this show. Superheroes and antiheroes, rooting for the bad guy who's kinda good has always been one of our things.

Kaitlyn repositions herself to lie horizontally. Then she rests her head on my thigh, settling deeper into the couch as she uses me like a pillow. Even the most platonic touch has me growing hard. I look down at her, and she smiles up at me. When the episode ends, I'm tempted to bend her over the side of the sofa and fuck her raw. The look on her face tells me she wants it too, but I push away the desire.

I'm a man of my word, regardless if she's testing every

fucking ounce of willpower I have left. But all the signals she's throwing at me—the mindless flirting, the innuendos, the way she eye-fucks me every single time I walk into a room—have me wondering if she wants more too. Is she afraid to make the first move and destroy the foundation she built our agreement on? We could be good together. Actually, we'd be fucking great as a couple.

But the moment I'd bring it up, there'd be no going back, and if she doesn't feel the same, I've risked it all for nothing. Once my feelings are out there and known, we won't be able to go back to just friends making a baby.

I wish I could say the risk would be worth it, but nothing is worth losing her in my life. Not after everything we've been through.

The episode ends, but several more are available, and they're all an hour long. "Want to watch the next one?"

I chuckle, running my fingers through her freshly washed hair. "You know if you keep pressing play, we're going to binge this season tonight. And I still need to shower."

She inhales my musk and grins. "I actually like the way you smell."

"I dunno if I should say thank you or tell you you're disgustin'."

A chuckle escapes her. "Both? I dunno, you smell like horses, hay, and leather, mixed with a hint of your body wash and sweat. It's…*sexy*."

I lift a brow at her. "Are you flirtin' with me?"

She laughs. "Flirting?"

Before I can respond, Kaitlyn sits up and straddles my lap. I grip her hips as she peers into my eyes. Then she rocks over my cock, and it's undeniable how fucking hard I am.

"No. *This* is flirting." She buries her head in my neck, planting kisses along my jawline.

"No, this is seduction," I say between gritted teeth, digging my thumbs into her skin to stop her from grinding against me. If I let her keep going, I'm sure she'd be putty in my hands and crumble just from the friction alone. "Don't test my willpower, Kate."

She stays planted on top of me and rests her arms on my shoulders but doesn't let her gaze falter. "I have a question for you."

I blink a few times, hesitant to answer whatever is on her mind. "Okay."

When her chest rises and falls, I notice she's not wearing a bra. Her nipples are at full attention, and her breathing is clipped. The pulse in her neck quickens. "Why haven't you given relationships another chance?"

I tilt my head, contemplating how to answer and choosing my words wisely. "Sometimes it's better to protect your heart until you find someone worth potentially breaking it."

"But you haven't given anyone a chance. Just a few hookups here and there even though some wanted more," she pushes, and I wonder what she's searching for. The truth? That she's the reason I haven't wanted more with anyone else? I'm not sure she could handle that truth, and I'm not sure I'm ready to fully admit it.

"I haven't, but I set my own rules in place to avoid making the same mistake of mixing business and pleasure. When everything happened with Edna and James, I had no escape, just constant reminders of what I'd lost. Eldorado is so small that I'm sure everyone would be up in my personal life, just like they were when I lived at home. I'm a private guy and like to keep it that way."

"That's understandable," she says, rocking her hips one time, but I quickly stop her.

"Why do you continue to push away men who are interested when you want a family?" I counter. She looks away before focusing on me again.

It takes her a minute before she responds. "My expectations are too high, and I'm afraid of rejection, especially after some have commented on my body. As much as I want a husband and family, I've been burned so much that dating just hasn't been worth it anymore. I figured out after enough times that not getting attached means I can protect myself from that kind of heartbreak."

I study her. "I guess we're not too different after all."

She laughs. "Totally cut from the same cloth. Probably why we're so good together."

Her words linger in the air, but they're not lost on me. I don't question what she means by that, even if my mind is already wandering.

She lifts her leg and sits down next to me on the couch, finally allowing me to adjust myself.

Kaitlyn notices the statue in my shorts but doesn't say anything. She knew exactly what she was doing– and how much I liked it.

"Do you think you'll ever speak to your stepdad again?"

"No." I don't have to think about the answer to that question. "He's emotionally abusive, and even if I tried, I'd never trust him. He's caused too much damage to my mom and me."

"But she stays?" Kaitlyn confirms.

"Yeah, and I've resented her for years for that. However, I'd love to try rebuilding my relationship with my mom. I miss her every day and make sure to text on her birthday and holidays, but it's always a brief convo." I stare at the wall, thinking about the last time we spoke. "I hope one day she comes to her senses, but honestly, I think she'd rather be with anyone, even a husband who's horrible to her, than be alone. After my dad died, Stan was there for her. Mom doesn't know what it's like to be alone, and I think that scares her. She was searching for what she lost when my dad died and thought she found it in Stan. Now, she's too committed to leave."

Kaitlyn looks at me with soft eyes. "That's sad. No one deserves to be treated that way."

"I agree, though if it's taught me anything, it's that if you can't be content being single, you'll accept anything in a relationship. I've been alone for so long that I'm content with it and don't need to be in a relationship to be happy. Some people do."

"I feel the same way. In my early twenties, I had a few friends who'd leave one guy and immediately be dating someone else within days or weeks. Being alone wasn't an option for them, which was fine, but I could never relate to that. Most guys are too much of a headache to deal with on a consistent basis." She chuckles. "Except you, of course. You only give me a headache once in a while."

I smirk at her playful tone. "It's because you're independent and know what you want in life. I think needing someone has a lot to do with self-esteem. I'd rather be alone than in a shitty relationship."

"Right, same. I honestly think my expectations are set so high because of my parents. They were childhood friends and grew up together, knowing everything about each other. Dad kept his crush on my mom to himself until the day she was set to marry another man. If my uncles hadn't tricked him into writing a letter while he was drunk, I wouldn't exist. And if I can't find love like my parents have, then I don't want it."

"I've heard that story a handful of times over the years, and it never gets old. Gotta admit, they're pretty cute together."

Kaitlyn glances at me. "There's a lesson in there somewhere—ahh yes, don't be a chickenshit."

Not sure if she's saying it for herself or me, but the message is heard loud and clear.

CHAPTER FIFTEEN

PAYTON

"ARE YOU NERVOUS? EXCITED?" Kaitlyn asks me as I put on my date-night boots. I can't remember the last time I wore them.

"A little bit of both," I admit, grabbing my keys so we can head to the rescue.

We somehow finished the fencing right at dark yesterday, just in time for us to break open a bottle of champagne to dedicate the facility.

"I told Grandma it was only supposed to be a small family gathering." Kaitlyn gives me an apologetic look.

I suck in a deep breath, shrugging. "Yeah, but you know how she is."

She chuckles. "That's the problem. She doesn't know what *small* means. Anytime she's involved in anything, it's bigger than Texas. But if they beg for a speech, I've got you."

"Thanks," I tell her. I'm glad she understands I don't like talking in front of a large crowd. It's not my thing. "Not sure you could outdo the one you gave at Kane's wedding, though."

"Ha! You know who my father is? He taught me how to talk shit before I knew my ABCs. Pretty sure I could riff on the spot."

"That's a fact."

When the pasture comes into view, my heart races. The number of trucks and cars parked on the side of the road only makes me more anxious. I look at Kaitlyn, and she shakes her head.

"I knew Grandma was gonna take this to the next level."

We drive up to the barn and, by some miracle, find a parking space. So many people are here, and I'm struggling with how to feel about it. A bright-red ribbon is draped across the main barn doors. All the Bishops are waiting off to the side, and I can see Patricia Stanley, the woman who writes all the local articles for the newspaper, standing by with her camera.

"Looks like they're all waitin' for us," I say, taking in a slow breath.

"Yep." Kaitlyn smiles wide. "Let's go!"

Her excitement rubs off on me as we climb out of the truck. As soon as her parents see us, their voices float toward us. "They're here!"

"In the flesh," I say when we're close.

Rose Bishop joins us too. She's wearing her Sunday best with her hair and makeup done. She's even got a sun hat on and sunglasses.

"Hope y'all don't mind. I invited a few people."

"A few?" Kaitlyn turns and waves her hand. "The whole town is here."

"Sorry, sweetie. Everyone wanted to come out and show their support." She opens her arms, and Kaitlyn falls into them.

When Kaitlyn steps back, she adds, "I'll forgive you this time."

"Can we get a picture of the whole family in front of the barn?" Patricia asks.

"Sure," I tell her as all the Bishops fall into place. Alex, Evan, Jackson, and John are standing by their wives. Handfuls of great-grandkids are sprinkled throughout, along with Kaitlyn's brothers, cousins, and all their spouses.

"We all gonna fit?" Kaitlyn asks, glancing around.

"Squish in just a little on the edges." Patricia points to the right-hand side. "If you can't see me, I can't see you."

A minute later, she snaps a few pictures, then moves Kaitlyn and me to the side for a small, uninterrupted interview.

"Honestly, all of this was Payton's idea," Kaitlyn tells her. "He's been working here for nearly a decade, and he's been my best friend ever since. My family has always tried to give back to the community, so doing something as monumental as starting a nonprofit will allow us to continue that mission. We just needed the right person to spearhead it, so Payton really deserves all the credit for his amazin' idea and contribution." Kaitlyn smiles proudly.

"Thanks, Kate, I'm honored," I tell her, then look back at Patricia. "Honestly, it was a group effort. Without the Bishops, this wouldn't have been possible. I couldn't be happier to partner with someone I respect so deeply. Kaitlyn has always had a passion for horses and riding. It's why she's one of the best trainers in Texas. Together, and with the help of those who have donated their time, we'll be able to make a true difference in the industry."

She grabs my hand and squeezes it.

"Can I get a photo of just the two of you for the front page?"

"Yeah, absolutely," I say, wrapping my arm around Kaitlyn and then waiting for the flash.

When Kaitlyn notices the crowd getting antsy, she leads me to the front of the barn.

She puts two fingers in her mouth and does a loud whistle just like her mom does. "Hey! Woo-hoo, over here." She lifts her hand and grabs everyone's attention.

"Appreciate you all being here today, but I'm sure Mayor Bryant has other things he could be doin', so let's get this party goin'."

The crowd laughs as the mayor steps forward with an

oversized pair of gold scissors. Everyone holds up their phones to record video and take photos.

"Thank y'all for having me here today," the mayor begins. "I appreciate so many of y'all coming for this dedication and amazin' project." He gives a heartwarming speech about helping animals and how the area has never had anything like this. "With all that being said, we're honored to celebrate with you and wish you tons of success. We know you'll make a difference, not just locally but also statewide."

He hands the scissors to Kaitlyn, and she stands closer to me, nudging me to grab them too.

"Let's do it together," she whispers, smiling.

"Photo first, please!" Patricia hollers, holding up her hand, so we focus on her. We smile, then once she's done, cut the ribbon. Everyone bursts into a roar of cheers and applause.

"I want to say something very quickly," I speak up, and everyone grows silent again. "This wouldn't be possible without Kaitlyn being my cheerleader and encouraging me to pursue this. It was always a pipe dream of mine, but with her and the Bishop family, they've helped turn it into a reality." I meet Kaitlyn's eyes and find they have tears threatening to pour over. Clearing my throat, I continue, "Just wanna say, I'm super appreciative and grateful to y'all. Thank you so much."

She smiles wide, and at the moment, all the people around us seem to disappear.

"Dreams come true if you let them." Kaitlyn pulls me into a hug, and for the first time in a long time, I feel something I haven't felt before—true happiness.

KAITLYN

After the dedication yesterday, I've been more tired than usual. Between my training schedule and the rescue getting up and running, my life will be hectic for a while. I have about fifteen minutes before I need to head to the barn, but I decide to go early because my nerves are getting the best of me.

Our first horse arrives today.

Payton submitted our contact information to the state along with our official open date, but I really didn't expect to have a horse within twenty-four hours.

On my way out to my truck, I pass my dad, who quickly stops me. "Want me to come with you?" He can sense when I'm overwhelmed and anxious.

"Nah. Game Warden Langston isn't supposed to arrive for another forty-five minutes," I explain. "Plus, Payton's meetin' me there to help unload the horse. Elle's supposed to show up and do a physical since we don't know what kind of condition Fancy is in. Elle said to imagine the worst, and you know how my mind wanders."

Dad studies me, knowing how sensitive I was as a kid when it came to animals. It's how I knew I'd never become a vet like my cousin Elle and preferred to focus on training.

"If you need anything, don't hesitate to text me. I'll drop whatever I'm doin' and head right over," he offers.

"Thanks. I'll keep you updated," I say, then go to my truck.

I selfishly hope to get to chat with Payton alone. He knows how to bring me back down to earth.

When I pull up to the bright-red building, I read the sign that Grandma Bishop insisted on being on the outside—Circle B Ranch Horse Rescue & Sanctuary.

It warms my heart to see it.

Payton turns into the driveway and parks next to me a few minutes later. My heart rate quickens as soon as he steps out of the truck and meets my eyes. His lips slide up into a cute grin, and I have to stop myself from reacting.

"Too bad we don't have time to celebrate this monumental day." I waggle my brows.

He immediately gets what I'm referring to, and even though we're out of my ovulation window, neither of us seems to care. Payton takes my hand and leads me inside the barn. The stalls are already prepped with fresh hay. He climbs up the ladder to the loft, and I follow him.

"What're we doin' up here?" I ask, noticing the hay is completely stocked.

Payton undoes his belt, then his jeans. The thought of him taking me here has me squeezing my thighs together. Electricity streams through me as he takes a few steps forward, hard as a fucking rock.

"Get naked, Kate," he says in a husky tone. "We don't have a lot of time."

I suck in a deep breath, needing this more than I want to admit. I move to the back of the loft just in case Elle or the game warden arrives, then I lower my riding pants and panties down to my ankles.

Payton follows, then spins me around and bends me over a hay bale. He eagerly rubs his finger through my wet slit before pushing the tip of his erection between my folds. Once he slams into me, I see white. I arch into him with each thrust, slamming back against his hips. As he fucks me hard, he wraps an arm around and fists my breast, adding pain to the intense pleasure my body craves from him.

I read an article that explained when you enjoy sex, your body prepares itself to accept sperm, so you'll get pregnant.

We set the rules, even though we're currently breaking one of them. No sex unless I'm ovulating, but neither of us seems to care. Now, we're teetering on the boundary line and fucking for the joy of it.

His grunts grow deep as he pounds harder into me. I gasp for air, my body trembling as the orgasm threatens to push me over the edge. Seconds later, he covers my mouth with his hand and brings his lips to my ear.

"Keep it down. You can scream my name later when my lips are between your thighs, you Little Devil."

"Say it again," I demand when he uncovers my mouth. I'm unhinged with pleasure, ready to explode on his cock.

"You're my Little Devil, always tempting me with your sweet pussy," he mutters, then slaps my ass while keeping his pace. My legs nearly give out, but he wraps his arm around my waist and steadies me. Then a moment later, he sinks deeper and fills my pussy. We stay connected, and I melt into him, enjoying how much his warmth consumes me.

When he pulls out, I flip and lie on my back, feeling drunk from the high. He falls back next to me, both of us gasping for air.

"That was so hot," I blurt out, turning my head to meet his hooded eyes. "But we probably shouldn't have done that."

"Do you regret it?" he asks, his expression flat.

I chew on my bottom lip. "No, do you?"

Without a word, he shakes his head.

Once we've caught our breaths, Payton pulls a pack of wipes from his back pocket, and we quickly clean up. I love a man who comes prepared. Just as I'm adjusting my riding pants, I hear Elle yell from the barn entryway.

"Hello?" she calls out, and I start to freak out that we'll get caught. Of course she'd be early.

"Comin'!" My eyes widen in fear as Payton steps back out of view. I try to flatten my hair as I rush to get my shirt on.

When I'm done adjusting myself, I walk to the edge of the loft. "Hey!"

"Whatcha doin' up there?" Her expression molds into a confused one.

"Oh, Payton and I were grabbing some extra hay for the pasture," I explain, turning to him, internally freaking out.

Seconds later, Payton throws two bales down, and they hit the ground with a thud. I move to the ladder and make my way toward her. Elle studies my face, and I hope to God my cheeks aren't red.

She pops a brow as we hold a silent conversation, but then she smiles. "Do you have everything ready for Fancy?"

"For the most part, yeah. She should be arriving in about ten minutes," I tell her as another bale falls to the ground.

"Do you have time to give me the grand tour of the place? It was so hectic yesterday, and we got so busy catching up with everyone, I didn't get a chance to check it out."

I show her all around from the offices, tack room, stalls, pasture, and corral. She's in awe at each thing I show her.

"When Grandma told me what y'all were doing, I was so damn excited. Please don't hesitate to call Connor or me if you need anything. We're happy to help however we can."

"Thank you, that really means a lot." We continue walking around. "I have cameras installed so I can watch them at night."

Payton walks up, his hair looking like he just got fucked, and smiles. "Hey, Elle."

She shakes his hand. "Nice seein' ya again, Payton. Love what y'all are doin' here."

Elle turns back to me. "I can tell you're anxious."

I let out a huff, happy she didn't see me before Payton fucked my brains out. "I'll be fine. Just jittery nerves."

"Don't be. You get to protect them from malnourishment, disease, improper care, and potential abuse. I saw some horrific things I'll never forget in vet school. This sanctuary gets to be their second chance."

I swear I see her start to tear up, and I can only imagine what she's witnessed over the years of being a veterinarian. Elle loves horses just as much as Payton and I do, but she was in the trenches during vet school, an experience neither of us really has. I've only worked with show horses treated like royalty that are fed the best diets and live in luxurious barns.

"I'm sure there'll be a learning curve," I say.

Payton nods. "Absolutely. Elle's right about us giving them a second chance. If they're coming to us, they've been through some shit, and we'll need to be careful."

"And as hard as it will be, please don't get too attached because these horses won't be healthy. Whatever happens to them after they arrive, just remember it's not your fault, and you've done the best you can." Elle's soft voice is meant to reassure me, but I'm still worried about what we'll witness.

"It's something I've been trying to tell myself. They warned us they'll be emaciated."

She frowns, nodding. "You know I'm happy to answer any questions night or day, so don't be afraid to reach out if you need anything."

I smile and wrap my arms around her. "You're the best cousin ever."

She laughs. "I'll take that compliment, considering how competitive that spot is."

When the sound of an engine pulls our attention, the three of us walk to the barn's entrance and watch the truck and trailer roll to a halt.

"Howdy," Game Warden Langston says, tilting his cowboy hat at us.

We exchange pleasantries, then he leads us to the back of the horse trailer.

"Meet Fancy," he calmly tells us while slowly opening the door. I swallow hard, immediately noticing her protruding ribs. An overwhelming amount of sadness and anger fills me.

In the past thirty years of being around horses, I've never seen anything like this.

Payton places his hand on my shoulder as I suck in a deep

breath. I walk around so she can see Payton and he can pet the softness of her chestnut-colored coat.

"Sweet baby," I say softly. "You're safe now." I look into her eyes as I gently run my palm down her nose. Her mane is severely matted.

Payton chats with Officer Langston while Elle starts her physical. She checks her hooves and teeth, and I help her measure different parts of her body. This allows us to determine what she should weigh and how much food she needs.

"She's malnourished. She'll need to eat one and a half percent of her body weight four to five times a day. Salt block. Alfalfa cubes soaked in water several times a day for the first two weeks, then you can decrease. Soaking it will help her digest it easier," Elle explains as she opens Fancy's mouth to check her teeth.

"Payton and I are going to take shifts feeding her. He'll do the first two during the day, and I'll do the others in the afternoon and evening."

Elle smiles. "Good plan. Y'all should be able to get her to a normal weight in about two months." Her voice stays soft and steady while she walks around Fancy. When she's finished her full body check, I hear the game warden's diesel truck start and the trailer bounce down the road.

Payton removes his hat as he comes over to us. "So how is she? Like your overall opinion?"

"Sadly, I've seen worse," Elle admits. "But before I can deworm her, she'll need to fatten up. Her teeth need to be floated and her hooves need trimming, but I think I'll need a radiograph of them first to make sure there isn't a bigger issue I can't see. I can get our best farrier out here to take care of it this week. With all of that being said, I think she'll be okay. Fancy's a fighter."

"She's in good hands now." Payton beams.

"I'll be back first thing in the mornin' before work to file down those teeth and give the primary doses of vaccines. After about a month, I'll administer the rest. Don't want to move too fast and shock her body because she's already so weak. When can y'all meet me tomorrow?"

"Whatever time works for you," I confirm.

"I'll text ya later after I look at my schedule. Probably gonna be at the butt crack of dawn," she admits.

"Sounds like a plan," I say just as her phone rings and interrupts us.

"Shit. I gotta run." Elle gives us a wave as she rushes to her truck.

"Thank you," I say, raising my voice.

"You owe me one!"

And then it's just Payton, Fancy, and me. Payton hooks a lead rope on her halter, then walks her into the open lush green free-roam pasture with a trough of clean water.

"We're not gonna let anything happen to you," Payton confirms when she starts grazing.

As I stand beside him, watching Fancy eat, he places his strong arm around my shoulders and squeezes. Being with him feels like home.

CHAPTER SIXTEEN

KAITLYN

PAYTON'S firm grip holds me in place as he thrusts harder, slamming my skull into the headboard. His intense stare holds me in place as I widen my legs and take all of him. Our eyes lock when he slides his hand up my throat, and we pant in sync.

Each time gets better and better.

My heart pounds in rhythm to our bodies slapping together.

"I'm so close," I tell him.

He lowers his face, his lips inches from mine.

"Come with me," he demands.

It doesn't take long before my body trembles and soars toward the ledge. Payton grunts and thrusts deep inside once more before we're flying high in the clouds.

My back arches as I chase the rush, and when Payton closes the space between us, he crashes his mouth to mine.

I don't have the willpower to remind him of our rules or break away because his soft lips are exactly what I've craved.

Even if I shouldn't.

"Payton," I murmur, breathing hard and wanting more.

"Kate."

"Payton."

"*Kate!*"

His loud booming voice jolts me upright in bed. Blinking hard, I realize I was sex-deep in a naughty dream.

About us *kissing*.

Fuck.

"You okay?" He squeezes my shoulder. "I heard you shouting and thought something was wrong."

Oh God, was I screaming his name?

"I'm fine," I finally reply with a deep exhale. "Just a weird dream, I guess."

It's the third one I've had since we fucked in the barn loft last week, but it's the first time it involved kissing.

"Could be a pregnancy symptom," he says, sitting on the bed next to me. "Some women get them."

Nah, it was just a sex dream about kissing my best friend when we agreed to no kissing.

And I wanted it…*bad.* There's no denying I've been thinking about us lately, but we made rules for a reason.

"Maybe."

"You're sweatin'. Sure you're okay?"

I wipe a hand over my face, then feel my forehead. Payton stares intently as if he wants to ask me something else, but since I've embarrassed myself enough, I quickly change the subject.

"I'm gonna get ready for work," I tell him, then look at the clock and see it's almost seven. "Don't you need to feed Fancy before work?"

"Already did. I got up early so I had time to come home and make you breakfast."

"How's she doing?" I ask.

"About the same, she's eating well. I can already tell she's gained a couple of pounds."

That's amazing, considering she just got here last week.

"Wow, that's great." I beam.

"Whatcha hungry for?"

"Um...you can surprise me."

He stands and heads for the door. "Okay, I made some coffee, but I was thinking of switchin' to decaf."

"Excuse me?" I glower. "Why would we do something so ridiculous?"

"It's better for conceiving and pregnancy."

"You can fuck right off with that."

He leans against the doorway with his arms crossed.

"Okay, how about we compromise at half-caf? That way, you'll get a little boost, but it's healthier for the baby."

I shoot him a murderous glare as I slide out of bed. "How about you drink decaf and I drink regular, then together, it'll be like half-caf."

One side of his lips tilts up. "That's not how it works."

I roll my eyes, digging in my dresser for clothes.

"I gave up briefs and added weird nuts to my diet, so I think you can manage to go without it for a while."

"Have you ever seen me without caffeine?"

"Oh, Kate. I've seen you plenty of ways."

I smack his bare six-pack abs when I walk past him toward the bathroom. Why does the man have to be so goddamn tempting when I'm still imagining his mouth on mine? Though I'm used to seeing him walk around half-naked, it doesn't help when he's reactivated my sex drive.

Then a thought hits me.

I should try kissing him the next time we have sex.

Assuming there is a next time.

That way, I can gauge his reaction, and if it's a negative one, I'll say I got caught up in the moment and promise it won't happen again. Then at least I'll know.

My gut tells me he wouldn't stop me, but it's obvious he won't make the first move when it comes to that. Kissing makes it intimate and real.

"Have you gotten your period yet?" He follows me.

"No, but I've also been late the past two months, so I'm not gettin' my hopes up," I admit.

He chuckles when we enter the kitchen. "I think maybe you should take one."

"Why? Because I'm having vivid dreams that make me shout in my sleep?"

"Your boobs look bigger too."

"Payton!" I instinctively cover my chest as he laughs.

"Nothin' I haven't seen, darlin'."

I open the fridge and grab my creamer, ignoring Payton's eyes burning a hole in my head as he watches me pour a cup of coffee.

"Trust me, you want me caffeinated."

I take a sip, and my mood instantly lifts. Payton shrugs with a smirk, then sets a pan on the burner.

"This better not be the fake shit, or I swear, I will hurt you."

He stays silent while taking the eggs and bacon from the fridge. I watch as he prepares our food and suspiciously drink my coffee.

"Here. Go take this while I finish up." He digs into his pocket, then removes a pregnancy test.

There's a sparkle of hope in his eyes, and I hate to disappoint him for the third month in a row.

"I haven't felt any symptoms," I explain.

Aside from the constant sex dreams.

"Not all women do right away," he confirms. "Based on what I read, only fifty percent of women have early symptoms." Then he hands me the pee cup.

Him and his research.

Inhaling sharply, I take it all to the bathroom.

After I stick the test in the urine, I set it down and wash my hands. Staring at my reflection in the mirror, I study my breasts.

Are they really bigger? Or is he messing with me?

I cup them, trying to decide if they feel heavier or not.

"This is crazy," I mutter. My boobs are the same.

Getting things ready for the horse rescue has occupied my spare time, so maybe I wouldn't notice the signs. Maybe I'm one of the lucky ones who won't get morning sickness all day.

Leaving the test on the counter, I walk to the kitchen and grab my coffee.

"Breakfast's ready." He sets the plate in front of me, and I sit on the stool.

"Thank you." I smile wide when he hands me a fork. Payton's made it a habit of feeding me before work.

"Don't forget your vitamins when you get to your office."

"I won't," I promise, then take a bite of my food. He's seasoned it with salt and pepper, just how I like it.

"I told Zach he could come with me to the rescue tonight. He wanted to try to save Fancy's mane, but I explained that it's too tangled and we needed to cut it."

"He already loves her so much."

"Mm-hmm. He's a Bishop through and through. I told him we could try to bathe her. Depends on her mood, though."

"Yeah, she might not take it well," Payton agrees.

He finally sits next to me and digs in.

"You gonna check the test?"

I sigh, finishing my bacon and last bite of eggs. "Yeah."

"You don't sound excited."

"I'm tired of gettin' my hopes up," I admit, putting my dishes in the sink. I don't know how women deal with this for years.

Payton stands and rounds the breakfast bar, then grabs my shoulders. "Don't get discouraged."

"I'm worried I won't ever become a mom. That there might be something wrong with me."

"Besides your caffeine addiction, you're perfect."

I stick out my lip, narrowing my eyes. "That was...almost a compliment."

He chuckles. "C'mon, we'll check it together."

Payton grabs my hand and leads me to the bathroom. I drag my feet, but once the test is in view, I freeze in place.

"You look," I tell him.

He drops my hand and walks to the counter. I wait as he picks it up and reads it. Though he's expressionless, my heart hammers in my chest.

"Kate."

My shoulders slump, and I squeeze my eyes to stop the tears.

"Just say it."

"It's *positive*."

"*What?*" I study his face as he stares at the test. Swallowing hard, I ask, "Are you sure?"

"There are two lines..." His face pales, and I worry he's going to pass out.

Stepping closer, I grab it and see two dark lines.

"Maybe I should take another one to be sure?" I mumble in disbelief.

I grab two more tests and rip them open. Payton takes one, and I take the other, then we dip them in the cup together.

We're too stunned to speak as we watch the tests' control lines appear.

"The second line has already appeared on this one," Payton states.

I look at the one in my hand. "Mine too."

The tears I'm holding back begin to fall.

I'm pregnant.

Payton pulls me close, tightly wrapping his arms around me as emotions pour through me. We stand holding one another for nearly a minute. Then he cups my face and stares at my lips. For a moment, I wonder if he'll finally kiss me, but then he buries his face in my neck, and I inhale his musky soap smell.

"I can't believe I'm really pregnant," I finally say, wiping my cheeks when he releases his grip. "I was sure it was gonna be negative. How'd you know?"

He shrugs. "Just had a feeling. I've been watching you for the past couple of weeks and noticed little changes."

Like my boobs.

I place my palm over my stomach, trying to imagine how it'll feel and look when it grows. Since I was tracking my days, I figure I'm about four weeks along.

Holy shit, we're gonna be parents.

"Does this mean I can go back to briefs?" He flashes a crooked smile. "And stop eating those nuts?"

I roll my eyes. "Well, they worked, didn't they?"

"You don't know that that was the reason."

"Well, regardless, you're released from duty."

"Hardly." He scowls. "Just because you're carrying the baby doesn't mean my job is done. I'm gonna take care of you and help prepare. That's *our* child in there."

Maybe it's the hormones, but holy fuck is Payton hot when he's assertive.

"Sorry, that's not what I meant. I know you'll be with me every step of the way. Your *baby-making* duties are over."

I've never felt happier to finally be pregnant, but that means my intimate time with Payton is over.

And that actually makes me sad as hell.

CHAPTER SEVENTEEN

PAYTON

KAITLYN'S BEEN extra irritable for the past week, and I noticed her breasts looked a tad bigger as if they were swollen. She couldn't tell, but it was obvious to me.

Still, seeing those positive tests was a heart-stopping moment.

I was so overwhelmed and happy that I nearly broke the rules and kissed her.

I wanted to.

But I knew crossing that line would ruin everything we agreed to. And we'd already broken one of the rules that neither of us had brought up.

However, I wasn't about to fuck up and bring emotions into it at the end.

My phone buzzes in my pocket for the fourth time, and I know it's Knox or Kane. I pull it out and see I'm right.

"Fuck. Your brothers are blowin' up my phone. They'll give me all the bitch jobs if I show up late again. I hate that I have to leave you right now."

"It's okay. Not a whole lot we can do anyway. I'll get my first OB appointment scheduled, and we'll go from there."

I lean down and kiss her forehead. "Call or text if you need anything, okay?"

She smiles. "I will. I'll probably tell Maize since she's known about it from the beginning. It'll prevent me from blabbing it too soon if I talk to someone else about it."

"Fine with me."

"Though we shouldn't tell anyone else until I'm out of the first trimester."

That's another two months away. Not sure she'll manage to keep it a secret that long, but I promise to wait until she's ready.

My phone vibrates with another message, and I'm not even late yet.

"I wish I could stay and celebrate."

"We will tonight!" she reassures me. "It's fine. I've gotta get ready for work anyway because I can't skip my training today."

I step closer, resting my hand over her belly. "Be extra careful."

She smiles. "Don't worry, BD. I will be."

I can't focus for shit.

Knox put me on cleanup duty for being ten minutes late. Not that I cared because it gave me time to work alone most of the morning.

I've always been concerned for Kaitlyn's well-being, but now I feel an intense protectiveness over her. Her job can be dangerous, especially if a horse spooks and she falls. Most of those she works with are well-behaved, but something could always go wrong when working with large animals. There's a risk involved each time she gets on that saddle.

Her parents break and train younger horses who sometimes get out of control. She's always prepared and takes safety seriously by wearing a helmet, but I don't know if that's enough. To ease my worry, I text her on my break.

Payton: Did you eat lunch?

Kaitlyn: Drinking a protein shake now, and before you remind me, I've already taken my vitamins.

Payton: Good! Do you need anything? Are you feeling fatigued?

Kaitlyn: I'm fine. About to get Malice in the arena before he's picked up tomorrow.

Payton: Don't overdo it, and drink lots of water so you don't get dehydrated.

Kaitlyn: I won't, and yes, I always do.

Payton: If you start feeling sick, take a break.

She doesn't respond, but moments later, my phone rings, and it's her.

"What's wrong?" I immediately ask.

"Payton, you need to chill!" She chuckles. "I'm fine, I promise."

"I'm just checkin' on you. I don't want you to be distracted while workin' with the horses and get kicked or fall."

"The only thing distractin' me right now is *you*. So please, calm down. You being anxious is makin' me anxious."

I blow out a steady breath, pacing. "Sorry. I hate that I had to leave abruptly this morning."

"I understand. This is all new to me too. Tonight, we can look up the baby's size at each stage and browse nursery stuff."

Hearing the smile in her voice puts one on my face.

"It's a date. I'll grab food and be home around six thirty."

After we end the call, I meet up with Knox and Kane for lunch. We sit at the picnic table outside the barn and chow down on the food Harper brought us. Ever since Knox found out she created a special club sandwich for Ethan, he's begged her to make them for him too. So now she brings some for all of us about once a week just to appease him. She probably just wants to shut him up.

I set my phone on the table, waiting for Kaitlyn's response about what she wants from the B&B since Maize has two different options on the menu.

"I'm gonna grab a water from the fridge. Y'all need anything?" I ask as I stand from the table.

They shake their heads as they stare at their screens, most likely chatting with their wives.

I head to the barn and return moments later. Kane's looking at something and laughing.

"What's funny?"

"BD? What's BD stand for?" he asks.

I tap my screen and see her message.

Kaitlyn: I'll take the beef tips. Thanks, BD!

Fuck. Nosy bastard.

"It probably means Big Dick, right? Now that y'all are livin' together, there's no way she ain't seen it," Kane continues.

I kick him underneath the table, nailing his boot. "Dude, shut the fuck up."

"Big Dick is a good nickname to have. I don't know what you're pissed about," Knox complains.

"Respect your sister," I warn.

"Oh, that's nothing compared to the shit she's done or said to us," he retorts, and Kane laughs in agreement.

I glower at the two of them.

Once I finish my food, I leave and go back to work. It's our busy season, and I want to get out of here on time.

"The baby's the size of a poppy seed!" Kaitlyn gushes. "That's so tiny."

We've been looking for a good pregnancy app for the past half hour. Since Kaitlyn has meticulously tracked her cycle, she can easily track her pregnancy progress. Right now, she's four weeks and two days along.

"Look how big it is at thirty weeks," I say, showing her the picture.

Her eyes widen. "Bishop babies are big too...would not surprise me if this baby came out at ten pounds."

I arch a brow. "For your sake, I hope not."

"So I called and told Maize during my lunch break. Her excited screams nearly made me deaf."

I chuckle. Sounds like something Maize would do.

"Do you think everyone else will have the same reaction?" I

ask cautiously. I know it's a sensitive topic since she's the only one having a baby without a boyfriend.

She shrugs, scrolling on her phone. "Once the shock wears off, I think they'll be stoked. I just hope you're ready for twenty questions about why we aren't together."

"Because we're just friends and don't want to ruin what we have." I repeat what we've both said since the beginning.

"Right! They'll get over it, eventually."

My heart sinks at the thought of her family not approving of the pregnancy. Though the Bishops have always been excited about a new addition, it doesn't mean they'll agree with our "one-night stand."

"Your brothers peeked at my phone when you texted me earlier. They asked what BD meant."

Her eyes widen as she looks up at me. "Oh shit. What'd you say?"

"I didn't say anything, told them to fuck off, but of course they ran their mouths and suggested it meant *Big Dick*."

She bursts out laughing. "Don't worry, I'll get even with them."

I snort. "You always do."

"Oh! My OB got back with me. My appointment is in four weeks. Do you wanna come?"

"Of course, I do. I wanna go to all of them. Just tell me the dates, and I'll be there."

Smiling, she rests her head on my shoulder. "You got it, *BD*."

Later that evening, after Kaitlyn goes to bed, I take another shower.

My hard cock has been aching for a release. Every conversation and thought about Kaitlyn being pregnant with my baby has made me eager to be inside her again. Now that I can't, I'm struggling more than usual to suppress my feelings.

Gripping my shaft, I stroke it hard and fast. Before our agreement, I'd jerk off to the idea of having her. Now that I know how amazing she feels, the fantasies of taking her again are torture. The memories of her riding me, of her bent over, and the taste of her lingering on my tongue have me coming in minutes.

Fuck.

Getting over Kaitlyn is gonna be impossible.

Especially since I'm already in love with her.

CHAPTER EIGHTEEN

KAITLYN

ONE MONTH LATER

Not only have I cut back on caffeine but I also have no appetite.

Which really sucks when I'm used to eating at the B&B every day, and people are starting to notice my absence. My brothers, parents, and a few cousins have asked why I haven't stopped in as much, but Maize has told them I've been extra busy with work lately.

I've personally been using the horse rescue and my training schedule as an excuse. Though they are keeping me extra busy, I'm also tired as fuck, so any breaks I get are spent napping in my office.

Payton still texts me throughout the day to check on me. I've only gotten sick a few times, but the nausea is the worst when I'm trying to sleep at night. I knew the first trimester might be rough, but it's even harder not being able to explain why my habits have changed.

I might not be able to keep it hidden for another month with all their suspicions.

On top of all my body's changes, I miss Payton's touch like

crazy. Maybe it's the hormones, but the sex dreams are still occurring too. We still hang out just like old times, except now, he eats in the kitchen while I sit on the couch. The smell of food makes me want to throw up, so he gives me space.

And the worst part—that I didn't anticipate—is the heartburn.

Everything I do manage to get down makes my throat burn. I'm chewing on antacids more than actual food.

At eight weeks, I'm bloated with swollen breasts. I didn't think I'd have this many symptoms so early, but at the same time, I'm relieved because it reminds me I'm having a baby. *Finally.*

I watch Fancy as she eats and am so grateful that she's getting healthier and stronger. Zach loves to come and talk to her. I swear, he's a little horse whisperer because Fancy perks up each time she hears his voice.

Because her mane was so tangled, we had to cut it, but it's finally growing back. Zach likes to gently run his hand over her Mohawk each time before he brushes her. It's their tradition, and I love watching them together. When Fancy arrived a little over a month ago, she was uneasy around people, but I can see how much she trusts Zach. While she still has a long way to go, we're pleased with her progress.

"Well, I gotta go to an appointment soon," I walk over and tell Zach as he wraps his arms around Fancy's neck and hugs her. "Do you want me to drive you home?"

"No, I'm gonna stay here for a bit, then I'll get my mom to pick me up," he says, patting his pocket where his cell phone is. "What kinda appointment do you have?"

Nosy-ass kid.

I hate lying, but Zach is too young to understand.

"Just a checkup at the hospital," I say.

"Maybe you'll see my grandma," he says. River works as a

nurse, and my uncle Evan and aunt Emily are doctors in the emergency room.

"It's possible," I say with a tight smile. *But hopefully not.*

"Anyway, see ya tomorrow, kiddo," I tell him, ruffling his hair.

"Hey!" He tries to squirm away from me, and I laugh.

As soon as I get home, I rinse off and change. By the time I start blow-drying my hair, Payton's in the shower. I'm so damn nervous that I haven't eaten all day, and even if I had wanted to, I wouldn't be able to keep it down anyway.

"Ready?" he asks, buttoning his jeans.

"Um...missing a shirt?" My mouth waters at the sight of him. Damn him and those abs and tattoos. Seeing him wear those tight dark-wash jeans and cowboy boots has me ready to beg him to knock me up all over again.

"Gotta grab it from the dryer, one second."

I study his back muscles as he goes to the laundry room. Quickly, I put on my shoes and grab my purse. Unfortunately, he returns fully dressed.

"Okay, let's go," he says, grabbing his keys.

It takes us an hour to get to San Angelo, and my anxiety is high at not knowing what to expect. It's too soon to feel any kicks or know if the baby is healthy, but I still want reassurance that everything's going well.

Payton grabs my hand as we walk into the hospital. "You were quiet for the whole drive."

"Just nervous."

He squeezes my fingers. "I'll be by your side the entire time."

I flash him a grateful smile.

Once I'm checked in, we head to the fourth floor and wait.

Five minutes later, they finally bring us back to the room. The nurse checks my weight and vitals before leaving me to undress. Payton turns around so I can strip, and I change into a barely-there gown.

"Thanks," I tell him, then sit on the table and pull the sheet over my waist. "You might want to stand by my head for the exam portion."

He chuckles. "Okay."

"Yes, I know you've already seen it all, but still."

"I didn't say anything."

I narrow my eyes. "You were thinkin' it, though."

As soon as the doctor enters, my mood shifts. Excitement takes over, and I can't wait to talk about the baby and find out my estimated due date.

After introductions are made, she does an internal exam, asks for the first day of my last period, and confirms that I'm eight weeks pregnant. Then she puts a heart rate monitor over my belly, and we hear a soft flickering sound.

"Oh my gosh." I tear up and look up at Payton. He's smiling wide and proud.

"It's faint, but it's there," the doctor confirms. "I would like to get some photos and a better listen of the heart, so I'm going to send you for an ultrasound. If it all looks good, I'll see you in a month for your twelve-week checkup and again at sixteen. Then we'll do a full ultrasound scan at the twenty-week mark."

"Is that when we can find out the gender?"

She smiles. "Yes, if you want."

After reviewing my list of symptoms, she makes suggestions for what I can do about my nausea and heartburn.

"Based on your period, your estimated due date is March thirtieth, but you could go into labor two weeks before or after that date. But I won't make you wait that long."

"Thank God." I groan.

"But up to a week late is normal, especially for a first pregnancy. We want you to be at least thirty-seven weeks to be considered full-term, but if you have any complications along the way, we'll keep a closer eye."

"What kind of complications should I be lookin' out for?"

"Bleeding, excessive cramping, early contractions, severe nausea or vomiting. Some women in your weight range have other concerns we can cross if we need to, but we'll have you do regular blood tests, too. We'll look for protein in your urine, excessive swelling in your legs, and high blood pressure because those can be signs of preeclampsia. Not super common, but it can occur in some pregnancies. You're not considered high-risk, but we'll keep a close eye on you because of your age."

I want to smack her tight-lipped smile right off her face.

First, she comments on my weight, and now I'm an old maid?

Once we go downstairs, I'm ready to get this over with and go home. I'm feeling more insecure than I was when we arrived.

"Kaitlyn Bishop," a young woman calls, and we follow her to a dimly lit room.

"I'm Analisa, and I'll be doing your ultrasound today. I just need you to remove your bottoms and put this sheet around your waist. Since you're still in the first trimester, a transvaginal ultrasound will help us get a better picture."

As soon as she leaves, Payton once again gives me privacy, then helps cover everything below the waist with the sheet.

"It's startin' to feel real," he whispers.

"Yeah, I'm excited to get pictures."

"Me too. It's gonna look like a little blueberry."

He chuckles. "Our little berry."

Analisa knocks before entering, then sits on the stool next to me. Payton stands on the other side of the bed, waiting and watching.

"If your husband wants a better look at the screen, he can stand over here."

"Oh, we're not married," I blurt out. "We're friends."

I don't know why I felt the need to reiterate that, but the moment I see her eyes light up and her gaze slide across his body, I regret my words.

"I'm the father, though," Payton clarifies.

"Oh. I'm sure she appreciates your support."

Is she kidding me right now?

I narrow my eyes at her but bite my tongue. Payton adjusts his stance like he's ready to hold me back, but I stay put. I don't need reassurance from her or anyone because I know how much Payton cares about me.

I reach over and take his hand.

"Here's the heartbeat," she says just as a loud fluttering echoes throughout the room.

We watch the screen, and my emotions begin to bubble over. I've been hormonal all day, but seeing the flicker on the screen and hearing the strong heartbeat is what I needed.

I look at Payton, and he shoots me a wink, then squeezes my fingers. The small flutter on the screen looks like a weird blob, but I've never been so happy to see anything in my life.

"I'm going to do a few measurements for the doctor, and then I can print off some photos for you."

"Great, thanks," I tell her and wipe away my tears of joy.

Another ten minutes pass before she hands us three photos and congratulates us.

Once I'm dressed, we exit the room and head toward the parking lot.

"I can't believe how small it looks," I mutter, squinting at the tiny bean.

"Small in size, large in attitude," Payton teases.

"Ha ha," I muse.

"Kaitlyn! Payton!"

My head pops up, and my heart drops when I see River coming toward us. I try to hide the ultrasound pictures, but it's too late. She's already noticed.

"Something you wanna share?" She eyes my hand curiously.

"Only if you can keep it to yourself?"

Wishful thinking on my part.

"You're pregnant?" Her tone isn't judgmental, but it's filled with concern.

I nod with a small smile. "Eight weeks."

"Wow, congrats. I didn't even know you were seein' someone."

Shifting my eyes toward Payton, I wait for River to get the hint.

"You two? Well, it's about damn time." She snickers.

"It's not like that." I quickly stop her before she can continue. "Just friends who had one drunken night together."

She arches a brow. "Oh. I see. Do your parents know?"

"Um...not yet. I was waitin' until I was twelve weeks to share the news with *everyone*."

Hopefully, she understands my emphasis.

Nodding, she crosses her arms. "Are you feelin' okay?"

"For the most part, just typical first trimester symptoms."

"That's good. Ivy and Kane's babies will be close in age to yours."

"Yep. They'll be able to grow up and play together."

"Yeah, that'll be nice. Okay, well, I'm off to work a twelve-hour shift in the NICU. Maybe I'll get to help deliver yours in seven months." She flashes me a wink.

I nervously laugh. "Ya never know!"

God, I hope not. I'm already self-conscious about pushing a watermelon-sized baby out of my vagina. I don't need my aunt witnessing it.

She pulls me in for a hug. "Take care, Kaitlyn. Text me if you need anything, okay? Don't wait too long to tell your mom. She'll want to share this exciting time with you."

"Just another month," I promise.

She tells Payton goodbye and then strolls off in the opposite direction.

"*Great*," I mutter as we walk out the doors.

I love my aunt, but I know better. It's only a matter of time before the entire town knows.

CHAPTER NINETEEN

PAYTON

My heart rapidly races, and I know Kaitlyn is having an internal meltdown. We get in the truck and sit in silence, staring at the hospital's front doors.

Kaitlyn eventually turns to me. "There is no way we can wait another month to tell my parents. Aunt River might be able to keep a secret, but I know she'll slip, and Uncle Alex will proudly tell everyone. I can't have them finding out from him. I should tell them today."

I suck in a breath because I wasn't fully ready or prepared to talk to Jackson and Kiera yet. I thought we'd have more time, but I know she's right. She wouldn't want her parents finding out the news through town gossip.

She pinches the bridge of her nose. "Why did we have to run into her today of all days?"

I grab her hand and squeeze. "Everything happens for a reason. I'm sure it'll be okay."

Kaitlyn rolls her eyes. "It's just bad timing on my part. But it's not like I can keep my pregnancy a secret for very long anyway. I'm already starting to notice the changes in my body and the way my riding pants are fitting. Or rather, *not* fitting."

"So to the training facility we go?" I ask, starting the truck and heading toward the ranch.

"Might as well," she mutters. "I wish I would've had time to get a cute grandparents gift together, but hopefully, they'll be excited enough not to care."

The whole drive back to Eldorado, Kaitlyn rehearses what she's going to tell them. She goes through a list of questions her parents might ask, and I crack jokes where I can to make her smile and ease her nerves.

When we arrive at the barn, I see Knox's and Kane's trucks parked outside. Kaitlyn lets out a roar of a groan. "Today really isn't my day."

"Hey, hey. It's gonna be just fine. At least you can get it over with by telling them all at once. And if they throw punches, I'll dodge them."

"Not funny," she snarls, then leans her head back on the seat and closes her eyes while taking deep breaths. "This is stressful, which I know is not good for the baby. But I knew I'd have to tell them eventually, so I might as well get it over with."

"Maybe it won't be as bad as you're anticipating," I tell her, hopeful for her sake I'm right.

She turns to me and forces a smile. "I just need like two minutes to compose my thoughts."

"Take as much time as ya need." I kill the engine, then cup her cheek. "Just because you're the baby of the family doesn't mean you're a little kid, Kate. They're going to be happy for you just like River was. They all know how much you've wanted this."

"And if they're not?"

"Well, then fuck 'em."

Kaitlyn cracks a smile. "Dammit, you're right. They *better* be happy for me."

"That's my girl," I say, noticing she bites her bottom lip before grabbing the door handle. We get out of the truck and head toward the group standing around and chatting. Kaitlyn leads the way, and when her dad meets my eyes, I grow more nervous. I don't want to disappoint her parents or any of the Bishops, especially after everything they've done to get the rescue up and running. I've tried so hard to earn their respect and approval over the years. The last thing I want is for them to kick me off the property or something. I don't think either of us fully thought out the consequences, but even now, I wouldn't change a thing.

Once we're a few feet away, she looks at her brothers. "What are y'all doin' here?"

Kane and Knox speak at the same time. Knox clears his throat and continues. "Dad asked me to drop off some paperwork. I just happened to have this dickhole with me."

"And that's why I'm the smart one," Kane says, rolling his eyes.

"Why are *you* here?" Kiera asks Kaitlyn. "Thought you were taking a half day?"

"Yeah, well…" She slightly hesitates, then just blurts it out. "I'm pregnant."

That's not what we practiced, but I roll with it. Sometimes it's better to just rip off the Band-Aid. Everyone's eyes grow as wide as saucers, and they talk over each other until Kiera whistles. The high pitch rings off the metal barn, and they all grow quiet.

"Now." She looks around, silently warning everyone. Kaitlyn looks like she's on the verge of tears until her mother takes a step forward and wraps her in a hug, then kisses her head. "Congratulations, sweetheart."

Jackson joins in, and it's heartwarming to watch.

Knox and Kane give Kaitlyn their sentiments, then Knox turns toward me. "You knocked her up, didn't ya?"

Kaitlyn immediately stands between us because he almost looks pissed and ready for a fight. "Stop it," she demands. "Yes, Payton is the dad. We slept together one night, and I got pregnant."

Jackson stares at me as if he's contemplating whether to hug me or introduce his fist to my nose. Before he can decide, Kiera pulls me into a hug.

"I always loved the idea of you two together."

"We're going to co-parent...as *friends*," I explain before Kaitlyn has to.

"Why?" Kane asks. "Why don't y'all just make it official?"

"It will make things less messy and complicated," Kaitlyn says.

The protests begin.

"This is what we want, so fuckin' respect it," she blurts out.

"Language," Jackson warns her, but he's smiling. "Come here."

He swarms Kaitlyn in his arms, and I swear I hear his voice crack. "You're gonna be an amazing mom."

Then he turns to me. "I guess if there were anyone my daughter was having a baby with, I'd want it to be you."

"Thank you, sir. We're excited." He shakes my hand, and I'm relieved he isn't punching me in the face with it instead.

"I still think y'all should just go get hitched already," Knox says.

"Or at least take her out on a proper date," Kane adds.

Jesus fuck.

"Alright, boys, that's enough. This is what Kaitlyn wants. She didn't interject her opinions into your relationships and what you should be doin'."

"Like hell she didn't," Knox argues. "But fine. Still think there should be a ring on that finger, but what do I know?"

"You don't know shit," Kaitlyn tells him. "Just mind your business and be happy for me."

"Well, since we're putting it all out there, I guess it's a good time to tell y'all Hadleigh is pregnant again, too. We just found out and were gonna wait to tell everyone this weekend. So act surprised when she announces it."

The hugs and handshakes commence again. Geez, this family populates like bunnies.

Kiera and Jackson look so damn happy to be having more grandkids, and it warms my heart to know that my baby will have amazing grandparents.

"Now all of our kids will be close in age." Kaitlyn grins.

"Were y'all trying?" Kiera genuinely asks Knox.

He shakes his head and chuckles. "Hell no. But we weren't preventin' either." He waggles his brows, and memories of him stealing my Brazilian nuts come to mind.

"Looks like we might need a triple baby shower between Ivy, Hadleigh, and me," Kaitlyn admits, and I can tell she's calmer.

"This is very true. Imma be a busy grandma next year. Can't wait." Kiera beams, happier than I've ever seen her.

"Might be time for us to retire, babe," Jackson says. "We'll have our kids and grandkids to run the place."

"Maybe so." Kiera laughs.

Kane's cell phone rings. "Shit, we need to get to the barn. Looks like Old Man Wheeler is there to drop off his mare."

"He's early," Knox grits out. "Sometimes I can't stand punctual people."

I chuckle, and we say our goodbyes. As I turn to follow Kaitlyn to the truck, Jackson calls me back.

"I'm going to respect Kaitlyn's and your wishes, but if you hurt my daughter—"

"I'd never. Kaitlyn's my best friend, and I only want the absolute best for her. I won't say it was a mistake because I believe everything happens for a reason. But this is what she wants—what she's *always* wanted."

"You're right. I know y'all said you'd raise the baby as friends and all that, but I can't seem to understand why. You can't tell me you aren't in love with her."

I blow out a breath, neither confirming nor denying.

"Kaitlyn's calling all the shots, sir. I'm just giving her what she wants."

"Ahh." He nods, then pats my shoulder. "She'll come around."

The horn blares, and we look toward my truck. Kaitlyn opens the door. "It's hot!"

"Guess that's my cue," I tell Jackson, and he gives me a smile.

"Don't mess with a mad pregnant woman. Take my advice on that one." He snickers.

When I crank the truck, Kaitlyn faces me. "What'd my dad say?"

"He threatened me if I hurt you."

She snorts. "I'd expect nothing less."

"Me neither. Where to now?"

Kaitlyn sighs. "We have to go to Grandma's house. If she finds out through the grapevine, we're both dead."

I chuckle. "Okay, okay. The last person I want on my bad side is Rose."

On the way over, Kaitlyn chats about her family's reaction. "It wasn't as bad as I thought it would be."

"Nah, they seemed very happy and excited." Just like I'd hoped.

"They did! It's a relief," she admits. "Maybe I worried for nothing."

"Maybe. Not like they were gonna blackball and ignore you. Your family loves you a lot."

"They love you too," she says. "I think they were happy to hear you're the dad and not some random dude I met at a bar."

"Even if it were, they'd still accept you and the baby, Kate. You're lucky. That's not something you should ever take for granted."

"I don't and won't, BD." She smirks.

We park in front of the big white farmhouse with the

wraparound porch, and now I might be more anxious than before.

"You know she's gonna expect a weddin' too," Kaitlyn warns when we get out of the truck and make our way up the steps.

"Oh, I'm well aware." I reach forward and knock a few times.

"I'm comin', I'm comin'." I hear from the other side. "Takes an old woman some time to make it across this big house."

Rose opens the thick wooden door and pushes the screen open. "Today must be my lucky day! C'mon in, kids."

Kaitlyn gives her grandma a kiss on the cheek, and I plant one on the other, then she leads us to the living room. Her house is the epitome of a Southern grandma, with the quilts and crocheted afghans carefully placed on the back of the couch. Makes me feel right at home.

"I just made some chocolate chip pecan cookies. Y'all want some?"

"You know the answer is always yes," Kaitlyn says. "I'll come help."

Kaitlyn follows her into the kitchen, and I hear them make small talk about the weather and the gossip Rose heard at church last weekend. A few minutes later, Rose walks in with a plate of cookies while Kaitlyn brings a platter with three large glasses of milk.

I take mine along with a few cookies. "They're even still warm."

As soon as I take a bite, I groan at how delicious it tastes. I swallow it down with the coldest milk I've ever had. "Best I've ever had," I say around a mouthful.

Kaitlyn follows my lead and moans. "Grandma, these are so good."

"I'll have to give you the recipe later," she says. "Now, why are y'all really here?"

Kaitlyn playfully gasps. "To visit my favorite grandma in the whole wide world."

Rose tilts her head. "Might've been born in the mornin', but I wasn't born yesterday."

I chuckle because it's something I've heard her say several times.

"I wanted to tell you some news," Kaitlyn finally says. "Before anyone else does."

"Y'all finally gettin' married?" Rose quickly asks.

Kaitlyn shakes her head. "No, but we're having a baby."

"Oh, thank you, Jesus." Rose stands and pulls Kaitlyn into her arms. "Now I can die a happy woman."

"No talkin' like that, Grandma. You're immortal," she teases, though I know she wishes that were true.

"I'm not goin' anywhere anytime soon, but I'm no spring chicken either. All I wanted was to see all my grandbabies have their own babies, and now it's happening." A few tears run down her cheeks, and Kaitlyn reaches forward to wipe them away.

"You're gonna make me cry," Kaitlyn says, and I can hear the shakiness in her voice as she speaks. "I'm already hormonal."

Rose stands a little taller. "So you're the father?"

"Yes, ma'am," I proudly say with a grin, and she gives me a nod of approval.

"Good. I was scared she was gonna get knocked up by some truck driver passin' through town." She gives me a pointed look that has me cracking up.

Kaitlyn gasps. "Grandma! Who do you think I am?"

Rose shakes her finger. "I've heard some of the things you've said, sweetie. Had me worried about ya. Well, when's the weddin'? Maybe a fall one? We could plan it quick. That way, you aren't showing too much in your dress."

"Uhh..." Kaitlyn stalls. "We're not gettin' married."

Rose sits on the couch and pats next to her so Kaitlyn will follow. "Yes, you are."

"We're not," Kaitlyn confirms. "We're going to co-parent and raise the baby as friends. We're already roommates, so it won't be much of a transition."

"I hear what you're saying, but I'm not listenin'," Rose states unapologetically. "I know you two are gonna get married regardless of how stubborn you're being right now. So much like your daddy, it's ridiculous. Worse than your brothers, honestly. You can say whatever you want, but I'd just like to request that you get hitched before I turn ninety. Got it?" Rose turns and looks at me. "That gives you a good five years to fall in love and have more babies."

I scratch my cheek, not wanting to argue with the queen of Eldorado.

"Well, since that's settled, do you know what you're having?"

"Not yet," Kaitlyn says, then pulls out the ultrasound photos from her crossbody purse. She was so busy trying to calm down her mom, dad, and brothers that she forgot to show them. "We got these today."

Rose studies them, and I can see the excitement on her face. "You know, when I was pregnant, we didn't have stuff like this. Stand up for me, sweetie."

Kaitlyn does, and Rose lifts her shirt without asking.

"I'm gonna make a prediction that it's a girl. Your bump is small, but it's high. We Bishops carry a certain way for each gender."

"Ya think?" Kaitlyn laughs. "That would be incredible, but I honestly don't have a preference. I'm just happy to be having one. And that our baby will have several cousins to grow up with now that Hadleigh and Ivy are pregnant." Her eyes go wide, and Kaitlyn quickly realizes she slipped.

"Hadleigh's pregnant again?" Rose gasps. "And they didn't come tell me first?"

"Shit, I wasn't supposed to say anything." Kaitlyn smacks her forehead. "Pretend you didn't just hear that."

"My lips are sealed, but this is why you're my favorite

grandchild. You actually cared enough to come visit, eat some cookies, then share the good news. But Knox's in trouble."

I laugh, knowing he's in for it now.

When I finish my cookies and milk, Rose offers me more, but I politely decline. Kaitlyn takes a few more, and they laugh and chat about the crazy cravings Rose had when she was pregnant with each of her kids.

"Peanut butter, maple syrup, *and* pickles?" Kaitlyn repeats. "That's disgustin'."

"You'd think so, but it hit the spot."

After the conversation comes to a lull, Kaitlyn stands, then we give hugs and say our goodbyes.

"Congratulations again. And thanks for stopping by. Y'all don't be strangers, ya hear?" Rose walks us to the door and gives us a wave. When we're back in the truck, Kaitlyn snickers.

"You're so wrong for tellin' her about Hadleigh," I tease, taking the gravel road toward the house.

"I really didn't mean to. I blame pregnancy brain. I'd apologize for slipping, but I'm sure I owe him for somethin' he did in the past."

"Seriously, though, I can't believe Hadleigh's pregnant," I admit. "Your parents are gonna have four grandbabies in the same year."

"Those Brazilian nuts are potent."

We fall into a fit of laughter, but Kaitlyn might actually be onto something.

"I'm just happy our little berry will have cousins their age to get in trouble with."

"Me too." She smiles, placing her hand on her tummy. "Me too."

CHAPTER TWENTY

KAITLYN

TWO AND A HALF MONTHS LATER

Now that the shock about the pregnancy has dissipated and it's no longer a secret, I'm enjoying it so much more. It helps that I'm not feeling as nauseous anymore and can eat actual food.

Payton has been the sweetest and makes sure I always have my needs met. Every night after work, he rubs my shoulders and feet. Then he makes dinner or picks up food from the B&B. Though I'm self-conscious that my stomach looks like I ate a Thanksgiving dinner instead of having a cute pregnancy bump, I'm still happy. When Payton rests his hand on my belly and talks to the baby while we watch our shows at night, I can't imagine doing this with anyone else. He really will be a great husband someday.

We've also looked at nursery furniture and have browsed for themes but won't make a final decision until we find out the gender.

Fortunately, that day is *today*.

Now that I'm halfway through my pregnancy, I'll have my twenty-week scan and find out if we're having a boy or girl.

Besides being excited about that, it's been fun sharing this experience with Ivy and Hadleigh and being pregnant together. Hadleigh's due date is a week after mine, and Ivy recently found out she's having a boy and a girl. Since she's only two months ahead of me, she's told me what I have to look forward to—the good and the bad.

Grandma Bishop can't stop telling everyone about her new great-grandchildren. She's always loved singing to them in her rocking chair. I can't wait for her to meet our little one so we can take tons of pictures to add to the others. On top of navigating baby stuff, the rescue has kept us busy. Since opening and getting Fancy, we've taken in five more horses. Zach loves each one, always eager to help and learn more about them. I wouldn't be the least bit shocked if he grows up and takes over one of the horse operations on the ranch. He's relieved some of the load off me while I've adjusted my training schedule so I don't overdo it. Gavin's also helped take some of my show horses since he's qualified in that area too.

"Ready?" Payton knocks on the doorframe, stepping inside my room.

"Does this shirt make me look fat?" Frowning, I turn and face him.

"No, it makes you look pregnant."

"That's not what I asked," I deadpan.

He comes closer, then kneels in front of me and places a palm over my stomach. "Can't wait to see you on the screen, baby." He presses a kiss above my belly button, then looks up and smiles at me. "You're beautiful. Now c'mon, we're gonna be late."

Groaning, I adjust my shirt and bottoms. "I'm about to burst out of these clothes."

His eyes go to my chest.

"Yes, I need bigger bras too."

He fights back a smile. "We should go. Kiera's waiting in the living room."

Everyone's waiting for my FaceTime call so they can find out the gender in real time. Since they didn't want a room full of people, we compromised.

As soon as my mom sees me, she swarms me in a hug and rubs my belly. "Let's go find out if I'm having a grandson or granddaughter."

She already has one of each from Knox and will have more from Kane, so I guess whatever I'm having will break the tie until we find out what Hadleigh's third baby is.

The ride to the hospital seems to take forever, but we eventually make it. I'm anxious as hell not to only find out the news but make sure he or she is healthy and growing on track. I've been checking all my pregnancy apps to see what stage I'm at and how big the baby is. Right now, it's the size of a sweet potato.

"Kaitlyn Bishop," a tech calls my name after five minutes of waiting. Mom gives me a warm smile, and I'm so glad she's here with me.

I stand, and my smile drops as soon as I see it's *her*.

Analise, the baby daddy flirter.

Her smile widens when she notices Payton. "You're back."

She ignores me as she leads us to a room. It's not until she gives me undressing instructions that she finally acknowledges me.

Once I'm ready, she returns, then flips off the lights and spreads gel over the wand.

I flinch, and she apologizes, "Oh sorry, it's cold."

No shit.

I watch the screen as she moves the wand around, taking measurements.

"So when do we find out the gender? I need to call my family so they can witness it in real time."

"Sure. Gimme just a second. Baby's movin' a lot."

I get Maize on the phone and tell her it's almost time. She's at the B&B surrounded by our cousins, aunts, uncles, and of course, Grandma Bishop.

"Well? What is it?" Grandpa blurts out impatiently.

Everyone laughs as we wait for the official announcement.

Payton holds my hand while my mom stands next to him, waiting. I hand her the phone so they can get a better view.

"It's a girl!" Analise finally calls out.

My eyes widen as my heart kicks up a notch. *A girl.*

Turning to Payton, I smile up at him and notice his glossy gaze. He stares at my lips, then leans down with his arm out.

Instead of hugging me, our mouths connect.

And neither of us pulls away.

His hand cups my cheek as he slides his tongue against mine. After a moment, he realizes what we're doing and jerks away. My mom's eyes widen in shock, and I realize everyone on FaceTime just witnessed it, too.

Just great.

No one is going to believe we're *just friends* now.

Tears well on the brim of my eyes as his kiss lingers, and I'm quickly reminded that we're having a baby girl.

"Congrats, Mom and Dad. Here are some pictures for ya." Analise hands us four ultrasound photos and wishes us the best of luck before cleaning up. She mentions my doctor will be in contact with me to go over the scan. But overall, everything looks great.

"I'll give you some privacy to get dressed," my mom says. She ends the call, then steps out of the room.

Payton grabs my clothes, then turns around while I put them back on. He stares at the pictures as if he's trying to memorize them.

"I think she has your nose," he tells me.

"You can't know that already," I argue.

"In this one of her profile, I can. Like a mini you."

I smile, trying to squeeze back into my jeans and growing breathless while doing so.

"How're ya doin'?" he asks, glancing over his shoulder.

"Yeah, just great." I groan, kicking my legs out to stretch the fabric.

"Stop being stubborn about maternity clothes," Payton says.

"I'll wear them when you do. It's only fair."

"I think you're gonna have to give in eventually." He smirks when I fight to pull up the zipper and lose.

I point at my stomach, then to him. "This is your damn fault."

"Excuse me?" He raises a brow, crossing his arms. "Care to explain? Because I'm pretty sure it takes two to—"

"You're always making delicious food or bringing home carbs from the B&B and serving me desserts."

Payton shakes his head, laughing.

"And you're always reminding me to eat!"

"Kaitlyn." He steps toward me, then rests his hands on my shoulders. "You're carrying our daughter. Gaining weight is normal. She's healthy and growing. That's all that matters. So for now, either buy new clothes or wear sweatpants," he says the last part with amusement.

I grind my teeth, hating that he's right, and I'll need to cave pretty soon.

"Just help me button them, and I'll stop whining," I say.

"Alright." He chuckles, reaching down and struggling just like I had. But then after I suck in a deep breath, he manages to get it closed.

"See? They fit fine." I beam.

"Let's go." He takes my hand, and we meet my mom in the waiting room. She eyes me curiously before glancing down at our hands.

Great, now she's really going to give me a hard time.

That kiss was technically our second, but it felt nothing like the first one six years ago.

That was the night of my birthday party Knox threw for me. I blew out the candles, and one was left, so they told me I had to kiss one person. Nearly everyone in the room was either related or taken, minus Payton. So for funsies, I marched up to him, told him not to overthink it, and smacked my mouth to his. He had barely flinched, and we never talked about it again.

But that doesn't mean I hadn't thought about it a couple of times since.

The way he devoured my lips today had my body buzzing, which was something I hadn't expected.

CHAPTER TWENTY-ONE

PAYTON

ONE MONTH LATER

KAITLYN HASN'T BEEN FEELING the best lately. She's recently had some of her roughest days, and I hate that she's been sick. She woke up feeling a lot better yesterday, so I planned a surprise for her since it's Saturday and we both have off.

She's still peacefully sleeping when I sneak into her room. She told me not to let her sleep too late because it throws off her weekly schedule. Knowing how much she loves coffee, even if it's not the *real* deal with caffeine, I grind some beans and make a fresh pot.

Not wanting to startle her awake, I sit on the edge of the bed and lightly touch her arm. Her beautiful blue eyes flutter open, and she smiles. "What time is it?"

"A quarter after eight. Made you coffee with your favorite creamer."

Taking the mug, she smiles, then takes a sip. "Thank you. Mmm, it's good. Oh, crap. I gotta pee."

I chuckle, then move out of her way so she doesn't have to crawl over me. Looking around her room, I notice how cozy she's made it in here. For months, there was just a twin-sized bed and a pair of old boots. Now, it's full of her furniture, rugs, pictures of us, and some of her prize-winning horses. I like it, even if I wish she were sleeping in my room each night. But after my slipup at our twenty-week appointment last month, we haven't talked about it or broken any more rules.

Everyone questioned if we were secretly dating, and I explained the truth—we're just friends who were emotional and got excited about the news.

Regardless, they still didn't buy it.

"Sorry. I swear the baby uses my bladder as a trampoline. I barely made it." She smooths her hair out of her face.

"How's she doin' today?"

Kaitlyn places her hand on her belly. "I feel like it's gonna be a good day. I usually know first thing in the morning."

"That's perfect." I meet her eyes and smile. "Because I planned somethin' for us."

She gives me a puzzled expression. "I don't want to do anything too physical."

"No, nothing like that. Dress in something comfy." I look at the clock on the wall. "Let's try to leave in an hour."

A smile touches her lips. "Ohh, I like the sound of that."

I stand, then give Kaitlyn space to get dressed and ready.

After I shower, I throw on jeans and a long-sleeved shirt, then grab my jacket. Considering it's the middle of November, I even wear a beanie.

Before I can ask if she's almost done, Kaitlyn comes out with a scowl. "I look stupid."

"You look gorgeous."

She takes her empty mug to the sink and rinses it.

"And that ass," I offer with a smirk.

"At least I still have that. "

I grab my keys, hoping today will brighten her mood. "It's only temporary, Kate."

"Tell that to my vagina."

"I'll be happy to," I quip.

When she fully comes into view, I can't help but admire how pretty she is. Kaitlyn's wearing a red sweater with black leggings and adorable ballerina slippers. Pregnancy looks good on her. Knowing it's my kid in there makes her even sexier.

"Am I dressed appropriately?" She swings out her arms.

"Yep. Perfect."

"I guess we should go, then."

When we drive down the gravel road and the B&B comes into view, I slow down and ask if she wants to stop and eat.

"I want donuts. Like glazed, chocolate, blueberry, and raspberry filled."

"All at once?" I say.

"Wouldn't that be amazing?" She laughs. "And a pickle, too."

"With the donuts?"

She shrugs. "Your child is makin' me crave the weirdest things."

Chuckling, I shake my head. "Why am I not surprised?"

I drive past the B&B and continue until we get to the county road. When we get to Eldorado, I head downtown to one of the donut shops on the corner. Kaitlyn's face lights up when she spots it. I love how something so simple makes her happy.

After we get a dozen donuts in all flavor combinations, we grab two bottles of milk, then sit at a small table by the front windows.

"These are so good, I just had a foodgasm," she says around a mouthful.

I burst out laughing, grateful no one else is in the lobby area to overhear us.

"So you gonna tell me what you have planned for us today?"

"Thought we could do a little shoppin'."

Her jaw drops, then her face splits in two. "I swear. It's like you're downloading my thoughts. I was just thinkin' I needed to start my Christmas shopping."

I shake my head. "This trip is for you. Thought we could work on our registry, maybe get some baby things, and you a new wardrobe."

She tucks her lips in her mouth. "I might cry."

"Oh no."

"Sorry, I'm not used to feeling so emotional over every little thing. Thank you." A few tears spill down her cheeks.

"If you keep that up, people are going to take away your hard-ass card," I tease, though I enjoy seeing this vulnerable side of her.

That makes her snort. "You better keep my secret safe."

"Always." I wink.

When we're done eating, we head to San Angelo. On the way, we chat about the rescue and how well Fancy's improving.

"Zach's really attached to her," she tells me. "I swear I overheard him telling her all about Lilia and how he can't wait to see her at school."

I laugh. "What a stud. Makes me happy he's grown so close to her," I admit.

We pull into the mall, and I love seeing her excitement. I'm tempted to interlock my fingers with hers when we get inside. I want the world to know she's carrying my child and I'm in love with her, even if she doesn't see it.

The first store we go to is full of baby clothes and toys. The many options are overwhelming, but Kaitlyn is like a kid in a candy store. I ask the clerk where we can register, and she directs us to a kiosk in the back. Once we sign up, we download an app on our phones, then start scanning things.

"I'm going overboard," Kaitlyn tells me after she's added at least fifty items.

"This is cute," I say, holding up a stuffed buck toy with a big rack. It looks majestic.

"It is!" She scans it. "This is the fun part of being pregnant. Oh my goodness, look at this."

Kaitlyn holds up a onesie with a heart and a pony on it. "I don't think I can leave without buying this. I'd have so much regret if someone didn't choose it."

"There's no regretting anything. We're gettin' it." I wrap my arm around her shoulders when I spot another one.

It says, *My Mommy is a Queen and I'm a Princess.*

"We're getting this one too."

She squeals. "That's so cute!"

After we've spent over an hour in the store, we purchase the things we couldn't live without, then hit up another one. It's the same song and dance as the first.

"I need to focus on things we actually need," she tells herself. "Or we're going to have a million clothes she'll probably never get to wear because she'll grow so fast."

"Or we can just have another girl and reuse them."

She meets my eyes and grins. "Our luck, it'd be a boy."

This makes me laugh. "You're right. No pretty princess onesies for him."

We look at the cribs, car seats, breast pumps, and maternity bras.

"Jesus, I never realized how much shit we'd need," I say when we pass several aisles of baby gear and furniture.

"Right? Just imagine how women did it before all this stuff was invented."

"And before air-conditioning," I add.

"Fuck that. These hot flashes are enough to burn our house down. I can't even imagine not having it."

I love how she calls it *our* house.

After stopping into a few more places, Kaitlyn gets tired. So we take a break for lunch, which always seems to give her more energy, then make our final stop at the maternity clothes store.

"I might spend all my money in here," she says, touching the different shirts and jeans. This is the happiest I've seen her in a long time.

"I know you bought some things off the internet that you hated, so I thought maybe you could find a few cute-ass outfits."

She laughs. "Will you help me?"

"I'd love to."

One of the associates comes over and helps Kaitlyn. They laugh and make jokes about some of the patterns of clothes. Considering Christmas is just around the corner, there are a few sweaters with candy canes and reindeer that look like uteruses.

"Can he come inside the dressing room with me?" Kaitlyn asks.

"Absolutely," the associate says, unlocking one of the rooms. It's large enough for a family of five.

When we're inside, Kaitlyn reaches for the hangers I have in my hand and looks at them.

"This one is kinda sexy," she says, and I turn to help her change. She huffs and groans, but when she's dressed, she tells me to look.

"Okay, this is adorable," she admits.

"Looks great on you," I tell her, smiling at how happy she looks.

She places her hand on her belly. "This is so comfy and slimming. I'm actually excited to try on everything else."

Each time she changes, I put the clothes back on the hangers. The last outfit is a maxi dress with long sleeves, but it makes her tits look huge.

Kaitlyn notices me stealing a glance. "The girls look great, don't they?"

"There's no denying that, but then again, you've always had perfect tits."

She chuckles. "Serious question…"

"Shoot."

"Would you have sex with a pregnant woman?"

Heat rushes to my cheeks, and I smirk. I know exactly what she's asking, but I refuse to give her the answer she wants. "Depends."

"On what, exactly?" She gives me a finger swirling motion, and I turn again.

"So what's the criteria?" she pushes again.

I suck in a breath and exhale. "Well, if it was my pregnant girlfriend or wife, absolutely. Nothing sexier than a woman carrying your child."

Kaitlyn stills, and I wish I could see her face. But then she drops it. I'm determined to keep the boundaries after my slipup in front of her whole family.

We ended up buying every outfit she tried on. She tried to pay, but I yanked her wallet out of her hand and told her it was my treat. Mama deserves to be pampered, and I'm more than happy to spend money on her. In fact, I'd spoil the shit out of her every day if she'd let me.

When we get home, Kaitlyn lies on the couch and falls asleep. As much fun as we had, she's exhausted. While she naps, I unload the bags.

I place the few things we picked out in the room that's starting to look like a nursery. Leaning against the doorway, I envision exactly what my daughter's room will look like and how she'll decorate it over the years. A smile meets my lips, knowing how many happy memories we'll make and how much she's already loved. There's no doubt in my mind she'll have a better childhood than I did. That's something I will make sure of.

After a few hours, I make dinner, then wake her up to eat.

"You know this is my favorite," she sing-songs, twirling the spaghetti noodles around her fork. When she notices the big dill pickle I set on a plate, she bursts out laughing.

"Our baby is thankin' you right now." She crunches into it and moans with delight.

"Gotta keep my girls happy."

"Thank you for such a good time today. I was dreadin' having to wear maternity clothes, and you made it a good experience."

"It was my pleasure to take you. Now, we'll just have to plan a day to go Christmas shopping."

"I'm down for that. Preferably sooner rather than later because today kicked my ass, and the bigger I get, the harder it will be to stand on my feet for long periods."

"I'll look at our schedules and plan something."

After dinner, Kaitlyn decides she wants to take a bath, so I offer to draw it for her. Then I decide to light a few candles and sprinkle in some salts. When it's ready, I grab her hand and lead her to it.

"This is so sweet," she gushes. "Will you help me undress?"

I give her a puzzled look because she's always demanded privacy. "Are you sure?"

She nods, taking her hair out from the ponytail and allowing it to fall around her face. Slowly, I slide my fingers into the elastic band of her pants and lower them down along with her panties. Then I take my time lifting the sweater over her head. I meet her heated gaze as I reach behind her and unsnap her bra. Her supple breasts fall, and I swallow hard, wishing I could suck on her taut nipples.

"You're hard," she states, studying the large bulge in my jeans.

I clear my throat, readjusting myself. "Do you need help gettin' in the tub?"

"Yes, please."

I hold out my hand to help her, but she stops in place. "Touch me, Payton."

Cautiously, I step closer and place my hand on her hips.

"Not like that. You know what I need."

"I can't," I whisper. My words nearly destroy me.

Defeat washes across her face. "Why not? Am I not your type?"

Placing my hand on her cheek, I blow out a breath. "My sweet Kate, you're so goddamn beautiful, the prettiest woman I've ever met. But you made the rules. I'm just following them."

"Fuck the rules," she hisses.

I shake my head, trying to stay strong even as she pushes the limits. "It'll only complicate things, and you know that. We've gone this far. I don't want to ruin what we have."

She groans. "I'm horny as fuck, Payton. Do you have any idea what that's like?"

A chuckle escapes me because she has no idea how many times I've wanted her more than life itself. "Actually, I do."

With one last attempt to change my mind, Kaitlyn wraps her arms around my neck and presses her breasts against my chest. "You'll either change your mind or regret telling me no."

I smirk at her seduction tactic. "Is that a threat, Little Devil?"

She leans forward and tugs on my bottom lip. "It's a fuckin' promise."

It takes every bit of strength I have not to bring her to my bed and devour her pussy like it's my last meal. But I can't budge on this. Everything inside me screams it'd be the best time of our lives, but she'd break my heart in the process. She wants me now because of her hormones, not because she's in love with me.

Instead of continuing, she lets out a frustrated sigh before moving to the tub. I give her my hand as she slides in, the warmth covering her immediately.

With her belly poking out of the water, she dips her head back until her hair gets wet, then sets one foot on the edge of the tub. Her eyes squeeze tight as she lowers her hand between her thighs.

"Fuck," she hisses. "You have no idea how badly I need to come."

I'm mesmerized by her as she continues down the slow path to find her release. Soft moans escape her lips, and she gently lifts her chin.

"I wish you were the one touching me," she nearly begs, picking up her pace. "The way you used to worship my pussy… shit," she groans out. "No one's ever done it as good as you, myself included."

My breathing increases as my cock fights to break through my zipper. "I should go."

"Watch what you do to me," she pleads, cupping her swollen breast, then twisting her nipple.

"*Fuck*," I whisper, though I hadn't meant to say it aloud.

"This is your fault," she murmurs, her movements becoming more intense as the water swashes. Just as I'm about to ask her how so, she continues, "Always touchin' me. Being so damn gentle and caring. Shit…I'm—" Kaitlyn's back arches, and her body convulses as she moans out in pleasure. She sucks in air as she continues teasing her clit. Once she shudders from the release, her body goes limp.

I cross my arms over my chest as her eyes flutter open. Her flirtatious gaze meets mine. "Enjoy the show?"

I pop a brow and lick my lips, not giving in to her seduction.

"Ya need anything else?" I ask before setting a big fluffy towel on the counter.

"Just to be fucked hard and ruthlessly." She flashes a knowing smirk, and I know walking away from her will be the hardest thing I ever do.

"It's not gonna work, Kate," I tell her, stepping backward toward the door. "Let me know when you're ready to get out of the tub, and I'll come help you."

She grabs a bar of soap and chunks it at my head, missing me by inches. It hits the bathroom door with a thud and falls to the floor.

"What the hell was that for?" I snap.

"Just makin' sure you're paying attention," she quips with a devious grin.

I grab the bar of soap and take it with me so she can't black my eye with it when I return.

Needing my own release, I go to my room and strip out of my jeans. Once I lie back on the bed, I roughly grip myself. Then I stroke my cock hard and fast as the image of Kaitlyn touching herself repeats in my head. Her trying to seduce me is something I'll never forget, even if it was only because she wanted to get laid. As guttural groans escape my throat, I imagine tasting her sweet cunt. When the orgasm rips through me, I picture Kaitlyn on top of me, squeezing her pussy as she milks every drop of come out of me.

"Goddammit," I whisper, knowing I won't be able to control my willpower much longer.

The last thing I'll be able to survive is getting my heart broken by the woman who will always hold it.

CHAPTER TWENTY-TWO

KAITLYN

CHRISTMAS with my family is a tradition I live for.

More food than a person can eat.

Decorations hang around every inch of the house.

Full stockings and wrapped presents cover the floor under the tree.

It's basically a Hallmark film.

There's always holiday music or a movie playing.

Grandpa's always stealing cookies before they've cooled.

Grandma's snagging a baby to hold all night.

People are spread out all over, snacking on food and eggnog.

The house echoes with laughter and fun story times.

And I love every second.

Luckily, this year is no different.

The only vast change is I'm pregnant and will be included in all the baby talk for once. Ivy's due to pop in less than two months, and since she's having twins, she's gotten uncomfortably big. Kane set his plate on her belly and thanked her for holding it for him. I thought the death glare she gave would set him on fire.

Payton knows better than to do something like that,

considering I'm still struggling with my body's changes. I'm excited we're having a baby, but between the hormones and feeling huge all the time, I didn't anticipate feeling insecure.

"We need to plan your shower, Kaitlyn," my mom tells me over dessert.

We started eating an hour ago, but we're still munching on all the sweets Maize baked.

"Well, we're registered, so feel free to plan away," I sing-song. Everyone in my family loves parties and will use any excuse to throw them.

"Did you pick a theme for the nursery yet?" Grandma asks.

"Well, I don't know if you'd call it a *theme,* but I wanted cute forest animals—bunnies, squirrels, foxes—and Payton wants deer. But not the Bambi type, the big bucks that you hunt. With arrows and guns."

A round of gasps echoes, and Payton glowers at me.

"Veto," Grandma says. "Sorry, honey, but killin' animals isn't exactly an appropriate theme."

I chuckle at Payton's embarrassment.

"That's not what I suggested." He directs his gaze at me.

"Close enough!" I argue. "A hunter hiding in the bushes while aiming his gun at a deer drinking from a pond is traumatic!"

"It was much cuter than she's makin' it out to be," he argues.

"My granddaughter will not be surrounded with camouflage anything. Sorry, Payton. Gotta agree with everyone else." My mom tries to give him a little sympathy, but it's not working.

Knox comes over, chuckling as he shoves cake into his big mouth. "Amateur."

Payton rolls his eyes.

"You'll eventually learn. They don't really want our opinion."

"That's not true," I argue. "Well, perhaps it is for you because you suck, but Payton actually has great suggestions."

"Ignore him," Hadleigh says, squeezing her way through the

crowd of people. For her third time being pregnant, she looks amazing. "He's just annoyed I won't let him hang dead animals in our house."

"Ew."

"You weren't complainin' when y'all came over and ate that yummy as fuck deer sausage a few weeks ago."

I laugh because he has a point. I'll eat it, but I don't want to see it.

Payton and I find a couch to sit on while we watch a Christmas movie. Dad's passing out beer, and Mom's pouring the spiked eggnog. When Dad offers one to Payton, he passes.

"Just because I can't drink doesn't mean you can't," I whisper to him.

He wraps his arm around my shoulders, pulling me in closer. "Nah, it only seems fair. You're sacrificing a lot for our baby, and I don't want you to feel alone."

"I don't because Hadleigh and Ivy aren't drinkin' either." I glance at his charming grin. "But you're too sweet for your own good."

"Just what every man wants to hear when they aren't gettin' any," Knox says, interrupting our private conversation.

"Do you *ever* go away?" I snap.

"No, ma'am. I'll be your pain in the ass brother for as long as I live."

"Ugh, God. Why do you have to make it sound like a death sentence."

"Because it is," Kane adds.

The room erupts with laughter. Even Hadleigh joins in although she's trying to act like it's not funny. She's well aware of Knox's behavior. Hell, she chose it.

Ivy sits next to me, and Kane cradles her to his chest, palming her belly and whispering in her ear. Her cheeks blush, and I hate that I'm jealous. They are too damn cute for their own good.

After Payton made it clear he wouldn't cross the line anymore, I've been dreaming about him nonstop.

By midnight, everyone's tired, and we make our rounds to say goodbye. My mom and aunts help Grandma clean the kitchen while the guys pick up the wrapping paper.

"Take care of my great-grandbaby," Grandma says, rubbing my belly.

"I will. See ya soon." I give her a hug, then wait for Payton so we can walk out to his truck.

"You gettin' tired?" he asks.

"Actually, not really. I think I'm getting my second wind."

He laughs, helping me into my seat. "Wanna watch a movie before bed?"

I smile. "Sure."

As soon as we get home, he tells me he's going to change into something more comfortable, and I do the same.

Except I don't put on baggy clothes like I typically do. This time I'm going to try something different.

"What're ya doing?" Payton asks when I walk into the living room twenty minutes later in nothing but a thin tank top and booty shorts. My makeup and hair are still done from the party, but I'm hoping he'll help me *mess* it up.

The last time I tried to seduce him, he used the *it'll complicate things* excuse. But after months of nonstop sexual tension, I'm tired of holding back.

"What do you mean?" I ask as I sit next to him on the couch.

"You warm or somethin'?" His eyes land on my chest, then lower down to my legs. "I can change the temp."

"No, I'm comfortable, actually. Though my vibrator died before I could finish, so I'm kinda mad about that."

He pauses for a beat before asking, "What kind of batteries does it take?"

"It's a rechargeable one, but the cord fried. Now I have to order another one and wait for it to come in."

He uncomfortably scratches his cheek as he processes what I've said. I'm hoping to finally make him snap.

"You could help me out until it arrives?" I wager, ignoring the TV show on the screen and hoping he will too.

"Kate..." His deep warning tone sends shivers down my spine.

"I can't help that my hormones are going wild right now. It's nearly impossible to get myself off anymore. What would you rather have me do? Ask you or some stranger at a bar?"

"You're not going to a bar at six months pregnant."

"Well, I wouldn't drink! I'd just find the first lonely man and ask him to take me home and fuck me raw."

"That's not happenin' either." His jaw ticks as he stares me down. "You're tryin' to push my buttons."

"That's not true." I flash him an innocent smile. "You haven't gotten laid since we stopped havin' sex, so I know you probably need it too," I add.

"I've gone longer than that."

"So what do you do in between? Jerk off in the shower? Or are you a *whack off in a sock* kinda guy?"

"Jesus Christ, Kate." He repositions himself on the couch as if he's waging a war with himself.

"It's just a question. You don't gotta get all squirmy."

He licks his lower lip as if he's contemplating what to do. I'd almost feel bad, but I know he wants this too. We've been dancing around each other for far too long, and my body misses his touch. Having him watch last month wasn't enough to make him crack, so I'm trying a different strategy.

After seeing how easy he fits in with my family and how great we'd be together, I'm tired of ignoring it. And I know he has to be too.

"What if you just give me your hand, and I'll use it on myself instead?"

"You can't use your own?"

"I can't reach down there as easily anymore. I have this whole baby bump thing goin' on, which is why I needed my vibrator."

"I guess you'll just have to wait until your new cord arrives."

My eyes lower to his groin as he noticeably gets hard. He can fight this all he wants, but he's craving it too.

"That's not fair because you can easily go take care of yourself," I explain, and he instinctively adjusts himself.

"Kate, what's this really about?"

"I want you, Payton." I spell it out slowly. "And I want you to fuck me."

"We set rules, remember?"

"We've already broken two rules."

His jaw ticks. "And would we still be *just friends* after?"

"That depends. Is that what you would want?"

"I'm asking you what you want."

"I want you to kiss me..." *And then fuck me six ways to Sunday.*

It's been a month and a half since we kissed in front of my mom, and I haven't stopped thinking about it. I felt the way he poured everything he had into it, and I ached for more when we broke apart.

But neither of us did anything about it after, and I'm tired of pretending it didn't happen.

"If you have zero desire to kiss me, then I'll drop it. But I don't think this is one-sided." My heart races as my confession spews out.

Payton stares at me like he's frozen in shock, and after several seconds pass, I'm convinced he's going to leave me high and dry.

Instead of staying and being humiliated by his silence, I stand to walk away. He's given me his answer by not saying anything at all.

"Kate," he murmurs, grabbing my hand as I step around him. "I'm not saying no because I don't want to kiss you. I do, but I'm terrified of losing you. You're in the mood for this tonight, but you might regret it tomorrow. I don't want it to seem like I'm taking advantage of you because I care way too much about you."

"Would you rather see me fall in love with someone else?" I ask but don't bother to wait for a response before I go to my room.

Now *I've* made it awkward and weird as fuck.

And my heart is shattered.

CHAPTER TWENTY-THREE

PAYTON

I CAN'T BELIEVE I just let her walk away like that.

After years of pining after the woman of my dreams, I froze. *Made excuses.*

Our relationship has shifted over the past several months, and I've tried to stay true to what she wanted in the beginning. But now I'm conflicted.

Does she actually have feelings for me, or does she just need me to scratch an itch?

My desire for Kaitlyn has been something I've pushed away for years, shoved to the back of my mind, and kept locked in a box.

And now she's *begging* me to break our rules.

The first time she brought it up over a month ago, I figured it was just a fluke and she'd never share the same feelings as me.

I hadn't expected her to bring it up again, and I really didn't anticipate her asking if what was going on between us was one-sided.

Fuck.

How the hell could she ever think I wouldn't want her?

As my head and heart fight between taking the risk or playing it safe, memories of us together flood my mind.

Were her feelings there all along? Or did they form recently? *Does it fucking matter?*

Getting to my feet, I head toward her room with my nerves on fire. It's now or never.

I blow out a breath, lean against the doorframe, then knock.

"Kate, open up," I say when she doesn't answer. "Please."

Footsteps pad on the other side, and I take note of her blotchy cheeks when she finally reveals herself.

She's been crying.

Her gorgeous blue eyes look at me as I stare down at her. Then she crosses her arms, refusing to speak. So I just blurt everything out.

"I can't tell you how long I've had feelings for you because I can't remember a time when I didn't have them. From the moment we met, I was drawn to you. Something unexplainable makes me want to be around you all the goddamn time. Once we formed a friendship, I was content with that because after my ex, I'd sworn off workplace relationships. But no matter what I did, my feelings for you didn't go away. They only grew stronger and harder to deny."

I blow out a relieved breath, feeling lighter from finally admitting it.

"And when you and I made this arrangement to have a baby together and co-parent, I was okay with it because that meant we'd always be in each other's lives. I accepted the fact that my feelings were one-sided and that I'd have to live with it. As long as I didn't lose you, I'd survive. But if you're telling me you have them for me too, that changes things. Hell, that changes *everything.*"

As Kaitlyn's chest rises and falls, I drown in the silence. I just poured out my whole heart to her, and as I wait for a reaction, I want to pass out.

"Say something, Kate."

She meets my gaze and swallows hard. "I never thought a guy like you would see me as anything more than a friend. You never made a move or gave me any indication that you had feelings for me, so I never considered it. I'm not sure when everything shifted. I think I've spent all this time denying it because I didn't want to lose you either. When I realized I couldn't bear the thought of you with another woman, I decided it was time to do something. Before I lose you to some other woman like the ultrasound tech or some rando my brothers try to hook you up with."

I fight the urge to laugh at her jealousy as if I ever considered being with anyone else. No one else ever compared.

"I don't wanna look back in ten or twenty years and wonder *what if*."

Stepping inside her room, I close the gap between us and palm her face. "There's never been anyone but you."

She blinks up at me, her bottom lip trembling. "Don't break my heart, Payton Jamison."

"You'd have to kill me first before I'd ever do that."

Then I crash my mouth to hers—something I've been dying to do—and pour everything I have into her.

She moans as our tongues twist together, and I taste her sweetness. My cock pushes against her stomach, and I realize I can't be too rough with her being pregnant.

"I don't wanna hurt you," I groan as she reaches for my erection.

"It's completely normal to have sex. Just don't squish the bump, and I'll be fine."

I smirk as she takes off her tank, and I'm greeted by her amazing tits. "Fuck, you're so goddamn sexy."

"I *knew* you had a pregnancy fetish."

"Only for the one carrying my baby."

"Fair enough." She walks backward and pulls me with her

until the backs of her knees hit the bed. Then she falls on the mattress, taking me with her, and our mouths collide.

Not wasting any time, I position myself between her legs, then yank off her shorts and panties. As I spread her thighs, I lean in and flick her clit with my tongue. She tastes just as sweet as I remember.

"Oh my God, how are you so good at that?" She threads her fingers through my hair. Her hips push into me as she arches her back and moans. Thrusting two fingers inside her pussy, I'm about to show her what she's been missing.

"Payton." She pants my name as she writhes against me, and I can tell she's inching closer to the ledge.

With a twist of my wrist, I drive in deeper. Steadying my pace, I push her completely over, and she cries out.

Swiping up her slit, I lap up her juices. "Fuck, baby. I've missed you."

My head is still trying to catch up that this is really happening. Years of craving her and months of being without her touch had me thinking it was all a fever dream.

But it's real.

"Show me," she demands, clawing at my clothes. "Get naked."

I chuckle at her eagerness, then rip off my T-shirt and remove my sweats.

She watches with hungry eyes as I stroke my hard cock. "Is this what you want?"

She bites down on her lower lip. "Yes, please."

"*Please*? Wow, such a good girl," I tell her. "You'll get it on one condition."

She frowns. "What's that?"

"Tell me, did your vibrator cord really break? Or were you lying to me?"

Her cheeks heat as she breaks into a mischievous smile and

leans up on her elbows to meet my eyes. "Are you really gonna punish me for that?"

"You really are a Little devil."

"For a good cause," she defends.

"You're lucky I'm already in love with you, or I'd punish you for that."

Her eyes widen, but I'm not sure which part shocked her the most.

"Or maybe I should anyway?" I tease, and she giggles when I lie down next to her. "Get on your side. It'll be more comfortable for you."

Spooning behind her, I lift her leg and rub between her thighs. Her head falls back on my chest as she moans.

"Yes, don't stop," she demands, gripping her leg to keep it up.

"Don't worry, I've got you."

I rub her swollen bud as I wrap my arm around her shoulders and cup her throat. Then I drag her mouth to mine.

"How badly do you want it, baby?"

"So bad," she nearly cries out.

I position my cock head to her entrance and coat the tip in her juices.

"Beg for it, Kate. Beg for my cock, you Little Devil."

"Damn, that's mean," she scolds as I tease her. "But fuck me, I need it."

Palming my shaft, I smack it against her clit, over and over until she screams my name.

"Payton, please. Don't make me seduce you a third time," she threatens, reaching down to pull me inside.

Chuckling, I do as she asks and thrust in deep.

"Holy shit, that feels amazin'. This position is incredible."

"I knew you'd like it," I murmur as I bury my face in her neck and suck on her sweet skin. "Fuck, it's always so goddamn good with you."

We pour months of sexual tension into our movements as our bodies rock together. Sensually touching and kissing her has me wondering how I ever went without it.

"You know this means you're mine now, right? I'm never lettin' you go," I whisper as my hold on her tightens.

"Please don't," she murmurs. "There's a reason it always felt right with you."

Those words have my heart somersaulting against my rib cage.

"How'd you know this position works for pregnancy?" she asks as I move my fingers to her clit and thrust harder.

"Read about it."

She releases a laugh. "You researched anything and everything, didn't you?"

I smirk. "Wanted to be prepared."

"Thank God you did. I'm so close." She leans her head back, and I capture her mouth.

"Come with me, sweetheart."

And moments later, we cross the finish line together.

After we cleaned up, we slid underneath the covers and, for the first time, snuggled after sex.

"What're you thinkin' about?" I ask while she traces my tattoos with her finger.

"How it's not fair that you have those sexy V muscles that

point right to your cock, and I've gained twenty pounds." She lowers her hand to my abs.

"You're stunning," I tell her, rubbing my palm over her belly. "Watching our baby grow in your belly has had me in a constant state of blue balls. The way I craved you was quite pathetic."

She laughs, inching closer as she brushes her fingers through my hair.

"Did you really mean it when you said you're already in love with me?"

I meet her gaze. "I thought I was clear, but if you need me to reiterate—*yes*. Madly, deeply, foolishly in love with you."

"I've never said those words to another man before but—"

"You don't have to say it just because I did. I've had years of pent-up feelings that you have to catch up to."

"I was going to say *before* you rudely interrupted..." she sasses. "But if there's any man I'm in love with, it's you. Being with you feels like nothing I've experienced before. There's a reason for that."

I cup her face, pressing my forehead to hers. "You have no idea how many times I hoped some day you would."

"We were both too chickenshit."

"To be fair, you've dated some idiots, and I figured that was your type."

She playfully smacks me. "It's slim pickings 'round here!"

"The only option you needed was right in front of you, baby." I shoot her a wink.

Her brows rise. "Too bad you waited so long to speak up."

"Could say the same about you."

We're at a stalemate as we tease each other, knowing we're both guilty.

"Was that a kick?" I ask, resting my palm on her lower belly.

"Yeah, she's wide awake." She giggles. "Always super active at night."

"I'm glad I don't have to miss this."

She places her hand over mine. "Me too."

"Of course now, I'm not going a single night without you in my bed."

"What about my bed?"

I contemplate for a moment. "We'll switch off, or you can just move your things into mine since it's bigger."

"You just hate my poster of Jace Macbride," she taunts, eyeing the five-time national bull-riding champion on the wall.

"Well, who in their right mind wants to stare at that?"

"He's sexy! Plus, have you seen how he rides?"

I roll my eyes.

"Is that..." She pokes my chest. "Jealousy I detect?"

"No." I grab her wrist, closing the small gap between us. "Nothin' to be jealous about when you're naked next to me."

She laughs, kissing me.

"My family's gonna freak the fuck out."

I haven't even considered everyone's reactions. This all happened so fast that I've barely steadied my breathing.

"Your brothers are gonna kill me, aren't they?"

"No more than when they found out you knocked me up."

"They're gonna gloat so fuckin' much. I can already hear all the *I told you so*'s." I groan.

"Oh, you know they were placing bets," she adds. "I wonder who's gonna win."

I chuckle in amusement. "*Me*. I'm definitely the winner here."

Then I wrap an arm around her body and position her on top of me. She slides down on me, and we simultaneously moan in pleasure.

"I love watchin' you ride my cock, baby." I give her ass a little smack, then gently squeeze her hips. "Yes, just like that."

She leans forward, resting her palms on my chest. I tweak her nipples and feast on her tits.

"I hope you know what you're in for." She slams down on me harder. "I have six months' worth of hormones to feed."

"Take whatever you need, sweetheart. I'm all yours."

CHAPTER TWENTY-FOUR

KAITLYN

ALTHOUGH I'M a little over six months pregnant and tired most of the time, I refuse to let this New Year's go to waste. It's my second favorite holiday after Christmas because it usually contains drinking and dancing. While I don't anticipate staying on my feet for hours, I will shake my ass at least once.

"Almost ready?" Payton asks, stepping into the bathroom. I've got a pile of clothes on the floor because I can't make up my mind. I'm standing in my bra and panties and am two minutes from having a complete meltdown.

"Everything looks stupid on me." I pout, sitting on the toilet because I'm exhausted from changing so much.

Payton walks over and drops to his knees. He cups my cheeks and paints his lips over mine. "Can I help at all?"

"Find me something to wear that doesn't make me feel like a blimp and isn't itchy or too tight." I frown, then add, "Or too hot."

He chuckles. "I feel like Frodo searching for the one ring. But gimme about five minutes."

"Thank you," I whisper, and he kisses me again before going on his mission.

Instead of wasting time, I finish putting on my makeup and curl my hair. Since my lower back is sore, I brought in one of the breakfast barstools so I can sit while I get ready. Just as I finish my mascara, Payton walks in with his hands behind his back.

"It took me a little longer than expected, but I think I found the perfect outfit," he proudly tells me, then looks over my face. "You're so goddamn pretty."

"Thank you, but let's see what you picked out for me first before declaring that."

He chuckles, then hands me a black sweater with 3/4 sleeves along with one of my favorite maternity jeans.

"Alright, I'll try it on and see." Though I'm not getting my hopes up, I do appreciate him trying. "Thank you for helpin'."

He leans in and slowly kisses me, swiping his tongue between my lips and groaning as we lose ourselves in each other.

When he pulls away, he immediately looks in the mirror and checks his face.

"This lipstick isn't going anywhere." I laugh and press my fingers against my lips. "Matte ColorStay. Permanent like ink. Could probably give ten blow jobs and it wouldn't smear."

His eyebrow pops up with interest. "We should put that shit to the test. You know, for research purposes."

"Hmm. I might be able to make that happen."

I slip on the shirt and look in the mirror. "Okay, okay. I'm liking this," I say, grateful I don't look like a loaf of bread.

When I bend over to put on the jeans, Payton smacks my ass. I turn and glare at him over my shoulder. "You're gonna pay for that one! I'm front heavy!"

He laughs, motioning with his hand he's going to do it again. When I pull up my pants, I'm thankful for the elastic band that slides easily over my belly. I move toward the full-length mirror. "Hmm, I actually like it. I think you might have a new job title."

"I'll also undress you every single day if you want."

I chuckle because he knew exactly what I meant.

Payton pulls me into his arms and runs his fingers through my hair as he kisses me. I melt into him, wishing we had more time for him to *actually* undress me, but we're already over an hour late.

"Mm," I moan, reaching forward and rubbing my palm against the statue in his jeans.

"Keep that up, and we won't make it to the party," he warns, lowering his mouth to my neck and sucking.

"You're right." I sigh, leaning into him. "Just need to finish curling my hair and then put on my shoes."

"If you wear those Crocs, your brothers are gonna make fun of you."

"They're comfortable on my swollen feet, so they can kiss my pregnant ass."

"I don't make the rules. I just play by them." Payton winks. "Sometimes."

I slide my feet into them anyway.

Once my hair is done, I take one last look in the mirror before we head out.

We arrive nearly two hours late, and the place is packed. If I didn't know better, I'd say the whole town was invited to this little shindig. Grandma insisted we host it at the B&B because it can hold more people. Maize went all out, per usual, and made tons of appetizers and sweets.

The music blares as we walk in, and then I notice Dad in the corner with a DJ booth setup.

"Y'all are letting him choose the music tonight?" I ask, shouting over it.

Mom shakes her head. "They have no idea what they've agreed to. You look adorable, by the way."

"Thanks, Mom." I smile. "You look fancy yourself."

"Thank you. You look handsome too, Payton." She pats the shoulder of his navy-blue sweater.

"Thanks, Mrs. Bishop."

"You can call me Mom, too, if you want." She winks.

"You mean, Grandma," Kaitlyn teases. "You need a cooler nickname, like Gigi or Memaw."

Payton snorts.

All my cousins, aunts, uncles, and grandparents are here along with some family friends. I look around the room, seeing all the smiling faces, and nearly burst into tears.

"How ya doin', baby mama?" Payton asks as we move to the table with the giant spread of chips and dips, sandwiches made on croissants, and mini cheesecakes in all different flavors.

"I'm okay. Just getting emotional again," I admit, adding a bit of everything to my plate. "I know I'm living the good ole days right now, and it won't always be like this." My eyes slide to my grandparents, who are slow dancing in the middle of the living room. The way they look at each other is so sweet, it's something I always hoped for, and now that I have it, I can't help feeling so grateful for it. My grandpa's hands linger down to Grandma's ass, and she giggles like they're seventeen all over again.

"Aw, sweetheart." Payton wipes the tears from my cheeks. "Just have to cherish each moment we can, ya know?"

I nod, but they won't live forever, and that makes me sad.

When we sit at one of the empty tables, Ivy and Hadleigh join us.

"That's a cute as hell outfit, Kaitlyn. You look so cute pregnant," Hadleigh gushes.

"You should talk. Look at your bump with baby number three, lookin' like a snack."

Hadleigh snorts, lifting her feet and putting them on the chair across from her.

I bump my shoulder against Payton and grin. "He picked it out for me."

"Aw," they both say.

"After I spent forty minutes changing clothes," I clarify.

Ivy scowls. "Maybe you should teach our husbands a thing or

two. You'd think mine would offer, considering I've got two of his children in here." She points at her bump, which is somehow the same size as mine. Ivy's always been petite, but I'm jealous as hell of how small she's stayed.

"I heard that," Kane says, popping a brownie in his mouth, then taking a seat next to her.

Knox howls. "If I'm choosing Hadleigh's clothes, she's wearing her birthday suit."

Hadleigh shakes her head. "And that's why I dress myself."

"Ah, c'mon, babe. Don't be that way," he says, carrying two cupcakes on a plate and pressing his lips against hers.

I laugh and then a yawn escapes me.

"None of that," Payton tells me. "There's just over two hours before the ball drops."

"There's a joke about balls in there somewhere, but this pregnancy brain is gettin' to me right now," I admit, taking a bite of a cannoli. "I'll probably think of it at three in the mornin'," I say, and Payton chuckles.

As soon as Maize walks up with Gavin and their three kids, she looks at Knox, Kane, Hadleigh, and Ivy. "When y'all payin' up?"

My mouth falls open. "Wait, you were in on the bet? That hardly seems fair…"

She laughs with a nod. "Yep. And I've got about two grand to collect between these four, plus Ethan, Harper, Rowan, Diesel, Riley, Zoey…"

I look at Gavin. "You allowed her to do that?"

He shrugs. "You know I can't control this woman."

"Isn't that cheating?" Payton asks her. "You were in on it."

"Whoa…wait a goddamn minute." Kane sits up straighter, already trying to weasel his way out of it.

"Nothin'," I quickly say, liking the idea of my brothers paying up after all their shit-talking. "Nothing at all. Get your bank, girl, just remember who your favorite cousin is when you go shopping. So which one of you bet we'd never get together, hmm?"

I look around the table, and Hadleigh chuckles. "Oh, we all knew y'all were bangin'. It's just Maize was closer at guessing how long it'd take your stubborn asses to admit you were madly in love with one another."

"That's right," Ivy adds. "Maize was spot-on."

Knox narrows his eyes at her. "I ain't payin' a cheater!"

"I won fair and square, and if you don't give me my money, I'm gonna tell Grandma. You know her rules about payin' your debts." She flips her hair over her shoulder, then follows Gavin, who's guiding the kids over to the dessert table.

After we finish eating, Payton and I move to the main area where all the older folks are drinking coffee. Dad's playing the most annoying viral songs I've ever heard, and Grandma keeps telling him to turn it down because they have to yell over it to hear each other.

"So, you don't think it's cheatin' that Maize was gettin' a play-by-play of our relationship," Payton asks, and I grin wide.

"She swore on her own grave she wouldn't tell a soul. And she didn't, so I owe her as much, even if it kinda feels like insider trading." I shrug.

Payton throws his head back, laughing. "I don't even want to know what you told her."

"Mostly just trying to convince her that nothin' was going on between us. But we both know that was a lie."

He laughs. "You couldn't resist my charm and big dick."

I roll my eyes. "Shush. The music might be blarin', but the adults are nosy as fuck."

My uncle Evan and aunt Emily decide to ditch out early, and with only thirty minutes left, the crowd grows smaller. I'm determined to stay the whole time because it's the last major holiday I'll have before the baby comes in March. Time feels like it's speeding by at times but slowing down at others. I want to cherish every minute of being pregnant, especially since I have no idea if I'll get another chance, but I'm also eager to meet her.

Dad puts on some baby-making music that's easy to dance to because Grandma threatened to fire him if she heard one more fast-paced song.

Payton stands and holds out his hand. "Would you like to dance?"

I look up at him, smirking. "Thought you'd never ask."

I'm brought back to dancing with him at the wedding reception nearly a year ago, which really lit the fire for this whole ordeal. So much has changed, and I'm so damn grateful I double-fisted all that wine. If I hadn't practically thrown myself at him on that dance floor, who knows if we'd be where we are today?

"Ooh," I say, placing my hand on my belly.

"Is she kickin'?" he asks.

"I think she's excited," I tell him, resting my free arm on his shoulder as he dances with me in front of the fireplace.

"It's all those desserts and loud music," he says, then leans forward and crashes his lips to mine.

"What can I say? Baby has a sweet tooth."

I notice my cousins and brothers are dancing with their spouses too. I smile, realizing I finally have what they have—something I've wanted for so damn long.

"I love you," he mouths.

Unable to contain my happiness, I smile wide. "I love you too. Thanks for being the most perfect baby daddy." I place his palms on my belly so he can feel the little life we created.

His face lights up when he feels her using me as a kicking bag.

"Just a few more minutes and we'll be going home so you can get some sleep," Payton tells her.

Another kick.

He chuckles. "She has your attitude."

"I can live with that. Considering she'll be one of the youngest kids in the family, she'll need to be tough."

"You know what I can't live without?" He leans in until he's centimeters away from my mouth. "You."

"I'd die before letting that happen," I say, repeating similar words he once said to me.

My dad lowers the music and brings everyone's attention to the giant digital clock on the mantel that's been counting down all night. Grandma stands when there are only ten seconds left and starts the official countdown. Grandpa takes his time joining her, then hands over her noisemaker just as Dad plays "Auld Lang Syne."

The music echoes throughout the room, along with loud cheers and laughter.

Payton leans in and slides his tongue in my mouth. The kiss is deepened, and we lose ourselves in each other for a moment. I feel eyes on us when we pull away, but I don't care.

"Happy New Year's, baby mama," he tells me, laughing as I hold on to him like this moment might disappear.

"You too, BD. It's gonna be our best one yet."

"For the first time in my life, I truly believe that."

Although my feet hurt, we make sure to stay and celebrate with everyone.

When I find Grandma, she wraps me in a hug, then does the same to Payton. "So earlier when we were chattin', I was rudely interrupted by your father playin' that terrible music, and I forgot to ask...when's the weddin'? I know we discussed fall time before, so if that's the case, that gives me a good nine months to plan."

I laugh. "Grandma! Baby first."

She gives me a knowing look, one I've seen many times over the years. "But I can clear my schedule for then?"

"Grandma..."

Payton interlocks his fingers with mine, and Mom rescues us

before he can speak up.

"Sweetie, you should get home," she says. "You look exhausted."

"I know, I know," I say, then look back at my grandma. "Guess it's up to Payton. Okay, we're takin' off. Love you."

"Love you too, sweetie." She gives me a brief side hug, then pats Payton on the shoulder. "Buy that ring, Payton."

He's so used to her antics that he just responds with a smile.

When we walk outside, I suck in the fresh, cool air. I was starting to sweat because Grandma likes keeping it hot in there. Payton opens the truck door for me and helps me climb in. Once I'm settled, he reaches across and buckles me, then places his strong hand on my thigh.

"Don't worry, I always planned on makin' you my wife someday. Even when I wasn't sure I believed in love anymore, there was always somethin' about you."

"Yeah?"

"My first day workin' on the ranch, and you cut in front of me at the buffet line, I knew I was already enamored by you."

"Oh really? Because I was thinking about what a nice ass you had."

He chuckles, bringing our mouths close. "Glad it worked out the way it was always supposed to."

I press my lips to his. "Only took us seven years."

"And maybe in our eighth year, we'll get married."

"Don't mess with me. I'm hormonal and tired."

"A lethal combination," he cracks.

I playfully smack his chest. "You're hilarious," I say dryly.

"I know."

Rolling my eyes with a grin, I add, "Hopefully, our daughter gets *my* sense of humor."

"If she's anything like you, she already has me wrapped around her fingers."

"Like a true Bishop."

CHAPTER TWENTY-FIVE

KAITLYN

FOUR MONTHS LATER

"She's the spittin' image of you," Payton says as we stare down at the blond-haired, blue-eyed baby girl in my arms that we would, without a doubt, do anything for.

The unconditional love I've always heard about didn't make sense until the moment I found out I was pregnant. But seeing her, finally meeting the little one who's kicked me late at night and given me heartburn, is a feeling I can't explain.

"She looks like both of us," I correct. "But she does have your brooding eyes and my nose."

"And I'm willing to bet, your snarky personality and sass."

"Oh, without a doubt." I laugh, rubbing my finger over her soft cheek.

Twenty-four hours ago, I was miserable and begging Payton to put me out of my misery.

The *How to Induce Labor* article Payton found had a list of ideas to help do that very thing. And I did all of them.

Eating spicy foods.

Bouncing on a yoga ball.

Going for long walks.

And when those didn't work, we went back to how it all started.

Sex. *Lots and lots of sex.*

I told Payton he put this baby inside me, so he had to help get it out.

Sex hadn't been comfortable in my final month of pregnancy, but nothing was. Everything I ate gave me heartburn. Sleep was nonexistent, which made me exhausted and irritable.

And although nothing about my labor was easy, we have a beautiful nine-and-a-half-pound baby girl. Hours of slow progress meant not being allowed to eat. Eventually, the doctor broke my water, and that was when the real pain started.

Miserable didn't even cut it.

The pain was *unbearable.*

Pushing for two hours nearly made me pass out. At one point, I tried to tag Payton in so we could switch places. I was done.

But in the end, it was *all* worth it. I'd do it all again in a heartbeat if it meant meeting our little girl.

"Kaylee Bishop Jamison, you've already stolen our hearts," I tell her.

"That's for sure." Payton leans down and presses his lips to the top of her head, then looks at me. "So when can we try for number two?"

I shoot him a death glare. "Never thought I'd say this but keep your dick away from me for at least two months."

Chuckling, he scoops Kaylee out of my arms and rocks her. "Your mama couldn't stay away from my dick even if it was on fire and shooting fireworks."

"*Payton!*"

"Just wait until I tell her all about how you begged and seduced me to knock you up."

"You better not, and that's a lie. I was perfectly content findin' me a sperm daddy."

He narrows his eyes, holding Kaylee closer. "Thank goodness she came to her senses, right? You picked me to be your daddy."

I can't even deny how cute they are together.

My family takes turns visiting and holding the baby for the next several hours. Grandma and Mom soak up as much time as they can, then we take a handful of pictures.

Hadleigh's due any day and is on bed rest, so she couldn't make it. Ivy stayed home with the twins since they're only a couple of months old and on strict sleep and feeding schedules.

The hour-long drive back and forth would've been a lot for them. However, my brothers came and met their niece.

Once it's quiet and everyone's left, Payton's phone beeps with a message. He reads it, then looks at me.

"She's here."

He puts Kaylee in my arms, then leaves. Moments later, he returns with his mom.

I met her for the first time at Easter dinner two weeks ago. He finally reached out to her after New Year's to share the news, and when she found out she was going to be a grandma, she cried. That was all it took for her to finally ask for help so she could leave her abusive husband.

Days later, Payton moved her into an apartment in Eldorado and helped her file for divorce. Then a couple weeks after, he introduced her to Kat, the bakery owner in town, and she was hired on the spot. Now his mom delivers baked goods and helps with inventory.

From what we're told, she loves it, and Kat says she's a great helper.

Payton couldn't be happier to have his mom back in his life.

"Oh my goodness," Carol gushes. "What a doll."

I place Kaylee in her arms. Her adoring smile is contagious as I watch her with her first grandchild.

"How're you feeling?" she asks.

"Meh. Like I just pushed a baby out of my vagina."

She chuckles. "It'll feel like that for a bit."

Carol stays for an hour, sharing stories of when Payton was born and what he was like growing up. Between him being the shy kid and me being the adventurous tomboy, it'll be interesting to see who Kaylee favors.

"See you soon, Ma," Payton tells her. She leans down to give me a hug, then he follows her out the door.

The nurse enters and gets me situated to try breastfeeding again. I haven't had the best of luck, but she's been a godsend in getting her to latch on.

"There we go..." The nurse coos.

I wince at the foreign sensation. "Is it supposed to feel that way?"

"It'll hurt for a little while until your nipples toughen up. She's learning too, but eventually, it won't be that painful."

I hold the curse words at the tip of my tongue at how hard she's sucking, but I'm relieved she's getting what she needs from me.

After five minutes on one boob, the nurse helps me get her situated on the other. "Make sure to switch, or you'll get lopsided."

When my eyes widen, she chuckles.

"Knock, knock," Aunt River sing-songs from the doorway. She was working when I first arrived but wasn't able to stay because of her patients.

"Come in," I tell her.

Payton walks in behind her, and River pulls him in for a hug. "Congrats, Daddy!"

"Thanks," he says, coming closer.

"She's precious, Kaitlyn," River gushes as she watches me feed her. I should be used to my family not having boundaries. Whether you're pushing a baby out or breastfeeding one, they'll stand right next to you, cheering you on.

"She really is. It's surreal she's ours. Like...we just get to take her home? I'm gonna need a more adultier adult to help me."

River laughs. "Your maternal instincts will kick in, trust me. And I wouldn't worry too much. Your mom and grandma will probably be camped out in the nursery to help."

Payton grunts. "Gonna need to change those locks if we ever want privacy again."

I snort. Over the past couple of months, my mom's been over a lot to help us set up the nursery and get the house ready. I hit my nesting phase, and we cleaned it from top to bottom. As much as Payton loves my family, he's an introvert who needs his quiet time and space.

"Privacy with the Bishops?" River mocks. "Good luck with that. When I was pregnant with Rowan, I woke up from a nap to Mama Rose measuring my belly. When I asked her what she was doing, she said she was trying to predict what I was having."

I burst out laughing. "That sounds like somethin' she'd do."

"That's mild compared to the years' worth of stories I have." River grins. "But we love her anyway."

Once Kaylee's finished eating, I hand her off to River while Payton sits next to me on the bed.

"Did your mom visit?" River asks Payton.

"She did. Actually, she left right before you got here."

"Oh, I missed her. That's okay. I'll see her in a few days for the bachelor auction."

"Speaking of, are there any bachelors left for it?" I laugh.

"A whole new generation of twentysomethings," River confirms. "I'm only goin' for Jessica's emcee commentary."

Jessica is Harper's mom, and she's hilarious.

"Yeah right, you're going for the same reason we are—sexy cowboys in tight jeans."

Payton clears his throat.

"You wanna participate?" I smirk.

"No, thank you. I've been humiliated enough from that."

"Well, technically, you're not married, so Mama might force ya," River explains. "Back in our day, the guys had to do it even when they were datin' their future spouses."

My eyes widen. "I can't imagine that went well."

"Oh we all fought for our men, throwing money and elbows so no one else won."

Since River married Uncle Alex long before his brothers got hitched, she's been around the longest and always has the best stories to share.

Kaylee starts crying, and River lifts her to her chest, patting her back. As soon as a loud burp releases, she stops.

"How'd you do that, and can you teach me?" I plead when River sets her back in my arms.

Payton chuckles, patting my leg. "Have confidence, babe. You're a natural-born mother."

I blow out a breath. Even though I've done so much research and read stacks of baby books, I still don't feel prepared.

"You'll learn as you go, just like we all did."

PAYTON

Watching the woman I love give birth to our child is a moment I'll cherish forever.

Kaitlyn was a champ, and even when she was exhausted, she pushed through until our beautiful Kaylee was born.

With my mom here and being able to see her almost every day, I now have everything I've ever wanted in life.

Almost.

Long after River's gone, the nurse takes Kaylee, and I follow along, per Kaitlyn's instructions. After she read about babies getting swapped in hospitals, she demanded one of us *always* be with her.

It only takes twenty minutes before I bring Kaylee back into the room. She's asleep and swaddled in a warm blanket, but instead of setting her in the bassinet, I place her in Kaitlyn's arms.

"How'd she do?" she asks.

"Didn't even wake up," I confirm. "Oh, but that weird hospital band they had around her ankle is gone." It's actually an alarm monitor that'll go off if someone tries to take her.

"What?" she screeches. "They're not supposed to remove that until we leave."

She sets Kaylee between her legs and unwraps the blanket to look for herself.

"It's not miss—" The words die on her lips when she notices the diamond ring on Kaylee's toe. "Payton."

When she turns to face me, I'm already on one knee.

"You are *not* proposin' when I look like I've been through a tornado," she exclaims.

Gently, I grab her hand and smirk.

"You're the most beautiful I've ever seen you, sweetheart."

"Don't lie to me." Tears well in her eyes.

Laughing with amusement, I reach over and take the ring. "You're my best friend and the love of my life. I'd never lie to you. But I do have a question to ask."

The dam breaks, spilling down her cheeks. I wipe them away before pressing my lips to hers.

"Marry me? And be mine forever."

Breathlessly, she furiously nods as she chokes back more tears. I cup her face and slide my tongue between her lips. Then I slip the ring on her finger.

"It's gorgeous, babe." She holds up her hand and admires it. "I can't believe you did this."

"I bought it a year ago," I admit.

She snaps her gaze to me. "I wasn't even pregnant a year ago..."

"I know."

"Was it for someone else?"

I scoff. "Hell no. I was checkin' out the jewelry store in town for a watch, and when I saw it, I just knew it was meant to be on your finger."

"What were you plannin' to do with it? Just randomly drop down to one knee and hope for the best?"

I chuckle, sitting next to her on the bed while she gets Kaylee situated back in her blanket.

"I was tryin' to find the nerve to talk to you about the night of your brother's wedding and decide if risking our friendship would be worth it. I'd already had a battle goin' on in my head long before that, but it was right before you mentioned sperm donors. When I saw it, I knew you'd love it. It's stunning, just like you."

"So you bought it in case we started dating?"

"Yeah, I guess you could say that. Or maybe I'd keep it for the guy you ended up with and let him give it to you. I just wanted you to have it. Even if I wasn't the one giving it to you."

"Dammit, Payton Jamison, don't do that." She squeezes her eyes closed, but tears stream down her face. "I can't control them today." She shrugs, aggressively wiping them away.

Smiling, I lean down and kiss her. "I didn't say I wouldn't have wanted to punch the bastard, but your happiness is all that's ever mattered."

"I'm glad you're that bastard instead," she muses, causing me to roar with laughter. "I love you."

"I love you so goddamn much, baby."

Once I take Kaylee in my arms, I sit in the rocking chair next to the bed.

"Who do you want to tell first?"

"I kinda just wanna wear it and see who notices. Maybe we should place bets on who we think will notice first."

"Oh, then I'm a hundred percent puttin' money on your grandma. She'll see it sparkling a mile away," I say.

She snorts. "I wouldn't doubt it, honestly. But I gotta pick Maize."

I hold out my hand, waiting for her to shake it.

"And what are the stakes?" she asks before taking it.

I think about it for a few moments. "Diaper duty for a week."

Her hand bolts forward to take mine, and I grin wide.

"Deal."

"It's on, baby mama."

"You're goin' down, BD!"

EPILOGUE
KAITLYN

ONE YEAR LATER

"Happy birthday to you! Happy birthday, dear Kaylee and Harlow. Happy birthday to you!" the guests sing in unison.

Hadleigh and I each hold up a mini cake with one candle so the girls don't burn themselves.

"Wait, sweetie," Hadleigh says softly when Harlow tries to reach for the flame again.

"And many more," Payton and I sing together, helping Kaylee blow out her candle.

Since the girls are only a week apart, we decided to celebrate with a joint birthday party. Kaylee taps the tray when I scoot her high chair closer, and Hadleigh does the same so they can taste their cakes. Like little savages, Kaylee and Harlow grab fistfuls, but most of it ends up on their face and in their hair instead of their mouths.

"Their cheeks are gonna be stained pink for a week." Payton looks at the mess as I take pictures.

I laugh as Grandma Bishop tries to take a photo with her giant iPad.

"Want a pic with them?" Payton asks her.

"Thank you, dear. Swear you're the only one takin' my hints."

I scoff. "I woulda helped ya!"

"Me too," Hadleigh adds.

"Well too late," she says, handing Payton her tablet. My parents along with Hadleigh's mom wait impatiently for their photo ops with the girls as Grandma leans between the two high chairs.

"Say cheese," Payton tells her, pressing the button.

As soon as Kaylee notices her, she reaches for her face. Grandma leans in, and Kaylee smears her cheek with icing.

"Oh no," I say, trying to stop it from happening, but I'm too late.

"It's fine." Grandma laughs so hard I think I see a few tears. Then Harlow pats the other cheek. "My sweet girls are gonna raise some hell. I just know it."

My family forms a half circle as we watch the girls enjoy themselves and get their pictures taken. I'm happy everyone's enjoying the party.

I'm grateful Knox is filming this. This is something I never want to forget, and one I want my daughter to see when she's older. The memories we're making are ones I'll cherish forever. Kane grins as he holds Isaac in his arms. Ivy's next to him with Isabella. The twins had their first birthdays two months ago, and it was a blast.

The older grandkids run around the B&B with water guns, and somehow, I know my dad's responsible for that.

"Mama, you're covered from head to toe," my dad tells her.

"It'll make a good story at church tomorrow. But we really have Maize to blame for this." She wipes a finger down her cheek, then licks the extra icing before grabbing a napkin. "Tastes good, though!"

"Sorry and thank you!" Maize says from the back of the

crowd as Payton gives Grandma her iPad back. She swipes through the pictures, smiling with approval.

Once we clean up the girls, Hadleigh and I serve sheet cake and ice cream.

"This has been a lot of fun," I tell Hadleigh after we've handed out one pan. Thankfully, Maize made three.

"It has. I'm glad we got knocked up at basically the same time."

I snort. "Ya know, I don't think I've told you this, but I made Payton eat these Brazilian nuts that are supposed to make the swimmers more potent. But Kane and Knox kept eating them when he'd bring them to work."

Her eyes widen, and she doubles over with laughter. "Oh my God! So you're actually to blame for this?"

"Well, Ivy was already pregnant, but it's Knox's fault since he doesn't know how to leave other people's food alone."

She snickers. "That's true. But hey, look at how cute our girls are. They're gonna be besties."

"I hope so. Unless they're the kind of friends who fight over the same boy."

Hadleigh deadpans, and I cackle. It was only six years ago when my brothers were fighting over her.

"They're gonna get into so much trouble together," I muse.

"I'm already dreading the teen years with our three so close in age." Hadleigh sighs. "Harlow already gives me a run for my money, and she's barely walking!"

"I thought the third one was always the forgotten child?" I say loud enough for my parents to hear.

"The third definitely gets away with shit the first two didn't." Hadleigh cracks up. "With the first one, you're always on alert and careful not to let them get into anything they shouldn't, but now, as long as I don't see blood, I'm not worryin' about it."

Once everyone's done eating, we set the girls up in the middle of the room and bring them their presents. Payton and

Knox help the girls rip the paper. Hadleigh's older kids, Hendrix and Hannah, run around, playing with toys and knocking chairs over.

Grandma and Grandpa have a front row seat to the action.

Once all the gifts have been ripped open, we pick up the mess, and the guys start putting the toys together.

When I look around, I notice Zach's not paying attention to anything but his phone.

"Havin' fun?" I ask as I sit next to him on the loveseat.

"Yeah," he says, focusing on the screen.

"Textin' your girlfriend?" I smirk.

He narrows his eyes at me and locks the screen. "For the last time, she's not my girlfriend."

He's almost thirteen now and has really been showing his little attitude. However, he's still a good kid. Six months ago, Fancy officially became his, and she was moved into the other barn, where he now takes full responsibility for her.

"But you somehow knew who I was referring to?" I arch a brow.

"Stop," he warns.

I wrap my arm around his shoulders and make a mess out of his hair, which only annoys him further. "No matter what, you'll always be my little buddy."

He scoffs.

"Ouch, you hurt my feelings." I pretend to be upset and stick out my lower lip, pouting. He rolls his eyes with a grin and bumps me with his shoulder.

Standing, I leave him alone to talk to his *friend* and start picking up dirty plates and empty soda cans.

"Don't work too hard, wifey. I need you to save some energy for tonight." Payton leans in, nibbling on my ear.

I snort. "What was that, hubby?"

"You heard me."

"Only if you're a good boy." I waggle my brows.

He smacks my ass before walking away. Even though we got married six months ago, I'm still obsessed with hearing him call me his wife.

We had the perfect fall wedding. The ceremony was beautiful, and the whole day felt surreal. I still can't believe this is my life and I married my best friend.

After another hour of chatting, people start heading out and saying goodbye. I'm so grateful they were all able to make it. When Kaylee gets fussy from her sugar crash, we put her in the car seat, and she falls asleep before we make it home.

Payton carefully takes her out and carries her inside without waking her up—a skill I haven't quite mastered yet. I grab all the gift bags and bring them into the house.

Once Kaylee is in her crib, Payton walks into the living room and sits next to me on the couch.

"She's gettin' heavy," he says. "I still can't believe she's one already. How'd that happen?"

"I have no idea, but at this rate, she'll be driving soon," I pout, realizing how much my baby has grown in the past year.

"I never realized how fast kids grow up until I had my own," he says, leaning his head back on the cushion and meeting my eyes. "Have I told you how much I love you today?"

"Not yet. But I'm listening."

PAYTON

"I love you more than I did yesterday. More than words could ever express. I love you more than spaghetti and homemade meatballs," I tell her.

She snickers. "I dunno if I'd go that far. Maize's cookin' is pretty elite."

A moment later, Kaitlyn stands and climbs onto my lap. She

rocks against my groin, and my cock grows hard with anticipation.

"Fuck," I groan, keeping my voice low and squeezing her hips.

"I have somethin' to tell you." Kaitlyn removes her shirt and throws it on the floor. I lean forward, unsnapping her bra and then sucking on a nipple.

"Is this what you wanted to tell me?" I waggle my brows after I come up for air. Right now, I want to lick her all over.

"No." She places her hands on both sides of my cheeks, forcing me to look into her eyes.

I wait with bated breath, her throat moving as she swallows hard as if she's nervous.

"Tell me," I urge.

"I'm pregnant," she blurts out.

My mouth falls open, and then I smile wide. "What? Seriously?"

"I took a test right before the party. Well, actually, it was more like five tests because I couldn't believe it. But yeah, Kaylee's gonna have a little sibling in nine months!"

"Wow, babe. Seeing you pregnant again and gettin' to witness our daughter grow is the best gift you could ever give me." Emotions take over, and our lips crash together, creating a beautiful symphony. Our tongues twist together, and when we pull away, I can see Kaitlyn's tears of joy.

"I didn't know it was possible to feel happier than you've already made me. I feel like I don't deserve it."

"You're an amazing friend, husband, and father. You deserve the world, and I love you so damn much. You've given me everything I've ever dreamed of."

I run my fingers through her hair and kiss her again. "We're having another baby," I say, the realization hitting me all over again.

"Yes, we are. Now, gimme what I want without makin' me seduce you, BD."

"But you're so goddamn good at it," I taunt. "I love hearing you beg for my cock."

"Mm...you're such a tease." She moves against me, rubbing her sweet pussy over my dick.

"Strip, you Little Devil."

She makes quick work of removing her jeans and panties while I lower my boxers. When she straddles me again, I wrap my mouth around her nipple as she coats me in her wetness.

"Fuck," I mutter as she takes exactly what she needs.

"Oh my God." She throws her head back.

"Keep it down, or we'll get interrupted," I remind her, wrapping a hand around her neck and pulling her mouth back to mine.

"I can't help it..." She pants. "It feels so good."

I smack her ass with my free hand and murmur in her ear, "Take all of me, baby. Fuck me just the way you need it."

"Shit, I'm close," she warns after I rub between her thighs.

And just like I've done dozens of times before, I send her over the edge while her pussy squeezes every drop out of me.

BONUS EPILOGUE
ZACH

FOUR YEARS LATER - JULY FOURTH

Zach - Riley & Zoey's son, age 17
Grandson of Alex & River
Great-grandson of Scott & Rose

Dear Zach,

As one of the oldest great-grandchildren, I want you to know how proud of you I am for always looking out for your brother and cousins. I know you'll continue to do great things and keep my legacy alive on the ranch. As long as you believe in yourself, there's nothing that you can't do. Your parents have raised a true Southern gentleman, and I hope whoever is lucky enough to get your love will appreciate everything our ranch and family have to offer. Follow your heart because it'll never steer you wrong.

Please continue to watch out for the younger ones. You're a natural-born leader, and I have faith you'll do amazing things in the future. I won't live forever, but when I'm gone, just remember I'm everywhere— in the wind, the stars, and in your heart. Always.

With all my love,
Great-Grandma Bishop

Today marks the second year since my great-grandma passed.

On her favorite holiday nonetheless.

She wrote me this letter six months before that, shortly after Great-Grandpa passed. It was as if she knew she wouldn't survive without the love of her life.

They were married for sixty-nine years and lived long, happy lives with five kids, twelve grandkids, and thirty-two great-grandkids.

And we still miss them every day. The ranch hasn't been the same, but we're still working, and it's operating like nothing's changed. Between my grandpa Alex and his brothers, they've kept it afloat, along with my dad and uncles. They're always finding ways to expand and grow the ranch.

July Fourth has always been a special holiday in our family, and although we're used to celebrating with a huge party and fireworks, that was halted the day she passed. But this year, we decided to honor her properly and keep the tradition alive. It's what she'd want, so we're going all out.

My grandpa's sister, Courtney, who lives in California, is here with her three kids, their spouses, and her nine grandchildren. The last time we saw them was at the funeral. So it's nice to get together for a happy occasion.

Dad put me in charge of grilling the meat today. Though Gavin and Grayson are usually the pit masters, I've been practicing for the past year to be just as good.

"Zach, you better get movin' if you're gonna get Lilia on time and make it back to start grillin'," my mom reminds me.

"I'm goin' now," I tell her, grabbing my truck keys and cowboy hat off the dresser.

She meets me in the hallway and smiles wide. "You look so handsome."

"Mom."

"What? You're handsome just like your daddy."

I roll my eyes. "I'm gonna be late."

She yanks me in for a hug and kisses my cheek. "Drive safe. See you there."

"Bye, Mom. Love ya."

Lilia lives fifteen minutes away in town, and although she has her own car, I prefer to pick her up. We've officially been together for two years, and although I just turned seventeen last month, I plan to marry her someday.

My cousin Amora is her best friend, but we all grew up together. Lilia and I were childhood friends long before we started dating.

As soon as I arrive and open my truck door, she flies out of the house and right into my arms. I catch her and plant my lips on hers.

"You look beautiful," I tell her, scanning down her floral dress.

"You're lookin' good yourself, Cowboy." She flicks my hat. "I love when you wear the black one."

I shoot her a wink, taking her hand and leading her to the passenger side. "I know."

On the way back to the ranch, Lilia blasts the radio and waves her arm out the window as she sings loudly to the music. I grin like a fool as I watch the love of my life. We might be too young to make lifelong plans, but I know without a doubt, she's the one. My great-grandparents married at nineteen and were high school sweethearts, and both lived to be eighty-eight. They knew each other most of their lives and set an example for all of us.

And I want to have a marriage just like theirs.

Lilia plans to go to college next year while I work full-time on the ranch. I knew I wanted a job with horses ever since I was eleven when Kaitlyn let me help her at the rescue. I was obsessed with getting my hands dirty and grooming the horses. I still am and continue to work as much as I can.

Since I'm staying, Lilia and I will do long distance until she graduates. She'll come home during all the holidays and in the summer. Once she graduates, I'll propose, and we'll get married and start our family.

I still plan to enjoy every second we have together during our last year of high school.

"I'm gonna say hi to Amora," Lilia says when I park in front of the B&B. I have to stop and get the meat, but everyone's already crowding into the house.

I quickly grab her hand and pull her across the center console. "Hold on."

Then I cup her cheek and brush my lips on hers. "Stay with me tonight."

My parents would never allow her to sleep over, but that hasn't stopped us from putting blankets and pillows in the bed of my truck. We park at the Bishop spot and hang out by the fire until we fall asleep.

But I want tonight to be *extra* special.

She licks her lips and nods. "I'll tell my mom I'm staying with Amora."

I kiss her knuckles, then we get out of the truck to greet everyone.

The parking lot is packed with vehicles, and the B&B is filled to the brim. I find Maize in the kitchen as always, and looking at the sweet desserts and food she's made for today makes my mouth water.

"You ready to man the grill?" Gavin asks, patting my shoulder.

"I was born ready." I smirk.

Grabbing what I need, I head to the back porch and set up next to the massive built-in grill. It's one of the many additions my dad and his cousins have made in recent years. The B&B got a complete remodel, and they added a huge backyard area with a flower garden and a few gazebos for the guests to enjoy.

It was a beautiful place to watch the sunset and kiss my girlfriend for the first time.

Once I've cooked all the meat, Maize wraps it in foil and places it in a warmer. Then everyone makes their plates, and we eat together. The family chats and catches up as if we don't see each other every day, but it's nice to hang out without worrying about chores.

"Ready for dessert?" Maize calls out. "I made every single one of Grandma's favorites."

We line up and look at the spread.

Blueberry pie, triple chocolate cake, blueberry muffins, sweet pecan pie, pumpkin pie, peach cobbler, carrot cake, and tiramisu.

"Dang, you baked up a feast," I tell her as I take a slice of cake for Lilia and two different pies for me. Lilia will say she only wants a little, but then she'll steal bites of mine, so I always get extra.

"Grandma liked to eat just like the rest of us." Maize smiles. "She taught me to cook and bake when I was your age."

"That's so sweet." Lilia grins, taking a forkful of hers. "Oh my gosh, this is delicious."

Maize beams with pride. "That's one of my faves too."

For as long as I've known, Maize has been the cook in the family, but I know her daughters are into it too. My cousins Madison and Mila are twins and a few years younger than me, but they're always hanging out in the kitchen with their mom.

"Your mama said you went on a college tour last weekend," my mom says to Lilia as she sits across from us. "That's excitin'!"

I hold back my disappointment because although I want her to chase her dreams, I'll miss having her so close.

"Yeah! It was awesome! The campus is so big, nothin' like here," she explains. When you grow up in small-town Texas, everything is bigger and better.

"Have you picked your major yet?"

"I'm still deciding, but once I figure it out, I'll narrow down which college I like the best."

"You know San Angelo has a great university," I tell her slyly.

She grins. "I know. I'm lookin' at that one too."

That's my choice because it's only an hour from here.

"Either way, you kids will be fine. Zach will be workin' during the week while you're in classes, and you'll still have weekends and holidays," Mom tells me as if that's supposed to lessen the blow of Lilia leaving.

But it doesn't.

She's not *just* my girlfriend. She's been my best friend since first grade. We've shared all our firsts together, and when I asked her to the school dance in ninth grade, she said yes, and we've been together ever since.

Amora plops down next to her, and they chat about their plans for next weekend. It's already bad enough I have to share her with my cousin, but soon I'll have to share her with a whole campus of friends.

"I wanted to say a few words and talk about Mama," John says as he stands. "Fourth of July was her favorite holiday for as long as I can remember. It's why we always brought it to the next level and made sure there were as many people here as possible. She loved her family and being around friends. As we got older, each year only got bigger and louder. Still, one of my favorite memories is when all five of us kids were teenagers, and Dad and Evan were in charge of lighting the fireworks. Evan lit a bottle rocket before the big show, and being a klutz, he knocked it over tryin' to get out of the way. That thang shot off and soared right at Mama. She spilled red punch all over her clothes. We were rolling because we knew Evan was in deep shit."

"*Evan Tyler!*" Jackson mocks in a high-pitched voice that echoes Great-Grandma's, and the room bursts into laughter. "Mama nearly strangled him for ruining her dress."

"You always knew you were in deep shit when she used your middle name," Evan confirmed.

The room booms with more laughter. Hearing stories of my great-grandparents is always fun. I wish I'd had more time with them, but they're talked about so much, it feels like I didn't miss a thing.

Kaitlyn and Payton walk around with Kolton holding their hands between them. He's three and a half and my little buddy. I've been teaching him all about horses and even got him in a saddle when Kaitlyn wasn't around. We made that our little secret. Kaylee is five and struts around like a little princess wearing sundresses and cowboy boots. She talks to the horses like she's the boss of them, which is pretty hilarious.

Later that evening, we gather for fireworks on the hill behind the big white house where they lived. My grandparents moved in there shortly after Great-Grandpa Scott passed away so she wouldn't have to live alone. She'd been perfectly healthy till the day she passed in her sleep.

Fortunately, she didn't suffer.

My dad and his cousin Ethan are in charge of the fireworks this year. Before they start, they whistle to grab everyone's attention.

"This year, we're gonna have the biggest show we've ever done, and it's all for Grandma Bishop. May she rest in peace and enjoy the explosions with Grandpa by her side. I know she's lookin' over us and is proud the entire family is here celebratin' her favorite holiday."

And then for the next hour and a half, booms followed by glittery colors fill the sky. Lilia sits on a blanket between my legs, and as I hold her tightly to my chest, I whisper in her ear, "I love you."

She looks over her shoulder with the sweetest smile. "I love you too, Zach Bishop. Forever and always."

We spend the rest of the night proving that love to each other in the bed of my truck. There's no doubt in my mind that we'll have a life just like my great-grandparents.

And I can't wait.

LILIA
TEN YEARS LATER

You'd think at almost twenty-eight, I'd have my life together.

Married with children and a career I loved.

Instead, it's crumbling more and more each day.

My boyfriend of two years just dumped me for his receptionist.

My children-bearing days are getting closer to the end with each year that passes.

And I got fired two weeks ago.

That one I should've expected, honestly. I've not been on my A game in a while, but now I'm struggling to pay my rent.

Going to college in California was supposed to be the jumpstart to my perfect life. I was going to marry my childhood best friend and high school sweetheart, have three to four babies, and use my finance degree to help him on the ranch.

All of that went to shit a year after I left.

Now I'm thousands of dollars in debt without my name on a diploma.

I lost the love of my life years ago.

And soon, I'll be homeless.

The only option I have left is to move back to Eldorado, Texas.

My mom has been begging me to come home, and it looks like she'll get her wish.

If only I didn't have to face Zach Bishop, the man whose heart I broke ten years ago when I told him it was over through a text message.

He's never forgiven me, and I don't blame him.

I did what I had to do for his own good.

But I have a feeling he won't see it that way.

Read Zach and Lilia's second chance romance in *Here to Stay*, book #1 in the Texas Heat series, a third-generation Bishop series.

WHAT'S NEXT

Read Zach and Lilia's second chance romance
in *Here to Stay*, book #1 in the
Texas Heat series

For fans of the *Bishop Brothers* and *Circle B Ranch*, Kennedy
Fox brings you the third-generation of the Bishop family in a
brand new nine-book Southern, small town romance series.
Each book can be read as a stand-alone and ends in an HEA!

When Lilia's down on her luck, she moves back to her hometown
and applies for a nanny position. The last person she expects to
see is her old high school sweetheart—the one she left ten
years ago.

Zach never forgot his first love who broke his heart, but when
Lilia begs for the job, he's desperate enough to agree—even if he
can't stand her.

As they fall into a new family routine, old feelings resurface, but
the past they've buried eventually catches up with them.

ABOUT THE AUTHOR

Brooke Cumberland and Lyra Parish are a duo of romance authors who teamed up under the *USA Today* pseudonym, Kennedy Fox. They share a love of Hallmark movies, overpriced coffee, and making TikToks. When they aren't bonding over romantic comedies, they like to brainstorm new book ideas. One day in 2016, they decided to collaborate under a pseudonym and have some fun creating new characters that'll make you blush and your heart melt. Happily ever afters guaranteed!

CONNECT WITH US

Find us on our website:

kennedyfoxbooks.com

Subscribe to our newsletter:

kennedyfoxbooks.com/newsletter

facebook.com/kennedyfoxbooks

twitter.com/kennedyfoxbooks

instagram.com/kennedyfoxduo

amazon.com/author/kennedyfoxbooks

goodreads.com/kennedyfox

bookbub.com/authors/kennedy-fox

BOOKS BY KENNEDY FOX

DUET SERIES (BEST READ IN ORDER)

CHECKMATE DUET SERIES

ROOMMATE DUET SERIES

LAWTON RIDGE DUET SERIES

MOCKINBIRD DUET

INTERCONNECTED STAND-ALONES

MAKE ME SERIES

BISHOP BROTHERS SERIES

CIRCLE B RANCH SERIES

LOVE IN ISOLATION SERIES

TEXAS HEAT SERIES

ONLY ONE SERIES

Find the entire Kennedy Fox reading order at
Kennedyfoxbooks.com/reading-order

Made in the USA
Monee, IL
28 August 2022

12687227R00163